TRANSLATING LIBYA

Ethan Chorin is an American businessman and writer. He was one of the first U.S. diplomats posted to Libya after the lifting of U.N. sanctions, and returned to Benghazi after the 2011 Libyan Revolution as co-founder of an organization working to build trauma capacity. In addition to *Translating Libya*, he is author of *Exit the Colonel: The Hidden History of the Libyan Revolution* (Public Affairs, 2012), a comprehensive account of the origins of Libya's February 17th Revolution. Chorin's features and Op-Eds have appeared in a number of international publications, including *The New York Times*, *The Financial Times*, *Forbes* and *Foreign Policy*. He is a frequent commentator on Libyan affairs for the BBC. A two-time Fulbright Fellow (Jordan and Yemen), Chorin holds a PhD from the University of California at Berkeley, an MA from Stanford University, and a BA from Yale University, with distinction in Near Eastern Languages and Literatures.

ETHAN CHORIN

TRANSLATING LIBYA

In Search of the Libyan Short Story

DARF PUBLISHERS
LONDON

Published by Darf Publishers 2015
Darf Publishers LTD, 277 West End Lane, London, NW6 1QS

Copyright © Ethan Chorin 2015

First published 2008 as *Translating Libya: Chasing the Libyan Short Story
from Mizda to Benghazi* by Saqi Books.

Cover designed by Luke Pajak
Cover photograph by Charles Cecil

www.darfpublishers.co.uk

Twitter: @darfpublishers
ISBN 9781850772842
eBook ISBN 9781850772866

Printed and bound in Turkey by Mega Basim
Typeset by Palimpsest Book Production Limited, Falkirk, Stirlingshire

Foreword

by Ahmed Ibrahim Fagih

I was very pleased when Ethan Chorin asked me to write the foreword to the second edition of *Translating Libya*. Chorin had approached me in 2006 for permission to include his translation of my short story *The Locusts* (Al Jarad), in a collection of work from 15 Libyan authors. I was happy that an American was interested in the story, and in Libyan literature, but I had no idea of the scope of the project, or where it would lead.

At the time of writing, *Translating Libya* is one of the few multi-author anthologies of Libyan Short stories in English.[1] While the book is not widely available in Libya, the book is known to a number of Libyan intellectuals, politicians and writers. This speaks to the impression the first edition has made, and the indirect value it has had in cementing U.S.-Libya relations.

Libya passed through two significant transformations in the last decade: the opening to the West, which lasted roughly from 2003 to 2010, and then the subsequent 17th of February Revolution and its aftermath from early 2011 to present, in which the Libyan people toppled the 41-year

rule of Colonel Gaddafi and then set about establishing a
new one, if so far imperfectly.

Translating Libya is like a time capsule where one can
trace the above transformations, and understand that they
were not completely conscious. Compare, for example, the
morbid resignation of Abdel Raziq Al-Mansuri's character
in *My Dead Friends* (Asdiqa Al-Mawti), which was written
before the opening with the West, with the more proactive
approach of the protagonist in Lamia El Makki's *Tripoli
Story* (Hekaya Trabulsia). Writing in 2006, El Makki
describes the impact of the new commercial culture in
Tripoli, and its impact on traditional relationships. While
new stories might have distracted from the main point of
Translating Libya, something more was needed by way of
explanation to put the stories in current context. I think
Chorin does this very ably in his new introduction.

Translating Libya is an expression of Libyan culture, but
also a lesson in how writers communicate in a repressive
regime, where heavy censorship and random, severe punishment are common. The stories reflect society past and
present. They even give voice to the sufferings and psychic
disturbances of the dictator, living in constant tension with
the people. Thus Sadiq Neihoum, many years ago a
companion of Colonel Gaddafi, depicted the agonies
suffered by the dictator in his story *The Sultan's Flotilla* ('An
Markab Assultan). A writer with such talent could only
follow his conscience, and write what his spirit dictated—
not what the Sultan commanded. As Chorin notes,
Neihoum's books were for obvious reasons 'almost contra-
band' in Libya but Gaddafi, like other Middle East strongmen,
tolerated some degree of criticism, as long as it was well
covered. Neihoum describes the town of Jalo, for example

(and with great irony) as a seaside town, when in fact it is well known to be deep in Libya's Eastern desert.

The cleverness of *Translating Libya* lies in its premise: the fact one must to look so hard for stories that *disprove* the thesis that Libyans feared to write about specific people and places, demonstrates the Libyan short story's political context. *Translating Libya* is therefore both a collection of 'apolitical stories of love and hardship' (as per the subtitle of Susannah Tarbush's review in *Al Qantara*), and a collection with great political meaning.

The idea of 'searching for place' is significant for other reasons. In Chorin's words, it committed him to visiting the very towns and sites mentioned in the pieces – some of which, even Libyans would have little reason to explore. Chorin's snapshots of the rich geographical and cultural diversity of Libya are also valuable. Libya is a vast country of 1,760,000 square kilometers. It has a number of very different environments, colours and flavours. Libya encompasses rich coastal areas, oases, mountains; its people are Bedouin, urban dwellers and rural folk. The reader of this book will gain, both from the stories and Chorin's commentary, a sense of this geographical and cultural variation in Technicolour.

I think it is important to emphasise that the writers whose work is included in this book did not write because they had nothing better to do. They wrote with a great sense of commitment and purpose, and a deep attachment to their culture and their country. Their work is directly impacted by the social and political events in the country— whether this is explicit, or not. How could it be any other way? Take *The Locusts* (Al Jarad). This was one of the first stories I wrote, back in the 1960s. It was inspired by a real event that took place in my hometown of Mizda when I was a boy. The story was interpreted by a highly politicized Arab community as a literary innovation, the first Arab use of 'The People' as literary protagonists – and a commentary on foreign occupation, which had ended in Libya several years before. In fact, when I wrote *The Locusts*, I was not thinking in any such terms, at least not consciously. But this is the condition a writer often finds himself in, and there is no escape. Libya experienced a highly troubled colonial past, a heroic resistance against Italian occupation, a long repressive dictatorship, and all the accompanying sufferings and hardships. When I started to write in the early 1950s, Libya was considered one of the poorest countries in the world. Only 5% of the population was literate. How could I, or any other Libyan writer, have been able to write, unaffected by the pain of friends and relatives and neighbours, focused only on perfecting literary turns of phrase?

At the time of writing, Libya is undergoing a period of tremendous turmoil. Law and order is absent in much of the country. Since February 2011, Libyans have been forced to confront dark questions: was 'freedom' worth the costs associated with the current harsh reality? What is freedom, exactly? The individual's answer of course depends: it depends on his or her current reality, and it depends on what happens in the future. Libya's past provides evidence of similar periods of fragmentation, chaos, and re-integration. The key is to make sure that the processes established now incorporate lessons from the past, so that we do not repeat the same old stories.

Chorin was present in Benghazi right after the Revolution, working on a medical project. In this context, he witnessed to some of the most traumatic events a foreigner could experience, including the attack on the U.S. consulate in 2012, which killed four Americans including another admirer of Libyan culture, Ambassador Christopher Stevens.

In his introduction, Chorin says he was caught off-guard by a question posed to him after a lecture. That question was, 'why should you put yourself in harm's way for a county that is so far away from you own?' I would like to conclude my comments by repeating his response: 'I am not sure I have a great answer to that question, other than that my years in Libya created an attachment to the place and the people, and a sympathy with their aspirations, that wasn't easily forgotten.' As a Libyan, and a writer of short stories, this is what pleases me most: the fact that someone like Chorin came to our country, was able to access our culture in the original language, and formed a bond with that culture.

Translating Libya is a very important contribution to Libyan culture, and the perception and knowledge of Libya outside of the country. I can only hope the reader will enjoy the collection, and I wish to say to him or her, all the best and God bless.

Cairo, Egypt, May, 2014

Introduction to the Second Edition

When *Translating Libya* first appeared in Fall 2008, many believed Libya, with a nudge and a kick from the West, could morph from brutal dictatorship to something approaching the 'kinder, gentler' oligarchic models of the Gulf and Islamic East Asia. While signs of subterranean pressures in Libya were not hard to find, no one predicted that the half-opening to the outside world would create a series of events that made the 2011 February 17th Revolution possible – if not inevitable.[2] Gaddafi must have had some time to regret his 'grand bargain' with the U.S. and the West, and perhaps, his more recent tolerance with respect to subtler forms of subversion.

I compiled and wrote pieces of *Translating Libya* (TL) while working as a diplomat posted to the 'New Libya', from 2004–2006. Libyan culture seemed to hold the foreigner at a distance. I was curious about the local literature – was there any, to speak of? What made this vast, lightly populated country, tick? All of this gradually led me into a world, not simply of 'stories', but of stories crafted to communicate in an environment where there was no such thing as 'normal communication'. Short stories themselves were, as in Abdullah Ali Al Gazal's story *The Mute*, messages in a bottle, meant to be read at a different time and place.

I left the Foreign Service in 2008 to take a job with a multinational company in Dubai. While Libya continued to surface in my professional life, it was no longer the focus. That changed in December 2010. I watched as protests spread from Tunisia to Egypt, skipping over Libya for the time being. I wondered how this could be happening – and if Libya would be next. A friend who had been holed up in Tripoli for the first twelve months of the Revolution told me a joke then popular among the opposition. It went like this: The Tunisians, who led the Arab Spring revolts, called out to the Egyptians, who followed them, over our heads (i.e., the Libyans): 'Get down you cowards, we want to see the *real* men on the other side of you (i.e., the Egyptians).' After February 17 the Libyans shouted back to the Tunisians and the Egyptian, in turn, 'We were just bending to tie our shoes, so that we could deliver a stronger punch than either of you.'

Several of the people I reference in the book (either under their real names or pseudonyms) reached out to me, even before the violent demonstrations in Benghazi of February 15, 2011. Libyan artist Mohammed Bin Lamin was one of these. He told me he was under surveillance and suspected he would be picked up at any time. He disappeared several days later. A friend called to tell me he had likely been taken to the notorious Abu Salem prison, site of a notorious 1996 massacre. A short documentary was made about Bin Lamin's imprisonment, and the drawings he made on the walls of his jail cell. He was one of a few survivors.

Christopher Stevens arrived in Libya a year after my

tour ended, as the Deputy Chief of Mission at the now U.S. Embassy in Tripoli. In March of 2011, he was appointed U.S. Envoy to Benghazi, and less than a year later, Ambassador. 'They had to give it to him', a former colleague gushed. 'Who else in the Department knew Libya better?' I called Stevens to congratulate him on his appointment as Envoy, and to wish him luck.

A few months before, in Fall 2010, I received an email from someone whom I did not know, but whose surname I immediately recognised. He said *Translating Libya* had given him some insight into a world he had left 35 years previously, and I was moved by that. We spoke, and discovered a shared interest in medical logistics. The conversation led to another, and another, and soon we were discussing the kinds of projects we might do together in Libya that might have an impact. About the same time, the original publisher of *TL* asked me to ask if I would consider writing a book on the revolution in progress. It was a timely offer, as that book, *Exit the Colonel*, made some of the humanitarian efforts possible, and vice versa. Neither would have been possible, in turn, without *TL*.

My colleague and I got as far as setting up the framework for a partnership between an American teaching hospital and the Benghazi Medical Centre (BMC), and witnessed, September 10, 2012, the signing of a Memorandum of Understanding that had potential to improve Benghazi's emergency care capacity. On the afternoon of the 11th, Ambassador Stevens told us he was thrilled at this progress. A few hours later, I received an alarming call about problems at the U.S. compound. A few minutes later, we heard the bang and shudder of RPG fire in the near-distance. I spent the rest of the night sitting in the corner of a room at the Tibesti hotel, lights off, listening to sporadic gunfire across the city. At dawn, things became eerily quiet.

During the following months, I had many more opportunities to talk about Libya, as I was to be promoting a book on the origins of the Libyan Revolution. I grew to dread some of these, particularly the television interviews, as the questions were predictable and had no safe answers. At a talk in California, however, someone asked me a straightforward question that, oddly, caught me off guard: 'Why would you take such risks for a country that is not your own?' The question initially struck me as absurd. 'But you don't understand', I started to say. 'How could I not?' My years in Libya created an attachment to the place and the people, that wasn't easily forgotten. When the revolution was going on, what I wished was to be there, in Benghazi, near the Qurena bookstore and Median As-Shajara, watching the Libyans reclaim their right to a more humane future, something other than the utter bleakness described in Abdel Raziq Al Mansuri's *My Dead Friends*, or Meftah Genaw's *Caesar's Return*.

In its first months, and year, the February 17th Revolution instigated a literary-intellectual renaissance. Within a short time, one had scores of new publications, the crown of which was *Miyadeen*, named for the squares that served as public gathering points during the Arab uprisings, and were reminiscent of *Libya Al Musawara* (Illustrated Libya), which contained some of the most interesting Libyan poetry and prose published during the Italian occupation. Miyadeen was a beautiful broadsheet, filled with interesting articles and amazingly candid interviews with artists, intellectuals and *thuwwar* (revolutionaries). Since Gaddafi had bombed Benghazi's main printing press, copy was sent to Cairo and came back in colour print. Less than two years later, militia culture and a resurgence of Islamic extremism had imposed a kind of repeat-censorship. If insulated from outside influence, I believe Libya may ultimately sort itself out, as it has in the past, during times of great pressure and turmoil. It will be interesting to see what literature emerges from the post-Revolutionary high, and subsequent lows.

I believe in the need for irrational optimism. The original idea for *TL* itself was somewhat farfetched: When I began, I could not be sure there would be enough compelling stories to translate, or that the underlying thesis would hold together. After the trauma of the Benghazi attack, a number of Ambassador Stevens' friends and former colleagues worked to bring Mohamed Bin Lamin, whom I met originally through *TL,* to California for a memorial art show, carrying with him the works of several other Libyan artists. Stevens had told colleagues he regretted not being able to visit Mohammed's gallery while he was Envoy – but Mohammed was able to make the journey from Libya to the event.

Why a revised Translating Libya?

The changes in Libya since 2008, of course, gave me the opportunity to say some things I couldn't while the old regime was in place, lest I put the authors in a difficult position. Post-revolution, I could make explicit some of the more 'subtle aspects' of the original, and add some additional context to a literary history that is experiencing shifts and mutations in Gaddafi's wake.

It is interesting that a couple of the people I interviewed for the original *TL* about their views on Libyan literature came into their own as writers subsequently, and also chose the short story as the medium through which to describe the changes swirling around them. A case in point is Azza Maghur, whose father, Kamel Maghur, is prominently featured in *TL*. A recent short story, *Shajarat Al-Zeitoun* (The Olive Tree) establishes her as a leading figure in modern Libyan 'realist-fiction'. I've included it here.

The final essays on the Libyan Short story as a genre, and psychological aspects, and the role of Libyan women, I've largely left alone. One reason is that I wish to highlight the ways in which the stories foreshadowed the revolution, and may explain what will happen to Libya in the future. One of the main messages one gets from reading snapshots of Libya's literary past is that the country has passed through numerous periods of deprivation and chaos, and yet managed somehow to pull itself together. In other words, while tragic, what we are seeing now is not wholly original. I added to the original text two articles that I wrote in 2011 and 2012, which describe the atmosphere in Benghazi before, during and after the attack on the U.S. compound on September 11, 2012.

Some of the travelogue that I interspersed with the stories had postscripts, which I've added here. The search for Wahbi Bouri's *Hotel Vienna*, for example, had a surreal ending in 2013, at a time when Benghazi was effectively off limits to Westerners.

I'm honoured for Libyan author and playwright Ahmed Ibrahim Fagih's introduction to this revised version of *TL*. His short story *The Locusts* (Al Jarad) was the essay that drew me in, and launched this collection. I corresponded with Fagih while editing *TL*, but our first in-person meeting was in Cairo, in the courtyard of a hotel not far from Tahrir Square, the epicentre of the Egyptian Revolution, on a sweltering summer evening in 2012. Fagih was more or less as I imagined him from his writing, and the occasional dust cover photo: a strong personality, witty and humane, with an artist's appreciation for the absurd. Several of Fagih's novels have been translated into English, including *Maps of the Soul* (Darf, 2014) and *Homeless Rats* (Quartet, 2011), which bears much of the charm of *The Locusts*, and is set in the same region. It too, in its own way, foreshadows the 2011 Libyan Revolution and its aftermath.

Ethan Chorin Berkeley, California April, 2014

TRANSLATING LIBYA

For my parents, and my Libyan friends

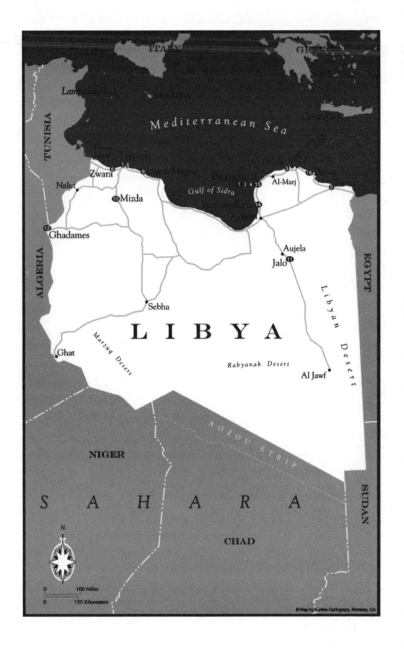

ITALY

GREECE

Lampedusa (It.)

TUNISIA

MALTA

Mediterranean Sea

Tripoli

Zwara

Nalut

Mizda

Ghadames

ALGERIA

Benghazi

Al-Marj

Gulf of Sidra

Aujela

Jalo

Sebha

LIBYA

Ghat

Marzuq Desert

Rabyanah Desert

Libyan Desert

Al Jawf

EGYPT

NIGER

AOZOU STRIP

SUDAN

SAHARA

CHAD

N

0   100 Miles

0   150 Kilometers

© Map by Eureka Cartograpy, Berkeley, CA

Contents

Stories from the South

Stories from the West

PART THREE: INTERPRETING THE STORIES

Introduction

With the renewal of US–Libyan diplomatic relations in July 2004, it was for many as if a space had reappeared on the world map. Within months of the easing of US sanctions that spring, a small team of American diplomats was back in Tripoli in temporary quarters, awaiting progress in relations that would ultimately lead to an exchange of ambassadors and a new compound to replace the one gutted by Libyan protesters in 1980. I served from August 2004 to July 2006 as the first permanently assigned, returning Commercial/Economic Attaché. The assignment afforded me an opportunity to travel and read into a place about which most Americans had ideas, but which only a tiny number could say they even began to understand.

Each short story contained in this book takes place in a different Libyan city, village or place of note, within three broader regions: Eastern, Western and Southern Libya, corresponding roughly to the pre-independence provinces of Cyrenaica, Tripolitania and Fezzan. In time, the pieces cluster around the major events of Libya's modern history, from World War II to Libyan Independence (1951), the discovery of oil (1959), Gaddafi's 1969 Revolution, the Sanctions Era

(1991–2003), up to the recent economic *infitah*, or opening to the West. Because many of the stories were so hard to find, the process whereby they were discovered is itself a story. Before each translation I have included a short historical essay or travelogue, in which I try to say something interesting about the place mentioned, as well as what it looks like today.

The collection's geographic and chronological diversity offers excellent fodder for a bit of social commentary. At the beginning of the book *Place and Identity* broaches the central mystery this book attempts to investigate: where did the people and places go? At the end of the book are six essays concerning specific social or economic problems or developments mentioned or implied by the stories: 'Three Generations of Economic Shock' looks at how little – and how much – has changed since the discovery of oil in 1959. 'Migration' describes how the movement of large numbers of people has contributed to shaping Libyan society. 'Minorities' examines the pre-1967 position of ethnic and religious minorities in Libyan society. 'Between Depression and Elation' looks at the emotional underpinnings of modern Libyan literature. Finally, 'Libyan Women' examines an apparent contradiction between the image of the Revolutionary Woman and the manner in which many Libyan women choose to live their lives.

This book is not a comprehensive analysis of the Libyan short story. Some works show a well-developed style, others are a bit rougher. Collectively, they are important less for being landmarks in the evolution of Libyan literature or use of symbolism, than for what they tell us – in a reasonably straightforward way – about the country, how it was, how it is and where it may be going.

Ethan Chorin
Tripoli, June 2006

Acknowledgments

Obviously, this kind of book is the product of the efforts of many people, not least of which, the translated authors themselves. Basem Tulti and I began this project together, and without his friendship, enthusiasm and knowledge of Libya – not to mention many of his contacts – this book would never have seen the light of day. Basem and I jointly translated Kamel Maghur's *The Old Hotel,*, Ramadan Bukheit's *The Quay and the Rain,* and Ali Misrati's *Special Edition.* My time in Libya would have been infinitely less enjoyable without him.

I owe a substantial debt to Professors Dirk Vandewalle and Robert Springborg, who greatly facilitated the publication of the original book. I would like to thank Darf Publishers, Ghassan Fergiani and editor Sherif Dhaimish for their patience, enthusiasm and careful attention, and my agent, Jessica Papin at Dystel & Goderich. I appreciate the efforts of the School of African and Oriental Studies (SOAS), and Professor Hassan Hakimian. I would thank Ambassador Richard Murphy, Laila Nayhoum, Azza Maghur and Eric Hansen for their advice and encouragement. The authors of the stories and/or their relatives were extremely gracious, both in providing copy and in giving me permission to translate and publish them. Othman Mathlouthi and Lamia El-Makki were invaluable assists with the Libyan dialect. Last but not least, I would like to acknowledge (in no particular order) Najwa Ben Shetwan, Abdelmoula Lenghi, Anne O'Leary, Mohammad Labidi, Abdul Rahman Neihoum, Mohammad Bin Lamin, Maryam Salama, Ambassador Ahmed Ibrahim Fagih, Ramadan Bukheit, Nureddin Tulti, Dr. Muhammad Mufti, Mohammad Kilani, Dr. Nouha Homad, Sammi Addahoumi, Fawzi Tweini, Ali Tweini, Judy Schalick, and Husni and Jalal Husni Bey. I was particularly touched by the fact that so many Libyans – close friends and just acquaintances – kept urging me to 'finish this!' I hope they feel I did the rich Libyan culture some justice in translation and observation.

PART ONE

Setting the Scene

Putting 'Libya' Back in Libyan Short Fiction

Reading through the modest body of work that is modern Libyan short fiction, a curious fact emerges: rarely does one encounter mention, let alone description, of actual places. It is as if one were to begin to walk through Kensington Gardens and suddenly realize that the usual crowd of sniffing, promenading canines is completely gone. Where did 'Libya' and the Libyan psyche go during the 1970s and 1980s? Will reforms mark the return of places to a country that remains, despite its proximity, largely unknown to the West?

Benghazi in the 1960s

The most distinguished Libyan writers from the 1960s were chroniclers, whose journalistic and legal training grounded them firmly in a realist genre. Through narrative and short story, they sought to log the changes that oil and foreign ideas brought to an extremely traditional and overwhelmingly rural society. Excellent examples include Bouri's *Hotel Vienna*, a love story set in a 'marvellous little hotel' on Maidan Al-Milh (Salt Square), Ramadan Bukheit's *The Quay and the Rain*, and Sadiq Neihoum's *The Good-Hearted Salt Seller*. If Bouri and Neihoum were the patron saints of Benghazi-based literature, Kamel Maghur was Tripoli's analogue. An Egyptian-educated lawyer with an impeccable resumé, including a term as Foreign Minister, Maghur set most of his stories in his family quarter of Al-Dahra. *Miloud and Rubina's Story*, a gritty tale about an itinerant Zwaran and a Jewess from Tripoli, has as its backdrop *The Old Hotel*, near the Old City's *souk al-hout* (fish market).

Why were so few stories written during this time about farther-flung Libyan locales? For one, the short story was largely an urban art form, and there were very few people living outside the coastal cities and towns. In the 1950s, the vast majority of Libyans were still illiterate. While the Gaddafi regime can be credited for teaching most Libyans to read and write, the fact that people could, did not mean they did.

The Place Moves 'Out There'
in the 1970s and 1980s

Travelling forward a decade one finds progressively fewer examples of nuanced, 'realistic' prose. Writers either stopped writing, or retreated into a kind of anodyne universe where allegory and alternate realities predominate. Indeed, Mohammed Salih, a writer and literary critic, calls the 1970s 'the age in which people before it wrote and people after it wrote'.[3] In the tradition of the Arab rationalist philosophers like Ibn Rushd, writers went underground – or at least, between the lines.

In the years surrounding the 1977 Libyan Cultural Revolution, Sadiq Neihoum's *The Sultan's Flotilla* ('An

Markab As-Sultan) constitutes, geographically speaking, a major find. An allegorical tale written in the style of the *One Thousand and One Nights*, *The Sultan's Flotilla* takes place in Jalo, a town in the Southeastern desert, once a major entrepôt on the north/south caravan trade route. In the story, an arbitrary, nail-biting sultan is persecuted by dreams of a toothy black dog, out for his hide. Ziad Ali engages in a similar technique with his *Saraya Castle* (Qal'at Saraya). In *The Sultan's Flotilla*, Jalo is visited by a plague, Sodom-and-Gomorrah-like. Sadiq Neihoum employs further biblical imagery in *The Good-Hearted Salt Seller*, where the wrestling match between the zanj and the Genie is reminiscent of Jacob's wrestling match with God, from Genesis 32. In Ziad's story, the Castle has retreated from the sea; it is up to the forces of good to bring it back.

If allegory didn't suit the writer's style in coping with censorship, outright evasion sometimes did. When reading Ahmed Fagih's short story about a Libyan's encounter with a prostitute in a Maltese hotel, or Ali Mustapha Misrati's lengthy piece about efforts to capture a monkey running amok in Tripoli airport, one begins to wonder whether the authors are laughing at their publishers, or their readers. During this bleak period, authors like Ibrahim Koni, Omar Kikli and Bashir Hashimi seem to have deliberately sworn off mentioning specific places altogether. Ziad Ali was one of many writers and artists who took himself, as well as his stories, elsewhere, preferring to write about Libya from Syria and Yemen. Interestingly, one essay devoted to the role of 'place' in Libyan fiction interprets the word in a Platonic sense, focusing not on places, but archetypes of place, e.g., 'the car' or 'the train'. Have authors been so

accustomed in this period to avoiding thinking of places
that vehicles begin to count?

The 1990s and Beyond:
Gradual Return of Places, but People Still Missing?

Encouraged by a loosening of economic controls, a general
amnesty for writers and the release of many journalists and
writers from jail in the 1990s, some exiled writers began
to return to Libya. A younger generation of Libyans, men
and women in their late twenties and early thirties, benefited from increased access to literature from abroad.
Moreover, the Internet brought quasi-underground sites
like www.*Libya-Alyoum.com*, which offered established and
aspiring authors alike both a vehicle to publish and a ready-
made readership. Of those writers remaining from the
'Golden Age', many begin to write again, encouraging a
new generation in the process. Kamel Maghur, for one,
wrote a great deal of new material in the few years before
his death in 2000.

Products of this period include Meftah Genaw's *Caesar's
Return* (Awdat Caesar), a creative invective against urban
decay in Tripoli. Genaw reanimates the story's protagonist,
a statue of Roman Emperor Septimius Severus, so that he
may return to Martyr's Square to chat up 'The Girl with
the Gazelle', a neglected bronze nude built into a corroding
fountain. Sick from their jaunt into past glory, the two
decide on the spur of the moment to hop on a ferry to
Malta.[4] The Western desert oasis of Ghadames is the setting
for Maryam Salama's *From Door to Door*, a protest against
continuing taboos concerning marriages between Libyan

women and foreigners. In *Tripoli Story* (Hikaya Trabulsiya) Lamia El-Makki describes social tensions that come with new money. The piece cites a range of Tripoli landmarks, including the upmarket neighbourhoods of Al-Jaraba and Gargaresh, whose relative opulence is a product of the latest economic opening. The piece is reminiscent of Bukheit's *The Quay and the Rain*, written during Libya's last boom. Bukheit's desperate longshoreman was one of the economic 'losers' of the 1960s; El-Makki's characters, while among Tripoli's new 'winners', are also losers in a sense, victims of their own greed. Even if commonly experienced, the feelings voiced by the quarrelling husband and wife are not the 'same old' dialogues, but evidence a twinge of sympathy for the predicament of the modern Libyan male, appreciated only for his role as a breadwinner. Abdel Raziq Al-Mansuri's *My Dead Friends*, a deliciously nihilistic work, tells the story of a man apparently so depressed he doesn't appear to care where he is. A.'s preoccupation is being memorable on the day of his death, by finding a comfortable spot in which to house visiting 'friends' (which he pays for with money saved for his sons' graduate education). While A. (note the absence of any name) is linked with a place, his identity is so weak it is practically missing.

The Twenty-First Century: Return to Reality?

The idea that Libyan society is not sufficiently complex to produce literature deeper than the short story rings hollow, for it is one of the most complex and contradictory in the Middle East, a region not widely known for its penetrability. As more Libyans travel, as exiled Libyans return, as pressure increases to implement Western-style press freedoms; as the older Libyan writers feel compelled to speak about complex and painful past experiences, 'place' will likely feature more prominently in Libyan literature. In a country where birth-place and tribal affiliation are so critical, acknowledging relationships in the printed word is key to sorting out issues of national identity. One might go so far as to say that only through claiming title to name, person and place, will Libyans be free to place themselves solidly into a unified concept of 'Libya', and to write longer, self-reflective works. The Kensington pooches are starting to return, but to where?

In Search of Stories

Where did this book come from? A series of accidents and coincidences, for sure, but first and foremost, a fascination with Middle Eastern culture and history. My interest in things Middle Eastern really began in 1990 with a summer of Arabic at the Institut Bourguiba des Langues Vivantes in Tunis, Tunisia. At the time, a few French and German friends and I made holiday trips to Jerba, thought to be Homer's 'Island of the Lotus Eaters', from *The Odyssey*, and the oasis of Douz. At the time, I remember very much regretting the fact that I was so close to mysterious Libya, but could go no farther. Thirteen years later, I took Ambassador Richard Murphy's early advice and applied to the Foreign Service.

The assignments process, elaborated in most Foreign Service autobiographies, is more or less a lottery, the results of which are announced in a ceremony at the end of a three-month training period. In July of 2004, as I was preparing to leave for a consular posting in Kuwait, one of my cohort passed me a cable calling for volunteers for assignments in what was then the newest American diplomatic mission: Libya. Earlier in the summer, while working

a bridge assignment in the press office of the Near East
Bureau, I would get a taste of things to come as an observer
of one of the first official Libyan delegations to the States.
I had absolutely no idea that a few weeks later I'd be on
a plane heading to Tripoli. Libya was exactly the kind of
destination I'd hoped for when I joined the Foreign Service:
Arabic speaking, interesting, culturally rich and wacky to
boot.

Background

In 2004, the small American contingent that was the USLO-
Tripoli (United States Liaison Office) was living in small
rooms at the Corinthia, the sole Western-standard hotel in
Libya. I was to report on economic events significant to
US interests in Libya, with particular attention to the process
of economic reform and developments in the oil and gas
sector. Because there was no representative of the US
Foreign Commercial Service in Libya at the time, I was
also charged with assisting US companies to enter (or
re-enter, as the case might be) the Libyan market. Given
the attention Libya began to receive in the wake of Gaddafi's
decision to give up weapons of mass destruction and the
upgrading of the 'Interests Section' to a 'Liaison Office', we
were for the better part of two years literally assaulted with
inquiries.

Passing over Corsica, Lampedusa and offshore platforms
marking the Bouri oil field, on 24 July 2006, British Airways
Flight 898 made landfall just beyond Jerba. Smaller Farwa
Island, pristine beaches and increasingly dense clusters of
scrub and palm-lined farms came into view just before

landing. As we drove to a reception at the British Embassy's 'Oasis Club', located on a small estate on the outskirts of Tripoli, the mission's interim political officer gave me a rundown of what he'd gleaned about the place in the previous two months. As we sat amongst a large group of festive Brits toasting the departure of my analogue, a British commercial officer winding up a two-year stint, I wondered what my impressions would be like at the end of my term here. The moon was so large it seemed almost absurd, and the sweet smell of olives and Jasmine hung in the air.

The atmosphere in the mission over my first six months was very different from that which prevailed two years later. In the summer of 2004 Libya was virgin territory for Americans. The Washington audience was hungry for information on everything from what people ate to how much they made and how they spent their leisure time. Libyans themselves were often startled (and interestingly, appeared downright excited) to meet an American. My office was my sleeping room. By January of 2005, I had use of a computer-equipped suite located one floor above. Thankfully, much of my day I spent outside the hotel, meeting with local businessmen and, where possible, government officials.

The way the process worked, if any of the resident diplomats wanted to meet an official of rank, a diplomatic note had to be submitted to the ministry in question, and the response took time. With commercial matters, however, many of the formalities fell by the wayside. Whatever I read or heard, if it had any value at all, was worked into a piece of analysis that was sent back to the State Department in the form of a diplomatic cable (essentially, a secure email). In the late afternoons, I'd sit in the hotel's groundfloor Tripoli Café, where the waiters weren't really waiters and the cappuccinos sometimes came with cryptic messages, including a pair of circles with dots in the middle, written in chocolate sauce on foam.

Before I left Washington, I was told I would have a Libyan assistant. I imagined he would be middle-aged and heavyset, perhaps with thick sideburns. I found instead a thin, wry and intense intellectual in his mid-thirties. Basem had acquired marvelous English as an undergraduate at Virginia Tech, and an obvious Scottish flavour during the few years he spent as a legal aide in Glasgow. After a few weeks getting my bearings in Tripoli, I asked Basem if he could recommend any good local authors. A few days later he handed me a paperback book containing a story he said he particularly enjoyed, Ahmed Fagih's *Al-Jarad* (The Locusts), the tale of a desert village's unconventional plan to combat an imminent invasion of voracious insects.

Whether the love was a self-love that came from the fact that I was able to read it unassisted by a dictionary, or the self-contained simplicity of it, I *loved* this story. Drowning my chops in a 1-Dinar plate of couscous at a sketchy joint a few minutes into the Old City, I spent the next few late evenings working to produce a solid translation.

I felt any study of local literature would be an excellent, more or less apolitical vehicle through which to give a foreign audience a sense of the place, and to educate myself about Libyan culture and geography. Basem and I discussed the idea of collaborating on a translation effort, and I suggested that we look for works that were descriptive, and mentioned specific places. Ideally these would be places we could visit, as about this time restrictions on the movement of American diplomats within Libya were lifting, and I wanted to get out and see as much of the country as possible.

After a few months of collecting and reading, it became clear there was just one – potentially large – problem with the idea: the vast majority of stories contained very light, if any, descriptions of cities, monuments or the like. This fact itself became a motivating factor. In a place with such rich history and natural beauty, exactly why was this the case? The proposed theme, i.e. 'place', immediately eliminated a few authors from contention, including two of the few Libyan writers already in English translation: Ibrahim Koni and Omar Kikli, both of whose works tend to be longer and very abstract. I had to bend the rules a bit even for *The Locusts* (Al-Jarad) for while the story gives a very vivid description of Libyan village life, the author mentions no specific place.

By mid-2005, my project library exceeded 200 books, purchased in practically every existing bookstore and outdoor market from Tripoli to Benghazi, borrowed from friends, etc. At least half of the stories came recommended. A number of bits – particularly toward the end – were handed or sent by email in draft manuscript. The few existing works of literary criticism provided some useful hints. After six months, I was discouraged not to have found any concrete references to Libya's desert towns. In this context, I was very excited to find in a paragraph referencing *The Sultan's Flotilla* ('An Markab As-Sultan) a short story by Sadiq Neihoum, in a thin volume of literary criticism.

Fergiani & Co.

With increased private economic activity and the appearance of a few quasi-autonomous presses, new titles have appeared, giving old bookstores something interesting to sell. I visited almost every bookstore in Tripoli at least once, most many more times. One of my early haunts was the original Dar al-Fergiani Bookstore (there are two, one on 1st of September Street, and its sister establishment on Mezran Street, both radiating off Green Square). Over the course of my many jaunts from the hotel over to Café Saraya, I enjoyed short conversations with Hisham Fergiani, the owner. Like many others trying to do business in the New Libya, Hisham was a dual Libyan/American citizen. Indeed, the fellow looked as though he'd have been equally at home in Brooklyn as in Tripoli. I told him about the evolving plan for this book, and within a few weeks he was offering suggestions, from bound volumes of old Libyan newspapers containing stories published in serial form, to newer books purporting to be critical studies of the genre. While none of the serial pieces made it into this book, many of the books I bought in Fergiani contained interesting background, upon which I have drawn in the end-pieces.

Al Mu'tamar and the Internet

A bit of the work of collecting and screening stories was done for us. In 2005, *Al-Mu'tamar*, a magazine of arts and culture, began to reprint Libyan literature and poetry dating back as far as the 1930s. While the series included many contemporary authors, many of the volumes were devoted to the stories and poetry of the older generation of Libyan authors, such as Wahbi Bouri (author of *Hotel Vienna*). It was in a *Mu'tamar* edition of Ahmed Lannaizy's short stories that I came upon *Mill Road*. In 2004, the independent Internet provider Libya-Online (then run by Moawwiya Maghur, another of Kamel Maghur's children) estimated as many as twenty per cent of the population of Tripoli had occasional access to the Internet. In a country with no independent newspapers and few other publishing outlets, the Internet has become in the last few years a place where Libyans go to find out what's going on, not only in the outside world, but at home too. *Juliana, Libya Al-Jeel* and *Libya Al-Youm* are names of some of the quasi-underground online venues where one can find Libyans writing about Libya.

Abdelmoula Lenghi and Maktaba Qureena

On my first visit to the eastern city of Benghazi, Basem took me to Qureena Bookstore on Omar Mokhtar Street, not far from the site of the original Hotel Vienna. The proprietor, Abdelmoula Lenghi, today more closely resembles a kindly grandfather than Moustapha Akkad's Lion of the Desert. It was as if he and his dusty books had been holed up here since the late 1960s – and they probably had. Qureena is a bookstore in the traditional sense, i.e. books are not an afterthought, and it is obvious that the person who runs the place cares about books as repositories of knowledge, not just commodities to be sold or traded. Amazon.com is a long way away. Perhaps half of the stories in this volume come from books I found rummaging through Maktaba Qureena. On my third and last trip through Benghazi, this time accompanied by Mohammed Labidi, head of the Benghazi Chamber of Commerce, I paid Sayyid Lenghi another visit. Abdelmoula asked after the translation project.

'I wonder if you have anything new that might mention the cities of Derna or Al Beida?' I asked.

'I do just!' Abdelmoula effused, pointing to a slim volume by the cash register. I skimmed through it briefly and added it to my pile of purchases. Only later did I read through the story *The Yellow Rock*, and find it appropriate to include in this book.

One of Many Detours: Souk Al-Juma

Tripoli's Souk Al-Juma, a region named for the eponymous Friday market, is a chaotic mess – everything and anything one can carry, spread out under the eaves of a freeway underpass to nowhere. Ibrahim, a friend and formerly a professor of Arabic literature, had suggested that I might find something of use in the 'book section' of the Friday market, where men sat cross-legged in front of piles of books, which they would more often sell by the pound than the title. I told Ibrahim what I was looking for, generally, and he and I split up to survey the terrain. I didn't find anything useful, but Ibrahim returned with a very dusty copy of Bashir Hashimi's *Collection of Stories* (Majmu'at al-Qisassiya), which, from the inscription inside the cover, had at some point been pilfered from the Libyan National Library. Hashimi's stories, most of which were based in Benghazi, were some of the most lyrical and descriptive I had read up to that point. None of them, however, mentioned 'places' other than in passing.

Laila Nayhoum, Poet

Nearly two years after Basem and I first began looking for published Libyan stories, I was just beginning to develop something of a reputation within the Libyan writing community as 'an American writing a book' and who was 'looking for short stories'. Laila Nayhoum had been a recipient of one of the US Mission's first International Visitor Fellowships, which bring artists of note to the States to network and present their work. She is a cousin of Sadiq Neihoum, two of whose stories we chose for this collection. I met Laila in July 2006, fittingly, in Café Saraya (see Stories From the West). Within a short time, she had already made a large contribution to this project. Two weeks before my departure, in attachments to ten emails from Laila, I had more quality pieces to sift through than I'd gained in many, many bookstore rummagings. It was Laila, for example, who introduced me to Najwa Ben Shetwan, whose provocative story *The Spontaneous Journey* (Al-Rihla Al-Awfwiya) also appears here. Born in Benghazi in 1961, Nayhoum did her undergraduate degree in English language and literature at Gar Yunis University. Upon graduation, she became a translator for *Thaqafa Arabiya* (Arab Culture) magazine. She is now editor in chief of two magazines, *Al-Beit* (The House) and *Kul Al Funoon* (All of the Arts), and runs the translation department at the Benghazi branch of the Libyan Press Corporation. She writes a weekly column of translations for *Jamahiriya* magazine on 'whatever's new in the world of Libyan literature' and recently started an Arabic-language blog (perhaps the first of its kind) focused on Libyan short stories and poetry.[5]

Mohammad Bin Lamin's Yellow Beings

A few weeks after I arrived back in Washington, Lamia El-Makki (author of *Tripoli Story*) sent me a link to the website of Libyan artist Mohammad Bin Lamin. I'd seen various pieces of Libyan art, some good, some not so good; all, like Libyan literature, somewhat haunting. Bin Lamin's work, however, was singular. I was struck in particular by a group of paintings under the heading 'Yellow Beings'. They were both outlandish and colourful, sort of a cross between Dali and Rothco, touched by desert and sun. One piece, depicting a creature walking with a staff, his hair wild, I imagined to be the kindly alter-ego of the evil Marabout in *The Yellow Rock*. When I asked Bin Lamin where his Yellow Beings come from, he was decidedly agnostic: 'They are spiritual creatures,' he offered, 'somehow bound up with the miracle of existence. Perhaps they are leaves which have fallen from an old tree that is no longer there, or people who have yellowed with maturity.' Bin Lamin insisted the Yellow Beings were 'not Libyan in particular', but in Bin Lamin and his work I thought I saw something quintessentially Libyan. If Bin Lamin were a writer, I'd no doubt have included his stories here.

Perhaps the Yellow Beings do indeed have some magic about them, for a month after I returned to the States, Bin Lamin inadvertently solved our last remaining problem when he asked if I would look over a few stories by a friend. At that point, Basem and I had basically given up on finding that one story with reference to the 'most beautiful place in all of Libya'. I thought I had come close when the septuagenarian owner of a newly opened used bookstore in Tripoli's Old City told me he knew someone in the area who wrote short stories, but it was not to be. With its timely and detailed descriptions of Derna and its environs, Abdullah Ali Al-Gazal's *The Mute* would constitute the final piece of our geographic jigsaw puzzle.

PART TWO
The Stories

Stories from the East

Benghazi

Bauhareshma

The Green Mountains

Tobruk

Benghazi and Environs

In deference to Eastern Libya's distinct role in producing Libyan writers and intellectuals, we begin our literary tour of Libya in Benghazi. The modern city of Benghazi had its origins in a fifteenth-century settlement, itself built on top of the ruins of an ancient Greek city. Story has it that the early village was named for Sidi Ben Ghazi, an itinerant Sufi. Benghazi first attained some regional distinction when the Ottoman Turks made it capital of the surrounding administrative district (*wilayet*) in the nineteenth century. All the same, prior to the late 1920s Benghazi was never really more than a village. In the years leading up to World War I and the Italian occupation the village become a town, then a city, working up from a pre-war base of about 20,000 people.

For hundreds of years, Benghazi's primary raison d'etre was as a terminus for the Trans-Saharan caravan trade – commercial agents from Egypt (via Jaghbub) and Tripoli met 270 kilometers away in Jalo, a staging point for the journey yet further south. They returned carrying ivory, ostrich feathers and hides. Further north, Jews were active as intermediaries, marketing the products brought by caravan to buyers from the northern Mediterranean. In addition to being a transit hub, Benghazi was also a major centre for trade in salt, which Wahbi Bouri, in a 2006 article on his hometown, called 'the life of Benghazi'[6] Salt had been one of Libya's prize exports since the third century BC, when Egyptian pharaohs imported the mineral from Fezzan's salt-fields (*sebkhas*) where the sun caused salt pools to boil. The resulting crystals were harvested and shaped into cylinders for transport by camel.[7]

After the Italians invaded in 1911, they built up Benghazi's infrastructure to support their colonial ambitions. Major works included construction of a new port, administrative offices, hotels and gardens. Maidan Al-Milh (Salt Square, named for the salt-sellers that congregated there at one time), Maidan As-Shajarat (Tree Square) and Hotel Brindisi on what is now Omar Mokhtar Street, were built in the early years of the occupation. This wave of Italian construction crested in the late 1920s.[8]

One effect of furious Italian construction was to divide the city in a more obvious fashion, with the Western, 'foreign' area increasingly distinct from that of the 'locals'. In 1951 the city was named the second capital of independent Libya.[9] Following Gaddafi's 1969 September Revolution, Benghazi lost its capital billing and Tripoli became the administrative focal point of an independent Libya. Oil exploration began in earnest in the 1950s; the resulting early revenues prompted an expansion of Tripoli town and its banlieux.[10] A great deal of hope and apprehension surrounded these developments. With high expectations that newfound resources would create employment and all-round prosperity, there was growing resentment at concomitant and dramatic social and economic changes, exacerbated by an influx of foreigners.

Stories written at this time are positively obsessed with these dynamics.

First Impressions of Benghazi

Basem and I entered Benghazi together in January 2005, a commercial reconnaissance mission of two. Our schedule included a visit to the administrative offices of the Great Man Made River (a thirty-billion-dollar endeavour that draws water from aquifers deep below the south-eastern desert to the northern coast), meetings with members of the Benghazi Chamber of Commerce, as well as courtesy calls on officers of the port authority. All in three days.

On a Friday, Basem and I arrived at Tripoli's Metiga Municipal Airport, where we boarded a dilapidated 727 for the one-hour flight over the Gulf of Sirte, renamed *Khalij at-Tahaddi* (Gulf of Challenge), after the dramatic over-water confrontation between US and Libyan fighter planes in 1981. At the time, Buraq Air was the darling of a private-sector-to-be. That Buraq was the name of the steed that carried the Prophet Mohammed to heaven struck the foreign passengers who made the connection as ominous, particularly as the planes were some of the oldest Boeings in operation, following a period of sanctions that deprived Libya of factory-authorized spare parts.[11] Flying into Benghazi from the West, we could discern nothing through the time- frosted windows but water, until the ancient vessel dropped itself onto the potholed tarmac. As we deplaned, a voice crackled over the intercom. 'Captain Bubeida and crew wish to welcome you to Benghazi International

Airport . . .' We recognized the voice of the airline's CEO, whom we had met in Tripoli two weeks earlier at the airline's new headquarters.

My prior notions of Benghazi came from pre-Revolution photos reproduced in the Congressional Research Service *Libya Handbook* – roads congested with vintage Carmen Ghias and Fiats painted solid colours; wide boulevards, lined with palm trees; smooth-sided apartment buildings painted beige and white. Those foreigners I'd met in Tripoli who'd been to Benghazi after 1990 described the place as dilapidated, dirty and mosquito-infested. Pressing through the crowds that waited in reception to catch glimpses of relatives, we flagged a taxi. The road from the airport into town is long and straight, with advertisements for washers and driers bearing the Korean 'LG' insignia on every lamp-post, each a piece of an endless message, à la 'Burma Shave'.

Indeed, the thing that strikes one first about Benghazi is how worn it is. There is nothing at all new in the collection of buildings that make up the city centre. Smack in the middle of the city stews a fetid lagoon that produces a foul stench, which many locals blamed for migraines. Walking in the vicinity of the bog, every so often one is struck by the profound absence of sound, as transient fowl engage in a collective moment of silence. The backfire of a car, or some other random event then provokes a massive airlift, as thousands of small, flying vermin assault the silence with a unified twittering. After one such moment, I stood mesmerized, watching as a thousand dots condensed into a single black mass, then expanded in an instant, like a drop of oil on vinegar, leaving a film of grey on the twilight sky.

Sadiq Neihoum spilled a considerable amount of ink defending his birthplace from those who claimed the place was depressing and dead. On a late Ramadan afternoon, the city centre has every appearance of being dead. Eventually one becomes accustomed to the city's invisible aerosol toxin and wear, and a certain charm pushes its way through. For all its lost lustre, Benghazi has a certain pulse – a closer look at the ground floors of old Italianate structures reveals neat and tidy microshops, protected by double or triple pane shatterproof glass. The goods are mostly European, mostly clothes. A bent, old man took us on a tour of what was envisioned then to become Benghazi's Cultural Centre-to-be, with stacked Ottoman-style balconies facing an internal courtyard.

In the afternoon of my first day in Benghazi, Basem and I walked from the Tibesti Hotel past Meidan Al-Shajara and the old Berenice Cinema before we alit at Al-Qafila Café (The Caravan), a loose collection of chairs arranged about a six-sided kiosk. A good two hours we sat there before the muezzin of a nearby mosque delivered the evening call to prayer. Shortly past eight, shutters were thrown open one by one with a loud clanking, and the square began to fill with people. By now I had formed the idea that Benghazi had more of a personality than Tripoli, whose ornaments and slogans and concrete structures scream conformity. Here, streets are wide, and lined with trees festooned with lights. Families with small children promenade past shops that in the early months of 2005 were filled with high fashion clothes worn by Chinese-made mannequins whose pointy features and gravity-defying nipples gave them an alien, even sinister appearance. With the Prophet's birthday a month away, the incessant, violent kerplow of fireworks (again the Chinese were responsible) made one jump nearly out of one's skin. One could see the projectiles whizzing in the air before impact, but somehow it did nothing to lessen the surprise at the resulting noise. I assume the nuisance was one of the main reasons the Libyan government added fireworks to the 'revised list of banned imports', along with ready-made clothes and transistor radios.

Sadiq Neihoum

The Good–Hearted
Salt Seller

Translated by Ethan Chorin

A long time ago there lived in Benghazi a well-built zanj[12] who roamed the city's narrow streets and ancient neigh-bourhoods behind his weighted donkey, his finger to his ear, calling out in a stentorian voice, 'Salt . . . salt.' The inhabitants of Benghazi called him Abdel Milh, or the 'Salt Seller'.[13]

While frightened by the zanj's appearance, the children followed his elongated frame with their eyes as he staggered through the alleys behind his hapless donkey. Resembling a looming palm tree, the zanj flapped his bright red tongue at the local children affectionately. They nearly died with laughter each time they heard his throaty voice, resembling the croaking of a frog. Every day without fail the zanj netted out ten ratls of salt into small, carefully-tied white bags, which he then packed into the donkey's saddlebag. Together, he and the donkey would move through the old quarters until they had sold everything. The zanj would then head for the vegetable market, where he always bought the same thing: five loaves of bread and two bundles of radishes. Groceries stowed, he stuck out his bright, red tongue and projected an inimitable, froggy voice. With a body like a great palm tree, lofty and rooted, the zanj returned to his house in Assabri,[11] where he poured out the radishes and loaves of bread before his wife.

While they ate, the zanj as usual mused aloud about the old city's alleys, the price of salt and the state of the vegetable market. His wife was uninterested, saying only that she was tired of poverty and his interminable stories. She bemoaned the fact that he didn't look for another job, one that used his strength, which was greater than a mule's. She reproached him for the fact that his brother had made something of himself, becoming the greatest wrestler in the Sultan's diwan . . .

'And you, you're just a black mule who hauls around loads of salt,' she said.

At this, the zanj lowered his head to the ground, and sat silently until his wife had spent her anger. Then, calmly, he lifted his head and said:

'Woman, salt is also the Lord's blessing. I don't want to make my living wrestling in the Sultan's diwan. Honest bread comes only from exertion.'

At that point, the zanj patted his wife's shoulder, looked up at the empty sky and, using his massive arm as a pillow, slept until night dissolved into day. When he awoke, the Good-Hearted Salt Seller walked back to the salt field, flanking one of Benghazi's principal roads.

He did not like rain, as it invariably scattered the piles of salt. As the zanj gnashed his teeth and spoke to himself, he suddenly spied before him a tall genie with sharp horns and nails, standing atop a pile of salt. He stopped for a moment to collect himself, then said calmly:

'Passers-by should not step on the salt with their feet, ya genie, for salt is the Lord's blessing.' The genie placed his hands on his waist and laughed until he was bent over, then said in a voice deep like thunder:

'Ya zanj . . . ya zanj, I came to engage you in a wrestling match, but you're killing me instead with laughter. Salt, which burns the throat, is not the Lord's manna. The *pearl*, ya zanj, the noble pearl that *resembles* crystals of salt is a blessing from the Lord. Do you care to wrestle me for a handful of pearls?'

The zanj bowed his head, and said with equanimity, 'I am not a wrestler. I am a salt seller.'

Again the genie laughed until he was bent over, then spoke in his booming voice:

'Ya zanj, ya zanj, you're going to kill me with laughter. A great hulk like you should not waste his energy selling salt. Come, wrestle me. If you manage to get me onto the ground, I will load you down with ten bags of pearls.'

The zanj raised his head again:

'And what would I do with pearls?' he asked. 'I sell salt.'

The zanj then turned around to attend to his bags. When they were full, he hoisted them onto the back of his mule and set off home, the small pale stars glittering on high through the gloom of the rainy night. That night he tossed open-eyed in his bed as his wife slept beside him. In the darkness, he extended his hand and placed it above her shoulder.

'Maybe salt is not the bounty of the Lord,' he said out loud. 'Maybe it is just salt, and I am just a cowardly and ridiculous zanj.'

The Good-Hearted Salt Seller turned onto his stomach, buried his hands under his pillow and slept. Lost in slumber, he heard the genie say to him in a thunderous voice, 'You are going to kill me with laughter . . . A great mule like you shouldn't be wasting his strength selling salt.' Awake once more, the zanj raised his head, looked over to his wife and said excitedly:

'Salt *is* a blessing from the Lord, just like wheat itself is a blessing from the Lord.'

Dawn found the zanj once again sleeping face-down, dreaming of a silver moon over the salt field and small white bags full of pearls. He dreamt of his brother, the greatest wrestler in the Sultan's diwan. Suddenly there he was, standing on the salt field. Wearing a leather belt ornamented with gold studs, the zanj's brother cut an impressive figure. The zanj heard him say to the genie offhandedly, 'Come forward, blessed Genie, I accept your challenge. My brother is just a mule who drags loads of salt . . . but I . . . *I* am a wrestler in the Sultan's diwan.'

Raising his head from slumber, the zanj cried out to his brother:

'Don't let him get you by the neck! Push him to the rear! There is a pile of salt directly behind him.'

At that instant, the zanj felt a sharp pain in his back. He opened his eyes to see his enraged wife looming above him. She began to kick him repeatedly. 'Indeed! The sun has reached halfway up the wall!' she screamed, reproaching her husband for his sloth. Once again she stormed off to lament her misfortune. The zanj didn't say anything then, nor did he speak to her when he returned from selling his load of salt. He just sat in silence, chewing absentmindedly upon chunks of bread. Leaning against the wall and using his massive arm as a pillow, the zanj again shouted in his sleep: 'Don't let him take you by the neck! Push him back! A pile of salt is directly behind him.'

On that day, the small, pallid stars overcame the gloom

of the rainy night. They watched the zanj as he crossed the field and perched on one of the salt piles. Today, he didn't bother to fill his small, white bags. The genie with pointed horns and nails appeared suddenly beside him. The stars overheard the two of them speaking loudly. Frightened by what ensued, they buried their heads in far-away clouds. Locked in a fight to the death, the zanj and the genie wrestled like two hyenas upon a field carpeted white with salt crystals. They staggered and scraped against each other in the gloom of the rainy night like two towering palms in the grip of a fierce storm. They struggled through the night, tearing a huge hole in the ground with their feet. They ripped into each other's skin like two wild hyenas. By the break of dawn, neither had gained the upper hand.

'Ya zanj, you and I must now part because I cannot leave my kingdom during the day. Come again tomorrow,' said the genie and, in the blink of an eye, he disappeared into the heavens. The zanj tried to follow him with his eyes, then turned back slowly without bothering to put salt into the little white bags. He was winded, and his back was as dried out as a wooden plank. With his head down, the zanj dragged his feet slowly behind him all the way home. Feeling as if he would expire, he fell upon his bed and immediately passed into a deep slumber.

Once again, Benghazi went without the salt seller's cry. For the first time, his wife inhaled a breath of morning air only to see the bags of salt she had brought the previous day still empty. She took her anger to her husband's bed, where she started to kick him in the back. She screamed at the top of her lungs to wake him, then cursed him. 'You drunk lout!' she cried, as she poured water on her husband's head, all the while cursing her bad luck. The zanj slept all afternoon, dreaming of the genie and the pearls. He saw the silver moon rise over the salt field, and when the evening came he was refreshed, but also hungry and writhing with pain. Alas, there was nothing to eat. For the first time, there were neither bread nor radishes in the house. When the zanj's wife sensed her husband was awake, she began to upbraid him anew. His brother had become a wrestler in the Sultan's diwan! She told him she knew his dark secret – that he was a drunk! Gazing at the sky in silence, his eyes shielded by his massive arm, the zanj did not respond. When the time came and the rain-filled sky lowered a thick curtain on the area, he crossed the field of salt with his donkey.

Once again the genie with pointed horns and nails appeared before him. Once again, the two creatures struggled upon the white field covered with salt crystals, then staggered through the gloomy sky like two giant palms scraping against one another in the hold of a storm. Early in the evening, the zanj put out a heroic effort. He wrapped his impressive arms around his adversary's waist, and succeeded in doubling him over until the genie was on his knees. It did not take the genie long to regain his balance, however. Using his shoulders as an anchor, he rose slowly, then wrapped his arm around the zanj's neck, which he squeezed with gusto. As midnight came upon them, the zanj started to choke. Behind a veil of wet blackness, his eyes went dark and his legs began to fail. Sensing near-victory, the awesome genie began to press upon the zanj like a mountain of copper. The zanj's eyes went ablur. Feeling as if his lungs would dry up inside his chest like two old bags, he made a final push to free himself from the genie's oppressive weight. He felt like giving up and falling to the ground. Once his right leg began to fail him, he said to himself, 'It's absolutely no use. He's going to throw me on the ground. I am not a wrestler, I am just a ridiculous, dull-witted zanj.'

At that very instant, tired to the bone, the genie loosened his grip:

'Ya zanj . . . ya zanj . . . we must part now. I cannot be away from my kingdom during the day. Come back tomorrow.'

The zanj opened a pair of eyes burning with sweat, and drew air into his lungs. With dawn's lights dancing upon the horizon, he looked out at flocks of white birds and smooth threads of morning rain and steered himself slowly home, his arms dangling at his sides. Covered with empty bags, his donkey followed him.

The Good-Hearted Salt Seller was spent to the point of nausea. His face was almost at his feet, which were dragging lifelessly behind him. He was shattered. When he arrived home, he collapsed on the bed, only to feel death creeping through his bones like veins of frozen steel. Once again Abdel Milh's cry was gone from Benghazi. The zanj's wife woke at five in the morning and found the bags of salt empty, as they had been for the past two days. Blind with anger, she threw herself upon the zanj and began to rip into his skin with her nails. It was no use, for the zanj was like a rock in the depths of a mountain cave. Face down, frozen in place, he slept throughout the day. When the zanj awoke, he felt refreshed but unbelievably hungry. His wife was there to spit in his face. Sitting beside him, she cursed her bad luck. The zanj said nothing; shielding his eyes with his large hand, he scanned the heavens. When the rainy sky once more drew its curtains over the countryside, Abdel Milh took his cue to set off with his donkey across the salt fields.

As before, the genie with sharp horns and nails appeared, and yet again the two began to battle each other upon the salt-strewn plain. The genie put his immense hands on the zanj's waist and began to squeeze, exerting all possible effort to bend him backward. The zanj was exhausted and hungry to the extreme; his hands were chapped and pale. When, at the stroke of midnight, his right leg began to fail him, the zanj said to himself, 'It is still early, but my leg is already starting to fail. How I wish I had a better leg!'

Once again sensing victory was almost his, the genie raised up his arms and, using his shoulders as anchors, fell upon the zanj like a mass of molten copper. The zanj sank to the ground. Soon he was on his knees and just about ready to topple over. Just then, he opened his eyes burning with sweat and saw a pile of salt – a small, silvery pile gleaming under the light of the pale stars. The zanj had scraped the salt for this particular pile the previous summer from a nearby pond, so that he might sell it this winter. As he collapsed under the weight of his immense foe, his eyes remained transfixed on this small pile. Someone spoke to him. Indeed, the voice seemed to come from this very pile of salt, and it was oddly familiar:

'Don't let him take you by the neck! Push him back! The pile of salt is directly behind him.' In an instant pregnant with lights and voices, the zanj felt that no, he was not yet ready to give up the fight. He would not fall to the ground. It was as though he were now riding a great wave of energy. He saw his great black arms rise up into the air like two great wings, then watched as the genie suddenly flew backward, emitting a piercing scream as he crashed through the mound of salt. Perplexed, the small, pale stars plucked their heads out from behind the clouds and watched what was happening down there on the salt plain. They saw the genic raise himself from the ground, point to the pile of salt, then pat the zanj on the back. He packed the zanj's white bags for him and disappeared in the flash of an eye. The zanj stood above the pile of salt, looking as if he wished to communicate with it, then staggered where he stood like an old palm on the verge of tipping over. The Good-Hearted Salt Seller moved across the field, his salt-laden donkey following behind.

In the morning, the denizens of Benghazi's old quarters were treated to a most singular sight: the zanj's angry wife, exhausted, dragging behind her the same donkey and shouting, 'Salt . . . salt'. What can I say but this: sometimes ambition can create pearls from salt, but faith alone can sell them.

Source: Qisas Atfal, Tala Books /
Arab Diffusion Company, Libya, 2002 reprint.

In search of Sadiq Neihoum

Given that Benghaziites tended to be much more familiar with Libyan literature than their Tripoli counterparts, I took it upon myself to ask a few Tripoli-based contacts with Benghazi roots whether they might be able to procure me copies of Sadiq Neihoum's works. After a few weeks of hearing nothing, I'd given this up as a lost lead. One day, I received a call from the same contact.

'We found the book you wanted,' he said . . . '*An Markab As-Sultan* . . . Can I drop it by later in the evening?'

This, then, is how it came about that I met in the shadows of the Corinthia a feisty American of Libyan descent, who passed me a xeroxed copy of Neihoum's *Tales for Children* in a manila folder, itself covered by a paper bag.

'Keep this under wraps, you don't want to be showing this around,' he whispered to me, as if he were dealing in pornography or pork rinds.

I spent the next few nights reading *An Markab*, which, if not as saucy as all that, was a very interesting addition to our collection.

Two days later, while I was ploughing through dust-covered remainders and forgotten volumes in the back of a bookstore less than a block from the Corinthia Hotel, I found copies of *Tales for Children* tucked into a corner. Not knowing if I'd find them again, and at five dinars apiece, I bought the set. Over the coming months, we would find more of Sadiq Neihoum's works spread throughout the country, all of which belied any systematic attempt on the part of the powers that be to keep Sadiq Neihoum's literary product out of the hands of the general public. In early spring 2006, I managed to track down the executor of the Neihoum's estate, his brother Abdul Rahman Neihoum.[15] An engineer with Libya Arab Airlines, and by all indications a thoroughly pleasant fellow, Abdul Rahman seemed surprised that an American would be interested in his late brother's work.

Wahbi Bouri

Hotel Vienna

Translated by Ethan Chorin

After finishing dinner with his father and brothers and sisters, Nouri left home on foot. He passed through Souk al-Jarid, Maidan al-Haddad and Souk al-Dhalam,[16] where the city's residents made a habit of lounging once they closed their shops and dusted off the day's commotion. One couldn't miss the guards that congregated in particular spots in the market area in order to watch people's movements. Nouri avoided Municipality Square, which he knew at this hour would teem with café-goers, many of whom were acquaintances. Instead he took a livelier path to Hotel Vienna, through Via Derna and its bombed-out buildings.

Hotel Vienna is one of the most beautiful edifices of post-war Benghazi, which the war turned into a ghost town. As the city regained a semblance of its former self, and as steps were taken to decide its fate, there was not a single lodging fit for distinguished guests. Victoria Schultz, an Austrian, had the idea of renting out a traditional, spacious Libyan house on Via Derna. It was a marvellous little hotel, whose rooms opened out onto an ample square. Schultz ringed the hotel with all kinds of fragrant herbs and flowers. Within a short period of time, the place had become a small paradise amidst the devastation. To the sleeping rooms Schultz attached a bar, and engaged a woman named Christina to run it. Christina was the daughter of Count Yaruski, a Polish aviator trapped in Benghazi when the Soviets invaded Poland and the Allies took over direction of the Polish army.

News of Hotel Vienna soon spread far beyond Benghazi. If a guest spent a night or more in the place, invariably he recorded something of his experience. In his book *Tunis Eastward*, Richard Karington wrote that he didn't have a single good night's sleep during the course of his journey from Tunisia to Egypt – except in Benghazi, at Hotel Vienna.

Taking up his usual place in the corner of the bar, Nouri watched as unfamiliar faces danced around Christina, flirted and engaged her in meaningless banter. The patrons seemed to enjoy the magic of her eyes and her scintillating conversation, far more than they did the drinks they nursed before them. The scene annoyed Nouri. As he exited the bar through the front door, he ran into a group of policemen.

'Why all the fuss?' he asked.

'Mister Pelt,' one of them answered. Pelt was the United Nations representative overseeing Libya's transition to independence. From this, Nouri understood that Mister Pelt was a guest.

Nouri quickly developed an obsession for Christina. Every night, without fail, he would trek along Derna Street to the hotel bar, where he assumed his usual place in the corner. From this vantage point he played the voyeur, observing how Christina spoke with the customers, how she projected her flirtatious laugh and mesmerizing glances. At such moments, he was consumed with pangs of jealousy, which assumed an element of bitterness whenever he caught Christina smiling at someone – even if it was *his* gaze she was trying to catch. Emotions seeped into his psyche to trigger all kinds of involuntary reactions. Nouri had fallen hard for this woman, clearly, but why? Was it because she was so different from him? Christina was beautiful, for sure. He was painfully aware of the many factors that separated him from her. Some part of him acknowledged that, despite the feelings she aroused in him, he knew very little about her.

Behind the smiles and the light gestures, Christina nursed her own demons. She had lost her country and a privileged existence. Her fiancé had been prepared to compromise his social status for the chance to marry her. Christina worried about the future. She was attracted to Nouri. She loved his innocence, and the way she could read him like a book. She found herself thinking that perhaps he could provide for her a respectable, stable life . . . So what?, she thought to herself. So what if it was in Benghazi?

On one of those yesterday evenings, after the last of the clients had left the premises, Christina approached Nouri and grabbed his hand. Nouri suddenly found himself moving to brush tears from her face.

'It's time we spoke seriously,' she stammered. 'What is the nature of our relationship? I want to know if your feelings for me are real. Nouri . . . I'm asking you . . . are you thinking of marrying me? Can you offer me a comfortable life, can you offer me a stable future?'

Nouri was flabbergasted. It had never crossed his mind that it would be Christina who would broach the subject of marriage. Scrambling to collect his thoughts, he responded: 'Christina, I think you have an idea how much I love you. I cannot live without you. I did not ask for your hand, because I was afraid you would reject me. Come and eat at our home next Friday. My mother would like to meet you. She has promised to make us a place after we are married. I only pray that everything goes smoothly.'

So it was that Christina and her father joined Nouri's family for lunch in Dar bin Fadhli with its antique rugs and Arabesque furnishings. Nouri's younger sister spoke with Christina in flawless Italian on a variety of topics, some of which Christina found upsetting.

The following day, Nouri and Christina met in the sitting room of Hotel Vienna. Christina appeared a bit out of sorts. Her sweet smile and customary mirth had all but disappeared. Nouri asked her how she felt about the previous day's visit.

'I liked your mother. I appreciated the kindness, morality and directness of your family. I agree to marry you and to live with you here in Benghazi, in accordance with your customs . . . But there is one thing . . . what conditions has your family given you?'

'My family has no conditions . . . where did you get this idea?'

'Your sister asked me to convert!' Christina stammered.

'Maybe this is how my sister feels,' Nouri said, 'but, really, what is the problem with converting – even if super-ficially. You will then understand the principles of faith, and perhaps believe in it to some degree?'

Christina pulled out a small handkerchief to stem the tears that fell from her eyes.

'I was born Christian and I was brought up Christian,' she said.

'I believe my religion guarantees me happiness in this world and the hereafter. I don't want to abandon my beliefs, even if that means I never get married.'

'I understand your feelings and your faith. But you understand also, don't you, that Islam respects all of the Prophets and their revelations, and recognizes that the spirit of God rests in Jesus. Islam recognizes the Virgin Mary. We have one God. Why would you fear Islam?'

Christina sat silent for a few moments.

'And what about our children? What would their religion be?'

'Of course, they would take the father's religion,' Nouri said automatically.

'My personal happiness is tied to my religion. Do you believe I would deny my children this solace? We live in a world that embraces freedom and the right of the individual to choose his faith, his political orientation and his manner of life – why is it not possible for two religions that live together in one world and in one city to do so in the same house? If you really love me, take me as I am. Take from me nothing!'

Nouri's face turned pale. He felt a sharp pain all over and a fever beginning to course though his veins. Excusing himself, he promised he would return.

Nouri clung to his bed for two weeks, staging a kind of strike that he didn't end until his family, driven to distraction, finally relented. During all of this, Nouri didn't dare mention children. He didn't see an easy way out of that topic. Despite the drain of the previous weeks, Nouri left the house more or less undamaged. He headed straight for the hotel. Through the power of positive thinking, he had already begun to weave the threads of a future life with Christina. He imagined that her magic eyes, her smile and the embrace of her conversation would be his alone. He would offer her all the happiness and stability she deserved.

Nouri turned the hotel inside out searching for Christina, but could not find her. After a bit, the owner came out and led him to the sitting room, where she poured a cup of coffee. Her face was red; she stumbled over her words. She tried to dodge Nouri's questions about Christina, but soon buckled under his persistence. The pain of what she had to tell him seized her heart and filled her with pity: 'Christina left for Tunis with her father. They've gone to London.'

Source: Hadith Al Madina,
Ahmed Mohammed Al-Lannaizy,
Al-Mu'tammar, 2005 reprint.

Finding Hotel Vienna

Soon after I joined the Foreign Service, my mathematician father pledged he would visit me wherever I was posted, assuming it was possible. At the end of a year in Libya, I figured he might have to forgo the Great Jamahiriya. Visas were never easy to get, and my position might be a help or a hindrance. I decided not to try to go through official channels, and use a friendly visa expeditor instead. Amazingly, it worked. The Public Affairs Officer at the time arranged for him to address students and faculty at one of the local universities. So it was that I found myself standing before a crowd of a hundred or so young Libyans – mostly women – at Gar Younis, proudly introducing my father. It quickly became apparent that the crowd was made up of students of English 101, not Mathematics. My father's English, accented with Polish and French, must have given them an interesting impression of how English is spoken in the States, particularly as, for most, this was probably the first American they'd heard 'live'.

I had an idea that we'd do a tour of the Green Mountains, which I hadn't yet seen. The Libyan style of driving, one hand on the wheel, 120 miles per hour, cell phone to the ear, put my father off the idea, and instead, we – he, Basem and I – took the opportunity to traipse through Benghazi in search of various sites and landmarks mentioned in the stories translated thus far. First and foremost, I wanted to find Wahbi Bouri's Hotel Vienna, that 'marvelous little hotel, all of whose rooms opened out onto the ample square'.

After walking the length of the corniche, we comman-
deered a taxi to help us scout out a few of the places we
couldn't reach on foot, or about whose whereabouts we
were most unsure. The cab driver, a man of about thirty,
had never heard of Hotel Vienna. He seemed not to recognize most of the place names we gave him, save Souk
Al-Dhalam and Souk al-Jarid, where we had him take us
first, as neither were an easy walk from the hotel.

Souk Al-Dhalam today is a dust-coloured arcade, opposite a collection of nondescript, decaying shops whose
windows are filled with car batteries and dangling sheep's
carcasses. The odour of the place combines with the dust
kicked up by any number of ancient cars to produce a
gritty, pungent smell. A thin street perpendicular to the
main portico of Souk Al-Dhalam leads into the façade of
Souk Al-Jarid, named for the palm fronds that once crowned
the entry to the covered market, today jam-packed with
ready-to-wear clothing and electronics. The contemporary
sight resembles any number of Middle Eastern markets,
without being distinguished from them in any way.

As we continued back towards the corniche, Basem
rang his father, who repeated instructions as to where to
find Wahbi Bouri's hotel. Something odd struck me about
the two of us there in Libya, dragging our fathers into old
and new worlds, respectively. Superimposing Mr. Tulti's
vision of long-gone landmarks against the view unfolding
before us, within a short time we landed upon a ramshackle
branch of Bank Al-Jumhuriya, which sits on the opposite
corner of Maidan Al-Milh from the Al-Qafila Café. Once
inside the revolving front door, one can clearly imagine a
hotel lobby in the atrium where tellers now sit, cramped,
behind a wooden docket facing a set of high-set windows.

Old men sit on chairs below. To the right, a staircase leads to the second floor and a series of offices. The 'ample square' mentioned in the passage above, Maidan Al-Milh, after the salt market that was once here, is now replete with over-grown trees; on the opposite side to Hotel Vienna is the carcass of Cinema Berenice. Muhammad Mufti tells us the location is indeed correct; however, most of the building that was Hotel Vienna was razed in the 1950s: 'Now for some of yours and Basem's guesswork. Where the Jamahiriya Bank stands now, there was the auspicious Albergo Alitalia with four towers at the corners. I remember it was badly damaged in the early 1950s. Around 1958 it was demolished and the present bland structure was built. The Vienna building still stands, a simple one, in a narrow alley still known as Via Derna, close by.[17] We tried, but we couldn't find it.

Mufti, Basem and Bouri's son visited the elder Bouri one weekend to discuss the story behind the story: who exactly was this Christina? Did she really exist? Where was the hotel? *Hadraza fis-souk*, or 'Banter In the Market', is the sequel to 'Hadraza fi Benghazi' (Banter in Benghazi). The latter has become a bit of an underground classic in Libya. In it, Mufti recounts some of the differences between Benghazi in the 1950s and Benghazi in the 2000s. Bouri insists that Christina did exist, and that the story is 'all true'.

6 November 2005

Found: Hotel Vienna

On July 20, 2013, nine years after my first trip to Benghazi, I received an email with an unusual salutation. '*Dear Brother*', it began. The author introduced himself as a Libyan-American from South Carolina. *'You don't know me. I read Translating Libya'*. He said he had some photos that might be of interest. The next mail read; *'While my big toe keeps its distance from Tibesti's "pool" . . . . this place still looks mighty cozy. From Via Derna – Sammi.'*

It wasn't immediately clear to me what Sammi meant. It had been a busy workday in California, and Benghazi seemed to me very far away, physically and mentally. I opened the attachments to the email and found what was immediately recognizable as a block of Benghazi apartment buildings, in a familiar state of decay. It wasn't until a bit later in the day that it hit me: my new correspondent had said, 'From Via Derna!' Could it be that he had found Hotel Vienna?

I opened my mail, and enlarged the images. Lo and behold, the half-effaced lettering 'Vienna' could be seen clearly. I was ecstatic – it was as if Sammi had provided conclusive proof that there was life in outer space, and that it was friendly.

Sammi and I corresponded further over the next weeks. Every day seemed to bring another buoyant revelation. Subsequent mails had pictures of a low key Sammi, next to some of the luminaries of the Revolution – one photograph showed him and Fathi Terbil, whose arrest on January 15, 2011, is associated with the outbreak of demonstrations that began the revolt against Gaddafi. *'Enclosed is a picture of man*

you may have met and certainly have written about, Benghazi'
own, Fathi Terbil. I know that if I can't help . . . he can.'

The next day, after I asked if he had seen Mohammed
Mufti, and here again, was a picture of Sammi with
Mohammed, and a copy of his book, *Hadraza fi Benghazi.*
'*I know of Mohammed Mufti only from his recent political
activities post Revolution, though now I will seek him out, as I
understand he is still in Benghazi now. Every little piece of
knowledge about Benghazi or Libya that I can acquire and/or
share adds to my hopes of hoping to somehow help the country
in the long run. I love to rant and rave about Libya to anyone
that will listen. That is why I contacted you.*'

I couldn't help asking myself, 'who *is* this mystical
Sammi, that he can produce the Who's Who of Benghazi
in a matter of days?' Further mails showed pictures of a
church, the family-owned patisserie, a car bombing. I
mentioned Abdelmoula Lenghi's bookstore.

The next day Sammi wrote: '*I have passed by Mr. Lenghi's
bookstore a few times, but his early Ramadan schedule contradicts
my very late Ramadan schedule. He is only open from 10am–1pm
so I will see if I can't cross paths with him in either his store or
at Benghazi's Soccer Club, Nadi Hilal, where I heard he hangs
out. I like his use of Silphium . . . a touch of class.*'

Destroyed: Hotel Vienna

*From May of 2014, fighting in Benghazi had intensified between
radical Islamic militias, many under the umbrella of the 'Shura
Council', and forces loyal to General Khalifa Haftar, and his
'Karama' (Dignity) movement. A large number of Benghazi's residents had fled the city. Six months later, fighters loyal to the Islamic*

State (ISIS) and Al Qaeda and its affiliates, had taken control of large sections of the city – including the area around the epicentre of the revolution, the Courthouse and Cinema Berenice. By May 2015, most of the block containing Hotel Vienna had been destroyed.

Hotel Vienna, c. Fall, 2012. The word Vienna is barely legible **in the blue area**. (photo: Sammi Addahoumi)

Ramadan Abdalla Bukhoit

The Quay and the Rain

Translated by Basem Tulti and Ethan Chorin

With the setting of the sun, the surface of the sea grew to resemble a pool of blood. As the dockworkers moved en masse from the quay towards the company office to collect their daily wages, Khalifa threw an empty bag over his shoulder. It was one of those used to shield himself from the clouds of dust kicked up as he offloaded cement onto the quay. The platform was positively overflowing with bags of cement. Khalifa shuddered to think how much of it he had carried on his own back.

'Tomorrow, all of it will be gone,' he said to himself. More was likely to come. It was all being used to build massive structures in town, buildings that filled him with awe every time he walked past them.

Khalifa approached the gathering mass of workers. His clothes and skin were the same faded, cement-grey colour, which added a patina of sadness to his tired face. The men waited for the boss to call out their numbers, so they could collect their money. Hearing his number called twice, Khalifa pushed his way slowly to the front of the queue. His eyes were fixed on the boss and his thick, black moustache.

At one time, Khalifa felt something approximating awe

as he stood before this man. No longer. As he fell back out of line, Khalifa felt out the individual bills, one by one. For an instant, a trace of a sparkle might have been perceptible in his eye. Khalifa walked down the broad street, lit by bright lights. Luxury cars raced in front of him, as if fleeing ghosts. Occasionally he looked up at the immense buildings looming above him. He imagined they were ghouls, looking down upon him and his drudging step with contempt. Khalifa recalled each stage of construction, and every last bag of cement it took to complete it. Through his own hard work, bit by bit, that stuff called cement had morphed into these oppressive creatures, incubi that returned the favour by squeezing the breath from him, making him feel insignificant by comparison. The fact that he was aware of these feelings irritated him all the more. Khalifa quickened his pace and scurried to the end of the street. Was he really afraid the buildings would collapse upon him? He continued walking east towards the shops, whose owners he imagined were waiting expressly for him, eager to convert his hard-earned money into a nugatory quantity of canned goods.

'How ironic!' he thought to himself: as a dock worker, he was the first to touch the products he now received back in exchange for his entire day's wage.

Khalifa felt as though exhaustion would fell him before he made it back, but somehow he managed to move forward along the blackening road, past more shops, some of which were lit by weak and dying gas lamps. He smelled something rotten as he trudged through swamps and puddles whose surfaces sparkled under the moonlight. He didn't gag from the accompanying stench, for he was used to it. It inspired in him as little feeling as would the perfume worn by the wives of rich people.

At home, Khalifa found his children waiting with their mother for him to return with the usual paltry offering, the urge to eat competing with hunger for sleep. As he handed the burlap bag to his wife, she struggled to express the fact that what he brought home was no longer enough. Khalifa muttered excuses: the shopkeepers were raising their prices day after day. Some blamed the Jewish traders.

With the three children now asleep, the corrugated metal hut fell silent. Khalifa lay down, using his large empty bag as a pillow. His wife drew closer to him, and in a soft voice, told him about a rumour spreading through the neighbourhood: someone had bought the land. They would all have to move, because the owner wanted to build on it. A bitter thought crossed Khalifa's mind: the cement he offloaded earlier that day might belong to this new owner. He laughed out loud as he observed his wife praying softly, hands extended.

'. . . and give unto us as you have given unto others.'

'*He* didn't give to anyone,' Khalifa mumbled as he tried to sleep. '*They* stole from us.' His wife was only vaguely aware that her husband had spoken.

A few days later, Khalifa stumbled into an office filled with people who didn't look much different from him. He signed his name, and was given a *bitaka*.[18] The officials present explained that everyone needed a bitaka in order to get a job. Khalifa didn't waste much time thinking about the process, as his only concern was getting a good job, like the ones everyone talked about. He heard that the monthly salary could reach thirty dinars.

'Good God!' That would be wonderful. He could buy clothes for his wife and children. He could even buy his wife something made of gold or a silver bracelet. 'Thirty dinars!' Khalifa wouldn't soon forget the day he arrived at the desert camp.

From his first day, Khalifa had been confronted with groups of fellow workers screaming, 'Let us out of here! We can't stand it any more!' The commotion made him uneasy, but he didn't know enough about the circumstances to form an opinion. In the evening, the group was divided into teams of five.

That night, he was suddenly conscious of his wife's nudging.

'Khalifa, why aren't you asleep?' she asked. He sighed, and in a voice mixed with bitterness and sorrow, he said:

'Nafisa, I have to go back home. I can't stand it here any more.'

Nafisa did not hear him, for by then she had given in to sleep. Khalifa recalled the early days of that year in the desert. He had felt then as though he had been given a new lease of life. When he came back to spend his first vacation, his children were happy to see him. He brought them canned food, courtesy of the Company. They got used to expecting him at the end of each month, but he never forgot how excited they were the first time. When the Company stopped distributing these perks, Khalifa bought cans from the store, but it was obvious they could tell the difference.

The shimmering of the moonlight through the holes in the ceiling and the wind-induced shaking of the sides of the house reminded Khalifa of his first winter in the desert. How severe the conditions were then. In the mornings, he worked under the rain. At night he stayed awake for fear of being swept away by flash floods. Once, a powerful storm washed away all the tents, throwing the camp into chaos as workers chased their belongings through the blustering wind. As if a calloused hand squeezing his heart, he recalled a co-worker shouting, 'Help me . . . my leg . . . help!' Khalifa didn't know what had happened. The morning after the storm, he went back to work with the others. Most of the men were so spent they couldn't continue. When the Greek supervisor wasn't looking, a few took the opportunity to escape. The supervisor shouted a lot that day, urging them to work harder and harder. He threatened to fire them all, then and there.

This sequence of memories was interrupted by the whining of packs of dogs that roamed the neighbourhood. The whimpering reminded him of that tortured cry he had assumed belonged to one of the workers supervising the drilling machine. How awful! They found him on the ground, impaled upon a metal rod. Khalifa remembered how the sight shook him: he ran up to the body, lying in what looked like a puddle of black water. He could smell the tar coming from a pipe extending underground. As he carried the maimed worker to the tent, a black liquid gushed out. The disgusting smell was everywhere. He searched for the doctor, but to no avail. Everyone rushed to see that nauseating black liquid flow from the ground. From his bed, the injured man cried, 'I discovered it . . . oil . . . let me meet with the manager so I can get my prize . . . let me go!!'

Khalifa tried to comfort the man with his words, then left to find a doctor. When he reached the well, workers were crowding around it. He spied the foreman, arms crossed, his face redder than usual. Speaking through a translator, the man conveyed an awkward message. 'Now that we've found oil, your work here is done. Collect your wages and return to your families.' The word spread among the men, who began to drift away. The translator added, 'The manager says he would like to thank this fellow who discovered the oil.' Khalifa smiled as he remembered the man lying there in his tent, somewhere between life and death. The braying of the neighbour's donkey woke Khalifa. He saw the first light of the morning seeping through the cracks of the hut. Despite the fact that he had not had much sleep, he rose feeling invigorated. He woke his wife and said to her decidedly, 'Nafisa, gather our things. I'm fed up with this place, the cement dust and the awful smell of oil. We are returning to the land.'

Khalifa headed toward the first place he had reached in the city, the taxi station. Throughout the journey he whispered to himself, 'I must find a way to get out of here before I'm kicked out, like the first time I was kicked out of the desert. I couldn't take that again.' When he returned at noon, he found the family's worldly possessions all packed. He gave his children a bag of fruit with which to occupy themselves, then helped his wife gather their belongings. As they left their shack, the children whined persistently:

'Are we leaving our home?'

Khalifa tapped one of them on the shoulder and said:

'This isn't ours any longer. I have found you a better home.' The taxi moved quickly away from the city centre. When it finally came to a stop, they could smell the scent of fresh green grass. Khalifa, his wife and their children got out of the vehicle and headed toward a half-crumbled house, lying in the middle of an overgrown field. As the children ran for the place, the eldest cried out, 'It's our old house! Much better than the one we left behind.' He headed to a crumbled section and with his brothers started an impromptu process of laying bricks in an attempt to fix it. Khalifa looked out at them all with a certain air of contentment. Rain began to fall. As his family entered the old house, Khalifa remained outside. He extended his hands to collect the falling drops of rain, as if to welcome those who were welcoming him. As his wife called out for him, Khalifa insisted:

'Let me wash. I want to enter my house a clean man.'

Ramadan Abdalla Bukheit, Hikayat Al-Madi Al-Qarib,
Dar Al-Kutub Al-Wataniya, 1996

Abdel Raziq Al-Mansuri

My Dead Friends

Translated by Ethan Chorin

A. opened the door of his apartment and embraced the men before him affectionately, as was the custom in these parts. These were some of his oldest friends, and most had travelled from places far from Tobruk. After he had led them into the reception hall and undertaken the various statutory elements of a Libyan welcome, he asked with a smile, 'Who died this time?' Life had taught A. that friends his age didn't come to visit the living.

'F. passed away – you still remember him, I hope?' said one of them, smiling (for the gentleman was like that). A. recalled F., and those beautiful days they had spent together in Tripoli. Suddenly, he felt like crying. He had not seen F. recently, nor had he thought to visit him in over five years, even though the dearly departed lived close by. All the same, he didn't cry.

A. stood next to his friends in line at the funeral hall where the remains of the deceased were being kept. In lieu of prayer, he looked into the rough, open ground, where the coffin containing F.'s body was visible.

After three days of sitting in honour of the deceased, chatting about their boring lives, A. bade his friends goodbye.

Back home, he sat on the pavement outside his building, contemplated his narrow street and wondered where they would put the tent when his day came. Which of his friends would come to pay their respects? A. noted that the narrow door-frame of his building would surely make removing his casket a difficult task for his friends, when they did come to take him away (as was their custom).

A. did not fall asleep early that night, as he usually did. He rose from bed and, sitting on a chair in his office, looked up at the white wall above him, on which hung a diploma inscribed with his name in ornate lettering – the PhD he earned from an American university. A. took out one of the ledgers in which he kept track of all the money he had in this world, about 100,000 dinars. Until that night, the sum was untouched, set aside as a reserve for whichever of his sons might wish to pursue an advanced degree. The following morning, and after running a few errands, A. arranged to meet a local real estate agent. He told the man he wanted to buy a house, but with one condition: it had to face a public square. The request surprised the agent, as all his previous clients had been more concerned about the state of the property itself than where it was located. All the same, he told A. he would call him when he found something suitable.

About a month later, the call came. Could they meet this afternoon? The agent found a house meeting his sole condition. A. exited the car and stood in front of the house, while the dealer nattered on about some repair or other. So preoccupied was A. with the square that by the time he could collect himself to respond, the dealer had wandered off.

'The repairs don't concern me much.'

A. stood in the middle of the square, larger than a soccer field. The grounds were peaceful; along the perimeter stood six electricity poles, and on top of each pole were two powerful floodlights.

A. found the agent. 'It's a done deal, I'll buy the place' he said, despite the fact that he had yet to set foot inside. He was oblivious to the expressions of the agent, observing the movements of his strange customer. That night, A. signed the contract and forked out over 90,000 dinars. After sunset, he returned to the square, now illuminated with floodlights so strong one could spot a needle on the road. This made him happy. On that last night, in the old apartment that A. loved dearly, for the first time in over a month he was able to sleep, comforted that he now knew where they would erect the tent for his friends, those who would come on that day from all parts of this world.

Source: Libya Al-Youm.

Saleh Saad Younis

The Yellow Rock

Translated by Ethan Chorin

'A small yellow stone . . . light . . . and flammable! What sort of puzzle is this?' said the Sheikh as he combed his thick, white beard with the fingers of his right hand, and juggled the sleeping stone with the palm of his left. The Sheikh raised his eyes, stared at the two boys, then dragged one of them before him:

'Where did you find this thing?' he whispered.

Pointing with his finger, the boy indicated that it had come from the mountain behind the village: 'Over there, near the Hanging Cave.'[19]

The second youngster approached the Sheikh. 'This wasn't the first time we found rocks of this colour,' he said . . . 'We found a bunch of them a while ago – but this is the first time we found one that burns . . .'

The Sheikh was silent for a moment, before he mumbled something that caught the attention of those present:

'*This* explains the mystery of all those things that were crushed or smashed without clear cause or reason.' The crowd became agitated. People began chattering amongst themselves:

'This rock is a blessing from the heavens,' said one.

'It will stand in for candles until the government fulfils its promise to connect us to electricity.'

'The state won't do anything . . . it's just promises,' quipped someone else.

'The stone will solve our problem, even if it's just temporarily.'

'Yes, indeed, the stone is a blessing.'

The Sheikh stood up, leaned on his cane, then turned the cane's eagle-head crest to face the crowd. Silence fell, as the crowd was ready to gobble up whatever wisdom might pass from the Sheikh's lips.

'This rock is an affliction!' he pronounced, eliciting an incredulous gasp from the crowd. He shouted: 'This rock is a *mrabet*.[20] What befell this town was the result of a violation of its sanctity . . . the dry spell . . . the sickness . . . unexplained deaths . . . the visions!'

The crowd's eyes were transfixed upon the eagle's head, as the Sheikh vomited up his singular vision: 'I see sparks coming from the forest . . . the fire blazes on; the ghibli pushes it forward.[21] It demolishes everything in its way . . . all that's left is kindling. I see the sky covered in a thick smoke . . . rain pours down thick, black drops. The wells overflow and a black flood covers the land. Nothing is left, for our houses are destroyed, the animals have been swept away. The sky is tinted red.'

'Yallah, what a nightmare!' said a woman with an ugly face, an ugly name and a loud tongue.

The Sheikh snapped at her angrily: 'Old woman! Sheikhs do not *see* nightmares. Their visions are but shadows of reality.'

The three of them, the Sheikh and the fathers of the two young lads, stood a way off, while the people conferred among themselves. Old women chewed on jokes with their rusty teeth. The Sheikh raised his thick index finger in the face of the two men, and issued his sentence:

'Your sons committed a sin . . . look!' he said, pointing

to the black tears accumulating at the rock's base. 'This is a sin that can't be erased but with blood,' he continued.

'Shall we sacrifice an animal?' asked the first. 'The biggest we have?'

'The only cow the village owns,' said the second.

'No . . . no . . .' said the Sheikh. 'The sacrifice is a piece of both of their livers.'

The two men at first didn't understand, so the Sheikh made it painfully clear:

'The sacrifice, my friends, is the two lads.'

The two men didn't cry out, they did not say a word.

The throats of the two lads vomited blood, and their eyes ran with tears.

The sheikh continued his rant. Some stood with gaping mouths, their faces pale as stone.

'People, I regret to say the marabet is not yet satisfied. I believe it demands we burn the village, for my vision told me this. We need to leave with the first rays of light. If we do, we will be spared further affliction.' So it was the villagers set about preparing a caravan to flee the yellow rock. All were there, except the two boys who committed the sin. In his lifetime, that sheikh who leant on the stick never, ever laughed.

Al-Baida, Libya, 1999.
Saleh Saad Younis,
Al Hajar Al Asfar, Benghazi:
Dar Al Kutub Al-Wataniya 2006.
Published originally in
Al Jamahiriya *newspaper,*
no. 2842, 21 August 1999.

The Green Mountains

Repeating phrases that seemed to be part of some collective Libyan consciousness, Basem described his father's
hometown of Derna as a paradise on Earth, replete with
waterfalls, vegetation almost tropical in its thickness and
variety; homes built into the mountain with the utmost
care. It was far more difficult to find material citing towns
in the Green Mountains, than it was stories referencing
Tripoli and Benghazi. My guess is that there is in fact much
more, most of it buried in collections of old writings and
old newspapers, and in expatriate memoirs. Strengthening
this suspicion, a spate of old writings were republished and
a number of new writings on the East appeared in print
during my last couple of months in Libya, including Saleh
Saad Younis's *The Yellow Rock*, Najwa Ben Shetwan's *The
Spontaneous Journey*, and Abdullah Ali Al-Gazal's *The Mute*.

This up-tick was not limited to fiction: my own understanding of the area was greatly helped by the recent
historical works of Muhammad Mufti and Wahbi Bouri,
both of whom I have cited liberally in the end-essays.

For close to two years, I was not able to get farther
east than Benghazi. The new pieces came just in time for
me to exploit the last official US government holiday of
my stay in Libya to visit a couple of the places in these
stories. This 'last hurrah' would not have been possible
without the generosity of Mr Mohammed Labidi, Head of
the Benghazi Chamber of Commerce, one of those who
seemed to take it as a personal obligation not to let me

get away without a look at the Green Mountains, which were a 'wholly different face of Libya'. Indeed, ten minutes past Benghazi's city centre along the coastal road, one senses a difference: the air is clean; the chaos of bumper-to-bumper cars disappears, to be replaced by a country scene full of grazing livestock and dogs that loll about and lick themselves. Over the right shoulder, a cow, caught in barbed wire, tries desperately to free itself.

First stop: Tokra, where in the seventh century the Byzantines tried in vain to fight off the Arab invasion from the East. Here we passed through the abandoned remnants of an Italian square, circled by long-abandoned, pastel-painted shops. Labidi led me to Roman ruins marked with legible inscriptions in Latin. Around us, brightly coloured wildflowers were everywhere. We climbed to the top of a fort and, using binoculars, looked inland at a short plain abutting a rugged, brush-covered mountain.

'One can get lost here,' Labidi said. 'And people have. It's possible to walk for a day and not see another soul.'

We caught the curator of the local museum on his way to take his afternoon siesta. He let us in graciously, despite the interruption. Labidi spoke animatedly with the guide and the director both. Just as one encounters Libyans in the West with unmistakably Roman features, the East harbours similarly dramatic examples of Hellenic types. Our guide could have been a recent immigrant, one of the refugees from Crete featured in Lannaizy's *Mill Road*, or a descendant of the ancient Greeks themselves. The museum contains a few impressive mosaics and castrated, armless statues. In place of one severed inscription, a note: 'On tour with the Gaddafi Charity'.

Moving on from Tokra, we made a right turn and

wended our way slowly up into the hills, where we passed a long line of honey sellers' roadside shacks. The area known as Al-Marj, or the Meadow, is the Greek 'Barca', a settlement established in the sixth century BC. In the 1960s Williams described it as a 'pleasant, rather sleepy little town'.[22] With pride, Mohammad announced that it was here, in the land of the Labidi clan, that the Libyan resistance to the Italian occupiers began. A bit further along, in the Al-Kuhuf (caves) region, mentioned in *The Yellow Rock*, I was reminded of the Sierra Nevada town of Auburn, California, with its limestone caves flanked by anachronistic railway trellises. This area was the setting for *The Lion of the Desert*, the film biography of Omar Mokhtar. It is here that one starts to see signs of the yellow rocks mentioned in Saleh Younis's eponymous story.

Labidi pointed to a cluster of yellow flowers along the road.

'I'm certain that is related to sylphium,' he said, a reference to the long-extinct flower that the Romans and Greeks believed had magical curative powers. 'How could this plant disappear completely?' asked Labidi, pointing to the nondescript flowers. Was this *thapsia garganica*, I wondered, a plant 'with none of the qualities of sylphium, though it looks rather like it at certain stages in its growth'?[23]

Past Al-Marj the road gradually turned upward, and we came to Qasr Libya, home to an impressive set of mosaic panels, most of which had been lifted from the flooring of a nearby structure. The visitors' logbook contains the signature of France's Jacques Chirac, who, passing through Cyrenaica in 1976 on a State visit (as Prime Minister), wrote in the visitors' book simply, '*formidable!*'

Farther on, the Greek ruins at Cyrene (present-day

Shahat) came into view. Passing through another small winding road lined by the crumbling remains of more single-level Italian bungalows we came to the site itself, no more than a square kilometre in area. Here one has a spectacular view of the coast, stretching perhaps twenty miles in either direction. From this vantage point, Cyrenaicans would have had ample warning of a seaborne attack. Guidebooks were titillating in their descriptions of Greek maidens bathing in icy waters that percolate up from an underground spring. The area reminded me of the palace at Knossos in Crete, and only a couple of prominent palm trees provided a clue as to our location a few hundred miles further south. Closer to the sea stood a well-preserved amphitheatre, over which a few Libyan families had spread an afternoon picnic. Across from a clump of redolent fig trees, a derelict restaurant sold Egyptian trinkets. A bit further down the single-lane road was a museum that had been closed for several years, allegedly to disguise the theft of much of its contents. From Shahat we tumbled down the hillside to Sousse, 'Appolonia', where Cleopatra is said to have bathed in a stone basin built for her directly into the surf. The port had been recently renovated by the Greek-Cypriot firm J&P Construction – a gift from the Greeks, so to speak, but the baths themselves are awash in raw sewage.

'Shame on you, shame on us,' Labidi said to a group of watchmen, as he gestured to the surrounding chaos. The group shrugged off his rebuke with smiles and the refrain:

'Allah is All Knowing and All Giving.'

'Allah is indeed All Knowing, but He's not going to do your job for you,' Labidi responded. On the way out, through the stinking puddles, I looked up at an enormous, multicoloured billboard emblazoned with the slogan: 'From Libya Comes the Unprecedented'. So true.

Farther east, the water becomes more and more blue, and the scenery more dramatic. The area around Ras Al-Hilal,[24] while devoid of ruins, is nonetheless spectacular. An overhang of modest cliffs shelters white sandy beaches and turquoise waters, flanked by a more vivid version of the vegetation that had accompanied us since Benghazi. These lands were the crown jewels of the Libyan Social Security Fund, which owns much of the shoreline property from eastern Benghazi to the Egyptian border. A few miles further ahead the foliage is thinner, at least in part the result of a massive planned burn, which locals say the government effected in order to root out subversive elements said to be hiding there. Today, the area is a massive bald spot in an area that would otherwise be among the greenest parts of the Green Mountains.

Not far from the small town of Ras Al-Hilal is the site of another interesting experiment in small-scale capitalism, an inn unlike anything I'd hitherto seen in Libya. For 100 dollars a night, one can rent a furnished modern villa with a barbeque and of a stunning view of the bay. Labidi spoke enthusiastically of building telefriks to carry tourists to the top of the mountain, and a resurrected ferry service to Crete, the lights of which he insisted were visible on a clear winter night.

Spring 2006

Najwa Ben Shetwan

The Spontaneous Journey

(Al-Rihla Al-Awfwiya)

While I was away on vacation in the seaside village of Bauhareshma[25] it occurred to me to write you a letter. I would collect all my feelings in it, then toss it into the Mediterranean. In the letter I would tell the world about us. The bottle I would push on its way with breath from my lips.

For a time, I left memories of us behind me, in a place whose only export is dust, where half a thousand inhabitants work to sweep the alleys and clear sand from the narrow tracks that lead to the village. Despite the amazing quantity of dust that swirled around us, I was able to love you there, and to house you in the expanse of my thoughts. I did this despite the traps that arose before me, including warnings from the head of our household, whom the State charged with overseeing this dusty *baladiya*.[26] You linked the bloodlines of our two families, and penetrated me, as the sea would infuse parched earth.

Brooms and dustbins were the tools of life in our village. My mother cursed the day my father took us there, from a city in the distance crawling towards civilisation. It was my fate to meet you there, although your profession had nothing at all to do with sweeping. In our dusty village I not only found my heart, I found for myself a different path.

I must tell you, this place in which I am now is more a part of me than my own veins and farther from my eyes than something that is absent. The purest salt tastes of Bauhareshma, which to me resembles a sacred space of worship. Salt divides the wind, the sea and the sand, inhabited by a scant few Bedouin. We haven't seen them yet. We have only felt their presence from afar. The only evidence of human activity here was a few grape vines laden with ripe fruit. It is as if the sea from this side were devoid of people, and the vast, frightening sky is looking for ways to expand into the eternity that is life after death. Indeed, there is nothing here one could call 'life', except a few curious insects endowed with the power to struggle against oppressive heat and deprivation. People who live in villages and cities need air conditioning to manage. Personally, I believe this changes both their form and appearance over the long term.

Just now, my mother is kneading bread in the tent. My father just picked up a hatchet, which he'll use to gather firewood to heat the *taabuna*, an oven dug in the sand. He took my youngest brother with him, to teach him how to cut the dry branches without harming the living parts of the stubby acacia trees. The others had gone swimming, and were now searching for strange shells to expand their collection of watery relics, some of which decorate the salon of our house. No doubt they took the salon with them in their minds, so they would not forget terrestrial life.

I hear one of my brothers calling me. I will go to him,

I will leave my papers and my bottle here so that he does not stumble upon them. I send kisses to you until I return. Kisses to you until the very end. I am now far from my brothers, who are thrashing about in the water, tossing their voices to the heavens. Balmy Bauhareshma is devoid of all sound except that of the waves, our transient voices, and my eternal longing for you. There's a stirring inside me. I imagine it to be you, lying on the bed next to me. I begin to feel myself in a place we haven't yet experienced. It doesn't resemble us and we don't resemble it, except in the unified geographical categorization that is 'us'. I wonder if we can ever really be a part of it?

The smell of burning wood wafts overhead. Apparently my father has succeeded in lighting a fire. While my mother readies the bread, she calls for us to come and eat something. Maybe it will be *shakshouka* with jerked meat, or *sharmoula* with cheese.[27] Of course, there will be the ubiquitous red tea with mint. Mother asks us to keep our distance while the bread bakes, so that we do not disturb the sand and cake our feet with dough. She is kneeling on her heels in front of the subterranean oven, so she may apply bread to its surface and cover it with an iron lid, upon which she will rest coals, while assuring a perfect fit.

For the remainder of our stay here, my mother occupied herself with the cooking. So much so that she only went to the sea when she needed water, or to cleanse herself in preparation for prayer. In my brothers' absence she heaped food upon me, paying no heed to my desire to remain thin.

Near our tent is a small, shallow well. It was in the nature of this land that salt and sweet water commingled. Digging, one could find potable water at a distance of approximately one and a half arms-lengths. My brothers were close to finding it, when my father warned them against playing with God's Bounty. One of those who had been in Bauhareshma before us had put the tyres of a large truck over the mouth of the well, lest the accursed winds bury it with sand. It was a good idea, for it is in the nature of tyres to put up a valiant fight against the burning sun.

I used a jerry can bearing the insignia of a shell outlined in red as a bucket to draw water from the well. I attached to it a rope and put near the well some stones, upon which one could sit while washing clothes or bathing. Meanwhile, my brother gathered shells that salt and water had sculpted into remarkable shapes. We looked at them admiringly. If you had been with us, I thought, perhaps one of them would have morphed into the shape of a ship's captain. I took one of the shells. I whispered into it my name and yours and the name of our unborn baby. I thought about the fact that this object had never touched another human before us. It tries to get to know us just as we now grow accustomed to the scent of this place. The shell insists it knows you, despite the fact that you've never set foot in this place.

'What are you doing with my shells?' the family shell-collector protested.

Even my grandmother took part in the show-and-tell, breathing into the shells not for any interest in them, per se, but for the sake of *barakat*.[28]

After gathering the shells to his bare chest, my brother went away with them to say things that none of us wanted to hear. In the late afternoon my other brothers went a distance along the shore searching for the remains of one of those ships that had lost their luck – wrecks they had heard about, read about in books or perhaps were figments of their imaginations. When they disappeared from our line of sight, my mother became very anxious. My father tried to calm her by tracking them with binoculars. I left them talking to one another and went to the sea. In my hands, paper, pen, an empty water bottle and a bag containing some of my favourite food.

'Don't go far, you'll be afraid out there alone. Stay with the others,' my mother called after me. She didn't know I went to be alone with you, and to write my secret daily correspondences before darkness descended. The waves were high. Something had happened to the sea, which had turned angry. I saw many large crabs scavenging for food. I threw to them the remainder of a red melon and some soggy bread. I gathered my joy and rode the waves, fast and threatening. A passer-by might imagine these creatures crawling towards his bed, with the gloom of Bauhareshma tagging close behind. These creatures, white or yellow with a helical casing – were they really crabs? Most of them remained in the water, soaking up the brown essence – the same stuff that makes up the earth and our skin, even. The sun's disc is a blazing ingot, beating down those in search of gold. The mermaids comb their hair as they prepare for a wedding of a Mediterranean houri[29] to the Sultan of the Great Ocean.

In the bottle I put the letter I wrote to you, along with your address. Perhaps, I mused, someone would find it and take it to you, so that I could tell you in words what I cannot now convey in touch: how much I love you, how much I miss you, as I stand in the midst of this primordial isolation. It's as if we are held together in a different age, glorious and frightful, hewn from earth we know. Truly, I'd have loved you then too.

At night, Bauhareshma was a completely different place. It shut itself in our faces, buried its throat and drowned its face, ugly like the Ottoman sailor who for centuries poured into it fear, blood and excrement. In that realm just beyond the audible, sailing ships cross the Mediterranean. They collide and sink, abandoning their cargoes of gold, slaves, spices and dried goods. The reef-fish nibble on the ships' cargo. They amuse themselves with the bottle I sent swimming towards you.

Some nights my brothers and I would venture a way from the tent, so that Father wouldn't hear us. We'd sing, or have yelling contests. Memories came to me of my beloved's singing folksongs that first attracted me to the beauty of his voice, laced with personal trials that had left tracks on his youthful heart. The moon peered down at us like the blade of a fabled silver sword. It fell like a great mirror and washed itself in the sea. It listened to us as we sang out loud.

Tonight, as we sit around the fire, Mother is preparing tea. My father is near her, and my brothers are talking amongst themselves. My thoughts go to you. The night siesta over, my mother recites her nightly proscriptions to scare away scorpions and vermin and those unseen earthly beings through which spirits channel evil night and day. With her forefinger she traces a line in the sand. She starts with our beds, but keeps going until she's encircled the entire encampment, all the while reciting *ayat* of the Qur'an.[30] My father guards the tent. A 9 mm pistol by his side, he sleeps in the rear of our pick-up truck, parked at the entrance of the tent. He will be there to save us from whatever earthly or otherworldly danger might descend upon us. He is determined not to let the dark forces take his children from him. We offered our support, never ceasing to ask for assistance from God and the Prophets and Messengers and Companions of Land and Sea. Protect us till we get home! We were longing for a change from our daily life . . . Perhaps we just needed to ask?

On our last night in Bauhareshma my brothers could be found counting the shells and sea scorpions they had gathered, putting them in soda bottles of different sizes to show their friends. My father took inventory of his camping equipment and made sure the bullets were secure.

'Allah sees all who neglect their prayers,' Mother chided us. 'Not knowing the direction of the *qibla*[31] is not an excuse to leave your prayers. Those who are sincere can always ask, or follow the lead of those in the know.'

At this point my father interjected, in a bout of contrariness:

'If you put your back to the sea, children, you'll be facing Mecca. Nevertheless, you know in what direction to pray when you're home – you'll preserve your piety there.'

My eldest brother went off; he didn't bother to tell us where. He went to the sea. When he returned to enter his bed, I noticed he was carrying a bottle in his hand. I tensed when I saw it.

He said to me: 'Look, sis, look at what I found on the beach. The waves carried it here.'

I took the bottle from him and, in the darkness, tried to open it. There was a piece of paper inside. I jumped from my bed to look for a light, so I could see what was inside. The moon was pitch black; only embers remained of the fire my mother had made. It seemed for a few moments that, in this place full of angels and sultans and traps set for the *Saliheen*,[32] it would be impossible to read the note in a travelling bottle. We had to resort to my father's cigarette lighter to attain our goal, which turned out to be . . . none other than the letters I wrote to you during my first days in this place. No matter. I will carry them to you myself, as my brothers carry the things they have taken from the shores of the inimitable Bauhareshma, and in the same way my mother tried to curry favour with the Saliheen.

Abdullah Ali Al-Gazal

The Mute

Translated by Ethan Chorin

1

When she awoke, the girl was completely exhausted. Yesterday, her mother beat her with a stick. This morning her body was broken and sore. She felt a periodic, stinging pain. Out of bed, she raised her dress and reluctantly, and peered down at the bright blue stripes that branded her swollen thighs. She touched and prodded her abrasions, only to feel the pain grow. As silence groped the walls, she felt pain course through her body. As was her habit, the mute lingered by the window of her room, then climbed the stairs to the top of the house, where she could make out the sea in the foreground. Pockets of wind buffeted her body. Tall buildings took nearby mountains from her line of sight. How long had life in this place disoriented her!

From the depths of the sea a broad tongue of water penetrates the city, seeming almost to break the place in two; that is, if a dry projection of earth didn't block the way decisively, making way for a stretch of clay that widens slowly until it turns to scrub. To the west there are fields encircled by clusters of palm. There, the earth fuses with a thick jungle of vineyards and fruit trees. Halfway between the palms and the forest the roots of a massive tree grip the ground. Overhead, green mountains loom. A spring bubbles forth, its water falling to create a small, clear lake ringed by slabs of rock. The lake takes the water and pours it into two fast-moving brooks: the first wends along a sparkling green canal linked with tangled roots; the second courses through a rocky area before it finds the cerulean sea. The sandy, brackish part of the shore is littered with fishing boats and lean-to workshops. Along the wilder side of the shore, rocks group together to create a gradually rising, seaweed-covered wall.

2

From her vantage point on the roof, the mute contemplates both the sea and the expansive plain. She tracks the birds as they migrate through the seasons. Either by the eave or by the window she lingers, always silent, drawing into her chest newly-minted oxygen emanating from the mountain spring. She watches and listens as life, with its glitter and chimney smoke and voices, returns with the rosy dawn to mar the night's silence. Her gaze flows from eyes both compassionate and tender, crying for the return of something she cannot explain.

A few days ago, the sea expectorated the body of a giant turtle. Not long after, a pack of teenagers came to haul the carcass away. Two groups, each with its own rope, dragged the body over zigzagging sand formations to a shallow grave. The air raged with putrescence. The jocular

pulling left a blood-spattered trail, mixed with the colour
of the shore. Young men collected salt-infused sand to pour
over the turtle's hardened frame. 'Does everything really
return to its roots?' the girl asked herself. How many times
had she watched processions of freshly hatched turtles run
the gauntlet between the sandy depression and the great,
vast sea? How many times had she watched them march
toward the waves as shore-dogs and predatory fish waited
to pick them off, one by one? Invariably, a few of the
creatures managed to disappear into the murky water. Tiny,
they moved with odd and intimate gestures, as if propelled
by a magical force.

The mute watches as shore birds, unlike like any she'd
seen here before, scoop up the turtles crawling forward
with quiet determination. How many times had she seen
the bright white butterfly flutter about on diaphanous
wings, only to become entranced by the magic and gran-
deur of the flame? When those angelic wings sear and
crinkle, the air breathes with an inexplicable joy. How many
times had she gone out at night to the forest near the
mountain spring? Just how many times had she heard the
insects belt out their eternal, unintelligible anthem, even as
evil spreads through the shadows, drowning the world in
silence? Since childhood, these matters had never ceased
to occupy her thoughts.

Today, the girl in the window feels herself infused with
the joy of raucous birds. Their chirping rises to her. She
whispers back to them. They laugh with her, and seem to
flap a wave. As the streets spring to life and her avian
interlocutors return to their hidden world, she follows them
in her thoughts. The magical birds hover in space, performing
their eternal rites. The mute looks around at the fresh,

harvested fields as the sun continues on its habitual arc. Floating shadows create for her a bubble of tranquillity that she rides the forest canopy, where creepy-crawly things zip through the dry leaves. When she opens her eyes she sees the forest creatures staring back at her.

The collective wailing transports the mute into an alternate universe. With her soul enveloped by tortured melodies, she wails and moans in response. The secrets that grow in her breast are the same as theirs. The unknowable clattering gets louder. The mute curls up into a ball, then stretches herself out onto the mysterious isthmus. Birds call out in unison, their voices mixing into a cacophony of a thousand ageless melodies. These rhythms are recreated time and time again: the logic of ants, the cooing of pigeons, insects' nocturnal dirges and the gurgling of the mountains' distant spring – all speak in unison. The mute is overcome with anxiety, until sleep at last overtakes her.

3

When, many years ago, her mother learned her daughter was mute, she felt a shudder run through her. The elders rushed her daughter to clinics and the Issawiya sheikhs,[33] but even the wisest and most potent of the fortune-tellers were not able to decipher her incoherent moans. Little by little, the child with the rosy cheeks and mouth of honey became a woman. The outline of her gorgeous eyes projected a stunning flash. Everyone, young and old alike, was drawn to her. Her growing bosom drove the ships' crews to distraction, scanning the shore as they did for a glimpse of that perfect body. Walking on the sandy shore, her feet moist with foam, the mute bends to pick up empty shells. This girl that no one really knows is a symbol of both beauty and defiance.

These skeletons on the sand, next to her footprints, these strange, hardened creatures . . . where did their supple bodies go, the mute asked herself as she filled a box with shells. Occasionally she raised the shells to her ear so she could eavesdrop on their conversations, before moving along the stone berm to that place where the mountain spring snores.

When she was a child and her father took her on walks to the sea, the mute wore a blue dress. As she stooped to tie her shoelaces, she would look up to contemplate the fishermen's thick, cracked fingers. On their faces she could read the signs of years of wear and toil. She listened as they spoke irrationally, opening their mouths to reveal yellow, cavity-filled teeth. The men would joke with one another as they picked bits of seaweed and sticky grass from their nets. The mute was frightened by the obscure power they displayed as they wrestled small fish forcibly from the interior of the blue sea. She could hear the silent cries of the fish, their silver bodies flopping about under the sun. How they would wail, craving to return to the sea's bosom! Frightful creatures with immense hairy chests, the fishermen formed timeless armies walking half-naked on sand. They hammered steel girders into the frames of wooden boats, until sparks flew.

The mute sits alone. A brawl breaks out nearby, confusing her. It seems as if the sea is lathering itself up with foam, and the waterfall poised to overflow. Tears well up in her little eyes. She emits a half-stifled sob, while her innards echo with a profound lament. She imagines the wind beckoning her, as around her the shouting of men grows louder. Their voices fill her ears, infecting her with intense anxiety. Outside the walls of her secret world nothing gives her pleasure but watching wooden boats and the sea itself, that carrier of anonymous soldiers.

The mute looks on as the fishermen empty their nets. She stares at the silver beings, she stares into their dying eyes. Silence follows. As the men gather to gut their catch, and swarms of flies do battle, she begins to convulse. The fishermen smile at her, their blood-spattered knives dangling at their sides. At some point in the distant future, she muses, these fish will turn to stone. She imagines the dead fish are waiting for her. If she could only go over to them, their severed eyes and heads would shake and grow into living, sparkling beings, capable of making their way back to the blue sea.

The fishmongers cluster together in their own quarter. Stray cats greet the hurling of fish-parts into back alleys with yowls of delight. The midday heat cooks up a fetid stench, similar to the one that followed the giant turtle as it was dragged through the sand. There is always some commotion in the market, as voices and men crowd together. As the mute feels the familiar, dull pain rise within her, her spirit looks for an escape. Images of the mountain spring and the wide sea stay with her until her eyelids slacken and she succumbs to sleep. In her mind's eye, she sees spectres wrapped in white − the colour of water as it seeps from diaphanous shells, or sparkling glass. The mute struggles to understand why she sobs uncontrollably when she contemplates the sea, or when she passes through the twisted vegetation that surrounds the mountain spring. Often, she smells an odd scent, something like loaves of burnt bread, or the odour of burnt moths stuck to the glass sidings of hot lamps.

The fishermen's faces, which time has engraved with deep ridges, project a hideous sadness, not unlike the expressions borne by the severed fish-heads. They too seem to cry out in pain. The mute follows them to the mosque for Friday prayer, as she used to follow her father in his ample *jalbaba*.[34] Lying in wait until the supplicants' voices rise into space, she sidles up to the windows and takes a peek inside. For a moment she loses consciousness. In her trance, she sees fountains of holy light pour freely from spots on their foreheads, smudged brown from contact with the earth. Far off, the mountain spring continues to flash and sparkle. In the winter, the city lights and the lanterns of boat crews move together like points of a fine knitting needle, weaving clothes for the night. In the background, a fierce wind rages. With each strike of oars against the water's surface, waves glisten and glitter, creating an awesome shimmer.

From time to time, the mute dips her consciousness into her father's sub-surface abode. If she cocks her head just so, she can hear his gentle speech. He tells her stories of the sea and strange, faraway lands – stories about their forefathers' struggles against the Italians. Fierce battles to the death. Her mind takes in images of winters much more desperate and painful than what she has so far experienced. Her father tells her everything, responds to all her questions. Why do beings fight? Why do they kill one another? Against these questions her soul continues to struggle and chafe, like a pair of hands over a winter stove.

The morning her father went to sea for the last time, its surface assumed a greenish hue, similar to the colour of the horizon on a frigid day – a quilt made of green cloth.

The mute recalls feeling as if she were encased in orange aura. That afternoon, thick clouds gathered. The surface of the sea assumed a touch of her imaginary aura, the waves rose a frightful rising, and the wind whipped itself into a fury. She watched as the waves smashed against the quay with ever more violent blows. Wandering in her blue dress, the child heard a cry near the wharf that stopped her in her tracks. A fight had broken out between the women swearing at one another. One broke over the other's head a metal pole, and it landed with a decisive thud. More yelling and swearing. The mute's ears were crowded with voices, with chaos. As a crowd gathered to watch, she ran away.

The moment the sea swallowed up her father, the mute's mother became her sole guardian. The day the sea carried news of her father's demise, she had been wandering the shore, looking out both for him and for signs that winter was coming to an end. She waited a long time. A boat, its lights dimmed, returned to the wharf in the dead of night. The broken vessel had been battered for two straight nights by swells and torrential rain under a thundering and flashing sky. According to the rescuers, monster waves had stolen most of the crew. The next day, the clouds dispersed. By midday the sea was strangely quiet, its turbulent upper layer stripped away by tranquil air. Finally, the rain-soaked days passed. Ashen-faced, the mute returned to the sea to wait for her dead father, surrendering herself to a melancholy the likes of which her mother had never seen. Alone in her veiled world, she was terrified. She distracted herself by collecting shells, and awoke each morning to the fluttering of birds. She got to know them so well she began to understand their logic.

4

Spring has come. The rock cavities tremble with green grasses and colourful flowers. While the new season forced the cold back into the walls of people's homes, it buried in the mute's bosom two minute seeds. Hardening by the day, they broadcast a subcutaneous mumble and pricked her flesh like two small creatures fighting to get out. The discomfort was such that she began to dread the waking hours. One night a few months later, she felt her insides again gripped by a sharp pain. The prophecy was realized. As her mother sat in silence, the girl shook, her features contorted. A thin, warm trickle ran down her thigh. Rising suddenly, the mute raced to the next room. Her mother spied on her through a crack in the door, as she raised her dress and saw a line of red clinging to her leg. Catching the hint of a vague evil smile escaping from the slits of her mother's eyes, she quickly lowered her dress.

'Ah . . . are you afraid?,' her mother asked.

'You are becoming a woman. You are now an adult. You will marry. Yes . . . You will marry and you will have sons.'

The mute's thoughts ran wild: Marry? Instantly her mind conjured up images of the fishermen. As the two crouched by a heater as they used to during the long, murky nights of winter, her mother remained silent, observing with fear as her daughter's expression changed from raving to vacant.

'This . . . is one of life's secrets,' her mother offered.

The girl did not look up, but her mother could tell she was crying. She repeated: 'Are you afraid?'

The next morning the mute's mother let a feeling of satisfaction overtake her, even as her daughter remained gripped with a fear she would be forced to carry a while longer.

5

The rumour in town was that the mute had only spoken once. Not long before the accident, she accompanied her mother to the bustling city. There she saw the butcher decapitate a ewe and tear open its stomach with a knife. With blood dripping from his hands, the man continued to disembowel the creature, conversing with a large, pasty-faced man as if it were nothing. The girl ran away and twice threw up in the street. She cried, she fell face-down on the sidewalk in the middle of a puddle of her vomit, then passed out. For a full day she spoke only gibberish. Then, she began to speak in words and sentences. Her mother was beside herself:

'My daughter spoke! She isn't mute!' Like lightning the news travelled the tongues of neighbours and fishermen. Once she had recuperated, the mute fell back into silence. There are only a few who remember the incident now. Over the years, the question that coursed the interstices of her soul was this: her mother's breasts are also flesh. *How can people eat meat? How could they eat a severed breast?*

6

Before the place filled with street-noise and honking horns, the mute awoke into her peculiar world inlaid with dreams and visions. While she stretched out on her bed, her eager, loving spirit crossed the wide street, heading west. It flitted through the mountain foothills and down to the spring, where it bathed itself in water and darkness. The mute's amorous spirit fell in love with waterfalls tinted the colours of rosy morning and nectar-washed rocks. It made eyes at the sun, while bursts of air and fragrance pelted one another with calyxes of chrysanthemum and narcissus. From her faraway vantage point, the beautiful girl listened to noble whispers. In that place where perfume and flowers and watery lights unite, she moaned a melody in counterpoint with the forest pigeons.

Suddenly, the mute feels herself jolted from that state of innocence. From the room behind the walls of the city and the cement buildings, her conscious body summons her back. The languid air and low-lying fog have burned off. In a flash of the eye, she returns to her original resting place. Her spirit has dissolved into flesh. Her mother is calling her. Her spirit is tortured by these two competing existences: in one lives her mother and the stick. The other is filled with soft light and chrysanthemum flowers. Yet, somehow, the mute feels herself getting closer to the object of her longing.

In the autumn months, the branches begin to yellow. People's dwellings, the streets and the paths along the quay – all are alive with Technicolour leaves. Creatures preen and don binoculars, which they use to spot humans dressed in blue, humans wearing straw hats, humans sweeping with wide brooms. A few months on, the trees lose their cover and the boughs go bare. A grey tent covers the city. At night, the stars blaze brighter. Young men leave the seashore behind, and rosy, naked bodies abandon the waterfall. At times the great roar of the sea and the thickening foam seem to take control of the afternoon. In the rainy season, the fields whistle with the wind, and pigeons dangle from the upper reaches of the palms. As the glow of the heaters dies down and the lamplights are extinguished, the mute feels another wave of anxiety. A light, moist breeze passes through the palms' flapping arches and the pigeons' vacant nests. This evening, her steps become almost reverential. The mute notes how exposed the trees seem to be.

'It's all about nakedness,' she thinks to herself.

This time, when she hears the sounds of the waterfall, the hair on the back of her neck stands on end. She decorates her body with bits of flowers and leaves and scrubs her skin with wild grains. What sweetness! Freedom calls to her. The mute is acutely conscious of an eternal force beyond the physical body. Those questions still nag at her. Where do the creatures go when they die? Does everything inevitably return to nakedness?

7

On one of her recent visits to the forest, the mute found a small, hairless bird flopping in its nest. She watched the fuzzy sparrow as it turned over and over in the straw bed, struggling against a flood of sunlight. The little creature

appeared weak with exposure to the searing heat. She
poured a few drops of water over it, prompting it to shake
and raise its head. Through two little lazy eyes, it peered
up at her. Calmed by the girl's incomprehensible language,
it leant on her shoulder and slept. The mute walked a few
steps inside the dark forest until she could hear the ranting
of the chick's worried mother, flapping out an SOS in bird
logic from above. After returning the little bird to its nest,
the mute sat by the edge of the spring. For the very first
time in so many years, she dared enter the water, and
allowed her body to disappear into the spray. Legs pulled
together, she gave her spirit freely to the erupting spring.
Water cascaded over her closed eyes. A voice arrived on
the wind from afar, startling the sparrows. The mute lingered
at the spring, under branches teeming with beaks. When
she returned at nightfall, far past the usual time, her mother
beat her with the stick. The girl did not comprehend her
mother's shrill rants – all she knew was pain.

'Where were you?' her mother screamed. 'Did you want
to bring shame upon us? Where were you?' The mute stared
at her mother with a blank look tinged with compassion,
or something else, perhaps loss . . . forgiveness . . . entreaty?
From then on, the mother locked the door at night so she
couldn't escape, but it was no use.

8

The longing summoned her. The mute's window reflected
streetlights and the headlamps of early morning cars long
before it was possible to distinguish squares and rectangles
from the black of night. As she pressed her elbows on the

sill to get a better view of the street below, tufts of hair fell down around her shoulders, framing her beautiful face. Moist, virgin morning air filled her lungs. Life's secrets passed through her mouth to her cheeks. She took in another gulp of air. For the first time in a long while, she smiled. As if to commemorate this event, her mother forgot to beat her. The morning breezes infiltrated the opening of her dress just under her throat. As she crossed the secret void, her breasts pinched her, infusing her perfect body with sparks of sensation. She drew her arms out wide, as if to protect the secret of her unknown love.

The sun began to soften. The mute climbed the stairs to look out from the roof, then set out. Pausing by the waterfall for a moment, she crossed to a clearing, where she lay in the moist shadow of the palm. A lattice of palm fronds filtered the sun to create a waterfall of light. A bird watched the waving lines of light from the edge of the rocky basin, gilded with bits of shell. The bird took two sips of water, then, flying off, gave the surplus to the sky. A drip of magic water fell into the clear pond, distorting its surface with little wavelets. She imagined this was the same bird she had returned to its nest a few months before. When she returned to the house, her mother scolded her. The mute went to her room and closed the door.

From her window she saw a flock of laughing city girls head towards the sea. She trailed them from afar. She watched them as they played in the open waves, then surrendered their bodies to the waterfall. The next day, again she followed them. The mute played the voyeur, watching as water poured upon human meat, as a cool breeze caressed the *houries'* radiant bodies, as goosebumps rose upon bodies redolent with the fragrance of rock–flower.

As the girls laughed and joked with one another, as they became more and more aroused, that old, dreaded feeling rose in her chest. Catching sight of the mute, they beckoned from afar. 'Come closer!' they shouted. The young girl clung to the roots of the naked tree, pointing to a gull swimming through layers of the void above, as her mother's voice dogged her relentlessly: 'You will have sons.'

The noise she produced now was more violent than that which escaped from her chest the day she stumbled upon a fisherman with a city girl in the shadows of the forest. She had been listening to the chattering of the sparrows in the midday heat when she saw two bodies approach, then slam together in a silent frenzy. It was almost as if they were enveloped by a halo of light. As he removed his belt, she could see the girl's face was flushed red, her hair all over the place. The girl guided the fisherman's large hand to loosen the knot of her dress, as he grabbed her breasts. After an instant she saw what was for her a strange sight: mud clinging to mud, moistened with sweat and pain. From her eyrie the mute imagined she saw an invisible ghost exit the girl's body, then disappear into the darkness. Then the girl pulled her clothes back on.

The mute's frightened eyes followed her mother, as she moved manically from one household chore to the next. Her anxiety propelled her to the land of chrysanthemums. The sun disappeared behind the green-wrapped hill, its absence spreading a long, cold shadow. The late afternoon twitter subsided. Calmer now, she sat in place until the moon's disc rose and projected itself onto the centre of the clear lake. Swarms of nocturnal insects rose with the heat that rose from the ground. Night crawlers rustled; sleeping birds fidgeted in their concealed nests. Glancing back and forth between the naked trees and the water, the mute was suddenly inspired to take off her clothes. As morning approached, the twittering of birds grew and the air bore a lemony scent. When she finally returned home, she could see a beating in her mother's angry eyes.

9

Is it a voice, or a sobbing she hears?

In the wee hours, the mute wakes suddenly. She feels the *jinn* whispering to her.[35]

Is it a voice or a sobbing? She is far from the forest, the mountain and the meadow, so what is this? What overwhelming grief permeates her body and spirit? The strange longing festers in her gut. It is a craving she can't sate. She goes out to the dark forest, where the sparrows and the pigeons hover.

Is it a voice or a sobbing?

Casting a wary eye at the rough sea, the mute crouches in a current of cold water. The water inundates her. As she loosens her head cover, brilliant locks of hair fall onto her back. She finds herself crying. Piece after piece of clothes she removes, until her earthen bosom is completely bare. The stream carries one last bit of clothing off to the sea, leaving her completely naked, her round buttocks shining like the crescent moon. A cold breeze blows. The moist grass shivers. Standing with a glazed expression on her face, the mute draws her legs together. The nocturnal *jinn* flap above her head, a sad flapping, as the calm water engulfs her. She doesn't feel a thing – neither shame nor cold, only a novel numbness.

The wind blows against her in stronger bursts, and the waves' whispers crescendo in a violent slapping. The sparrows are busy in the darkness above. They observe the tense, hard body below as pockets of cold water collide with it. The mute feels invigorated. After a preface of frightful screeches, the birds converse in their secret language. On her wet lips flash dawn's early light. She feels the numbness grow, all the while sensing the silent, diminutive creatures observing her from the branches above. The sea ceases its raging. The spring continues to pour its water over the mute's naked, aching body, washing away traces of dirt and clay. She hears the hidden river running through the mountain's depths.

The blood that runs in the mute's veins finally dislodges bits of a universal secret: the story of the first beginning and the last end is there before her. Imagining luminous tears pouring out from the eye-sockets of the perplexed birds, she surrenders herself to the spray. She imagines the avian twittering transformed into a frightful reproach: tales of worldly horrors, of painful journey – the wretchedness of the desert. The exile that separates the first instant of life and return to the realm of light. The birds spell out their goodbyes, as the Mute responds to the ringing in her depths. There would be no relief before she rid herself of her mud and sludge casing, she thinks to herself. It would be far better if she completed the last segment of her journey naked, than remain trapped in a shell reeking of an atrocious crime, of an ugliness infused with desolation and loss.

Is it a voice she hears, or a sobbing?

The mute climbs the smooth rocks that rise to the spring's source. She approaches the eye. The current becomes stronger. She clings to the rocks, waiting for a chance to plunge her head into the depths of the spring. The morning light falls around her like silver dust. The water sparkles, and she feels an imminent peace. Pushing her head further forward, she manages to squeeze herself into the pit of the spring's source, where the raging current wraps her like a warm blanket. It pulls her torso into the watery cave, which readily consumes her. On the other side, the fields of veiled paradise are laid out before her. Very soon, the city would suffer the mute's disappearance, for on this day, the spring ran dry.

Derna

In his book *Sahaari Derna*, Dr. Mohammed Mufti describes Derna as the Libyan city that arouses the most passion, perhaps for its place in imagination as the spot 'closest to heaven and paradise'.[36] Derna is actually five separate villages located a short distance from one another: Medina Al-Mushayad (meaning 'the high, lofty') is located on part of the mountain foothills and is the main agglomeration; Medinat Al-Magharat (named for a well located in the town's centre) sits a bit higher up to the west; Qareat Al Jabiliya is the portion nearest the sea; Abu Mansour Al Fawqani and Abu Mansour Al Tahtani are split by a wadi that overflows in the winter. Abdullah Ali Al-Gazal describes this geographical feature in *The Mute*: 'From the depths of the sea a broad tongue of water penetrates the city, seeming almost to break the place in two – that is, if a dry projection didn't block the way decisively, making way for a stretch of clay that widens bit by bit until it turns to scrub'. Williams describes Derna port, opposite the villages above, as 'ugly and not much used these days'.[37] Pacho mentions that the harbour is marked by an ample entrance, but is unprotected, so ships rarely lay anchor except during summer.[38] As with Benghazi and Algiers, and other spots along the North African coast, Derna is a stopover for migratory birds and all manner of wildlife, including sea turtles.

Derna: past and present

Mufti describes a kind of miraculous entry to Derna from the west: one's first impression is of a distinctive façade, different from that of any other Libyan city. 'The way is spread before you, an asphalt threat between the mountains and the sea . . . you feel like you're at the gates of Nice . . . or Monte Catini . . . or Beirut or Greece.' The surrounding orchards are full of all manner of fruits and vegetables: figs, peaches, pomegranates, apples and oranges. Onions, olives, tomatoes, large gourds and fragrant plants grow in the spaces underneath the citrus groves. The young traveller Jean-Raimond Pacho, was so impressed with this bounty in the early 1800s, he mused that at times he felt he was back in Provence: 'Dernawi houses have hanging gardens; grapes dangle from trellises that allow inhabitants to grab fruit in summer without having to leave their houses.' The feeling of uniqueness, Mufti says, disappears as one proceeds along barren corniche: 'The invasion of stone and cement does not leave except a few bushes here and a spot of greenery – all that's remained of years past . . .'[39] Williams, writing close to half a century before Mufti, has this to say about the same stretch: 'The last ten miles for Derna was absolute desert in summer, so that the sight of the palms and gardens of Derna made a satisfactory journey's end. In immediate approach, however, the town is ugly and untidy and the hills around it gaunt and repellent, with the road rising

obliquely Eastwards towards Tobruk and Egypt, a dark
ribbon in bare lion-coloured rock.'[10]

The progression of snapshots of Derna offered by Pacho,
Williams and Mufti underscores the malaise that has slowly
overtaken Benghazi and Derna alike.[41] Williams describes
the centre of the town in the 1960s as 'having character,'
a place 'where one can enjoy ice cream and lemonade and
beer in a shaded square'.[42] In 2003, Mufti writes 'today the
mosque straddles the central square – for the shops that
had been between it and the square had been destroyed.
[The mosque] and the cafe add a certain life to the place.'[43]
In 2006, a passer-by described the square as empty, with
the exception of official buildings and the Jebel Ahdar
(Green Mountain) Hotel, hidden behind a thicket.

In the 1940s, a very large number of Libya's best
teachers, professors and writers called Derna home. But
why is it that Derna – and by extension Cyrenaica,
Benghazi and the East – produced so much of Libya's
literary talent? The assertion is not in contention, and
various authors have speculated about its cause. Was Derna's
influence on Libya's early intellectual history due to the
proximity of Cairo's Al-Azhar University, the most pres-
tigious institution of scholarship in the Muslim world, or
the fact that so many of the latter's alumni settled here?
Was it due to the prevalence of chapters of the Sanussi
religious orders, which rode the backs of camels with
traders to spread Islamic teachings into deepest Africa?
Mufti believes the best explanation may be the fact that
large families, faced with dwindling land-shares, pushed
their children to acquire skills that might allow them to
make a living doing something other than farming. Some
of Derna's reputation for scholarship is related to policies

of 'outsiders' – whether the Turks or the Italians – who, while much vilified, were responsible for creating primary and secondary schools at the beginning of the twentieth century.

Stories from the South

Jalo

Mizda

Ghadames

Soluq

Sadiq Neihoum

The Sultan's Flotilla

('An Markab As-Sultan)

Translated by Ethan Chorin

In ages of old, Jalo was a port city. People called it the 'Jewel of the Seas'. Its waters teemed with the ships of pirates and traders. Caravans arrived at Jalo laden with elephant tusk; its markets were replete with spices, slaves, sandalwood – even Chinese porcelain. All of the people of Jalo lived like sultans, except the Sultan himself, who was condemned to endure a bizarre sort of apocalypse, a living nightmare so awful he couldn't bear to rest his head on his pillow or close his eyes at any time of day or night, for fear of dreaming of a certain black dog.

The dog was a hideous sight: putrid, offensive, with gouged-out eyes. Invariably it appeared to the Sultan above the hills of dry sand spread behind Jalo's ramparts. It reared its ugly head, howling in such a crazed state that the hills themselves appeared to drown in its odious inhalations. Upon some unknown cue, the black dog lunged at the bare heels of the Sultan, who then ran for his life, crossing parched sandy hills before vaulting himself over the walls of Jalo, whereupon he was then forced to jump over vine trellises and row upon row of houses. In the Sultan's dream, the enemy chased him as far as his marble castle, itself encased by ten iron walls.

In the Sultan's early dreams, the outermost wall kept the black dog at bay. Then on one New Year's Day it reappeared, and broke through the first wall. Exactly a year later the black dog returned and barrelled through the second wall. The Sultan watched all of this from his bed in a state of abject terror, his eyes wide open.

The meaning of the Sultan's dream eluded every last wise man of Jalo. They came to the palace, one after the other. Some branded the Sultan's head, others muttered incantations and created all manner of talismans, all to no avail. None was able to relieve the desperate Sultan, who by this time had lost all desire to sleep, took up drinking by night and by day staggered through his marble palace in a state of exhaustion. On the fourth New Year's Day, the Sultan fell to the ground in a drunken stupor, dreaming of the black dog that howled above the parched hills. Screaming in fright, he awoke and summoned the last of the long line of wise men that had requested an audience with him. He took it upon himself to cut this man's head off personally, then retired to his room to bemoan his wretched fate.

On that same day, there arrived to Jalo two strangers. One was a well-known *Fagih*,[44] the other, a lame farmer. The Fagih entered the city on a white mule from the Western gate; the farmer entered from the Eastern gate. The two met in the middle of a square on the road to the Sultan's marble castle. Thinking at first the farmer was from Jalo, the Fagih stopped to ask him the way. Then he noticed the man was barefoot, and that his lameness was of such severity that he bent at the middle. Moreover, the farmer was carrying with him nothing more than a sack of date pits. Concluding the person before him was in fact a foreign beggar not worthy of his attention, the Fagih struck him with the belly of his white mule, which he then steered at a clip towards the Sultan's palace.

At the palace, the Fagih presented himself to the Sultan, bade him long life, then said: 'Keep in mind, ya Mawlai,[45] nothing disgraces the wise man more than withholding good advice from his lord and master. Since the ages it has been said that wisdom is the chief of all virtues, and that the word of a judicious wise man is sharper than the sword.' An agitated Sultan began to bite his nails. He had gotten used to indulging this bad habit before the interminable line of strangers that came from near and far to offer their services. In fact, he became so engrossed by this activity that the diwan decided to hire His Majesty a slave especially to chew his nails. The slave was not present just then, unfortunately, so the Sultan could do nothing but chew them himself.

The Fagih then resumed his speech:

'Ya Mawlai, I have heard about your unhappy lifestyle and this dream of a black dog. So I consulted the ancient books, and looked up the wisdom of the righteous forefathers. I became one with the advice of the keepers of the most great secrets until such a time as I understood the root of your illness and its cure. With God's permission, ya Mawlai, in my hand is your cure, your health and your happiness . . .'

The Sultan took a moment's break from his nail chewing and said, matter of factly:

'O respected one, O man of great learning. I have heard this line a thousand times, and I have severed the heads of a thousand Fagihs. I have done this to the point where I am thoroughly sick of listening to Fagihs and cutting off heads. Do not let the devil deceive you, for I will cut off your head as well, if you brand my scalp in vain.'

The Fagih kneeled between the outstretched hands of the Sultan and replied:

'Not all that glitters is gold, ya Mawlai, and not everyone who wears a turban has the ability to cure a Sultan. I did not cross the wadis and deserts separating Jalo from the faraway kingdom of Zanzibar in order to brand your head. I came but to grant you a piece of advice and good consultation. I came to tell you that the black dog that you see in your dreams, ya Mawlai, is a warning of an apocalypse sent to you by The Great Destroyer.[46] I have come to warn you from a coming catastrophe, a catastrophe manifest in your unconscious . . .'

The Sultan bent forward in astonishment to ask,

'What catastrophe?'

The Fagih remained silent for an instant, then raised his head to speak:

'Mawlai, we have read in the books of our wise and learned forefathers that Jalo will be destroyed at some point past its Golden Age. God will send upon the town a searing wind from a blast furnace, a scorching hellion that will train through Jalo for a period of seven days and seven nights. Not a single plant will remain breathing, for they will have all perished, their roots shrivelled up in the clay. There will not remain on the vine trellises a single grape, nor a single apple in the orchards. All that will be left is a dust-swept, barren wasteland. There will be no more dwellings in Jalo, and God help whatever remains. Everlasting God be praised.'

The Sultan cupped his mouth with his hand in horror, then said after a moment,

'When will this happen, exactly, O learned one?'

'After seven years,' said the Fagih, coolly.'. . .After seven years, when the black dog breaches the wall and arrives to nip at your heels. Henceforth, you will not see the black dog except once each New Year's Day.'

The Sultan started at this news.

'Only once each new year? Only one time, you are sure of it?'

The Fagih confirmed it:

'Yes, Mawlai. The black dog will appear only to mark the passage of years, and on the seventh year it will break through the seventh wall, ready to bite your heels. That, ya Mawlai, will be the bite of misery and wretchedness that marks the vicissitudes of time.'

The Sultan interrupted the Fagih yet again:

'And what would you recommend us to do, ya honoured Fagih?'

The Fagih raised his hand to his head, kissed the ground between the hands of the Sultan and then said firmly,

'The idea and the wisdom are yours to offer, my lord.' After a short moment, he continued. 'However, Mawlai, I have read in the books of the sage forefathers and listened to the words of the great keepers of secrets, all of which indicate that Jalo will be destroyed from top to bottom. They say that God will forgive the city its sins and transgressions with the help of a decent man vested with a certain trust. Jalo will again be populous, and the caravans will come again on schedule. Its markets will once more bustle with slaves and spices. My opinion, ya Mawlai, is that you should make for yourself, your subjects and your army a thousand boats, as preparation for whatever contingency. When by the order of God the apocalypse arrives, you will load these ships with your luggage and possessions and sail out onto the wide sea, far from the wind and the heat, until the days of ghibli and despair pass. you will then return to your city, which will celebrate its time-honoured glory by rebuilding.'

The Sultan homed in on one point:

'And this decent man, ya honoured Fagih, this man in whose heart trust settles, the man who is destined to save the Sultan from the searing wind – where is this man now?'

The Fagih bowed his head humbly for an instant, then said matter-of-factly:

'Ya Mawlai, we have read in the books of the sage forefathers and heard from the great guardians of secrets that this man will arrive in Jalo seven years before the calamity. Consider in your eminent wisdom who that might be.'

From that moment, the Sultan understood the implication of the Fagih's words – that *he* was this man, in the flesh and blood. The Sultan did not allow himself to believe it, however, until he had fully investigated the truth behind the Fagih's words.

The Sultan retired to bed, instructing his servant to wake him if it were obvious he had begun to dream the odious black-dog dream. The sultan did not that night dream of the black dog. Rather, he slept the remainder of the day a heavy sleep, a sleep so profound it kept him in bed through the following day. When the Sultan finally awoke, he was so pleased that he summoned the Fagih, clasped him close between his arms, then kissed him between his eyes. So happy was he that he even married the Fagih to his daughter. As the Fagih sat beside him in a seat of honour, the Sultan announced to the people of Jalo the news. He asked them to begin building a flotilla. All of this is what ensued after a stranger arrived through the Western gate on a white mule.

Meanwhile, the lame stranger with the bag of date pits hadn't budged from the place where the Fagih struck him with the belly of his white mule. He lingered there until late in the afternoon, when he finally managed to pull himself together to gather up the dates, most of which had scattered on the ground. The lame stranger spat on the people of Jalo, then limped up to the parched, sandy hills, whose summit he managed to reach overnight. Once he'd arrived at the tops of those hills he did not sleep, but began immediately digging in the sand with his finger-nails and pouring date pits into the resulting holes. The next morning the lame stranger dug a well, and made himself a bucket from his sack. He then proceeded to carry water in this bucket to the palm groves, which were, of course, still just shrivelled pits sitting in sand. The lame stranger heard of the Sultan's command, and from his little sandy hill he observed the people of Jalo scurrying about in every direction, carrying planks of wood and carpentry tools. He saw them cut the material crafted for the sails, and work on building the boats, but he did not go to work with them.

News reached Amir Al-Haras[47] that one of the inhabitants of Jalo had been blithely ignoring the Sultan's order. With a hundred of his best horsemen, the Amir rode up those parched hills of sand, where he found the lame stranger. He stripped the shirt off his back and whipped him a hundred times. He then ordered the stranger to prepare himself to return to Jalo to work on the Sultan's flotilla, but the stranger paid no attention. Despite the lashing he had just received, he simply slipped his shirt back on and returned to the task of carrying water from the well and pouring it onto the palm orchards.

Amir al-Haras returned the next day and whipped him with yet another hundred lashes, before commanding him to return to Jalo to work on the Sultan's boats. The lame stranger simply donned his shirt once more, and returned to the work of carrying water from the well and pouring it over the palm orchards-to-be. On the third day the Amir visited him and set about throttling him, a great anger in his eyes.

'I will beat you to death, you crippled stranger. What gives you the right to countermand an order from the Sultan?'

And the lame stranger said simply,

'I do not want to work on the Sultan's boats, O Amir al-Haras. I am just a farmer, I know no calling other than the cultivation of palms.'

The soldiers traded quizzical looks; Amir al-Haras opened his arms in an uncomprehending gesture.

'What is this "palm" of which you speak, O lame stranger?'

For indeed, not a soul in Jalo knew what a palm tree was, having never seen one. From top to bottom, there was a not a single palm tree in all of Jalo. The lame stranger bent forward for a moment, lifted his head, averted his eyes from the glare of the sun, and said:

'The palms, O Amir, are brides whose earrings are made of ruby. Their crowns are fashioned from corundum that sprouts from the depths of the earth. They grow to the height of the clouds, so that those who are parched by thirst may see them, drink their fill and find their way home.'

When they heard the lame stranger's words, the soldiers laughed so hard they almost fell from their saddles. Amir al-Haras shook his head as he observed the lame stranger resume carrying and pouring water. He ordered his soldiers back in the direction of Jalo, and called out,

'Let this pig alone, as he is possessed by one of the devils. It is not worth the effort to burn his skin with a whip.' On the Amir's mind was the fact that, having once whipped a man similarly possessed, his son died the next day.

So a year passed, with Jalo's people working on the Sultan's flotilla. A second year passed, but the work was still not finished. The Sultan had been forced to press-gang most of Jalo's workers, and the orchards and vine trellises were totally neglected. Even the traders locked their shops shut, so they might work on the flotilla. The Fagih himself oversaw the massive effort, urging on the carpenters and boat-smiths with passages from the sura of Noah. The third year passed, then the fourth. Slowly but surely, one vessel after another sailed out from the port of Jalo.

The inhabitants of Jalo that evening observed the spectacle unfold. The lame stranger was also a witness, but he did not care for these large boats. He spent most of his time on top of the parched, sandy hills, where there was to be found but one well, from which he constantly brought water to his palm nurseries in a bucket he had made from his sack. The palms began to rise from the ground, unfolding massive fronds over the high hills. Not one of the citizens of Jalo saw any of these trees, so busy were they with work on the Sultan's flotilla. The fifth year passed, then the sixth, and by now most of the boats had risen in the port of Jalo. The Sultan's daughter bore the Fagih six children. At the end of the seventh year, she bore him one more son. It was then that the Sultan dreamed again of the black dog. He looked on as the dog broke through the final wall and came barrelling down upon him with gouged-out eyes to bite his heels with its poisonous tooth. The Sultan shouted out from his dream, his eyes wide with terror. He immediately summoned the Fagih, who issued the signal for the exodus to begin. The Sultan's flotilla sailed quickly from the port of Jalo, spreading its sails against the blue sky like a thousand white-winged hawks. The sight prompted the lame stranger to stop and watch in amazement from the heights of his sandy hills. He was now alone in Jalo.

Listen well, children. Listen, all you little men, as you stand above each sandy, parched hill watching the Sultan's flotilla. There came the scalding wind, as the Fagih had foretold, and whipped the streets of Jalo for seven days and seven nights. As the Fagih prophesied, afterward not a single grape remained on the vine trellises, nor a single apple in the orchards. Nothing was left but a barren, wind-blown wasteland. The sea itself dried up and retreated from Jalo, leaving the Sultan's flotilla to settle on the sand dunes.

Listen well, children. After seven days and seven nights, the wind abated, as the Fagih had said it would. Jalo was decimated. God did then forgive it its sins and transgressions, and the caravans did return, and the souks buzzed anew with trade in slaves and spices, all as the Fagih said they would. But the Sultan did not return, for the ships could not sail on the surface of the desert. *Know thee then well: if you turn your back on Jalo, Jalo will turn its back on you.*

Source: Qisas Atfal, Tala Books/ Arab Diffusion Company, Libya, 2002 reprint

Jalo: in Search of the Sultan's Flotilla

Where is Jalo?

There are many in Libya who themselves have no idea. Where does the name come from? This is also unclear. A web search produces the following bits of basic, random and wholly irrelevant information: on the face of the Earth, Jalo sits at Latitude 29° 01° N, Longitude 021° 34° E, at an elevation of 197 feet. It is approximately ninety-six kilometres from the city of Ajdabiyia, which itself is a bit more than 200 kilometres south of the eastern port city of Benghazi. Apparently, a family from Norway named their dog, a flat-coated retriever, Jalo, as there is an extensive website dedicated to the exploits of Jalo the dog from Norway. Those most likely to know where Jalo is – apart from those who once lived there or live near there – are the oil hands, for its proximity to petroleum-bearing Concession 102, linked by pipeline across the desert in 1967 to the northern port of Zweitina.[48] Libya's mining law no. 25 of 1955 divvied up the country into four areas. The oases of Jalo belonged to the third set, which included Aujela, Tazerbo and Kufra. Jalo was prime viewing ground for the 2006 solar eclipse. Apparently there are those searching for love in Jalo, as testified by a lone posting on the Internet, under the title 'Women Searching for Men': 'I am a 19-year-old woman searching for men in Jalo'. In a town of less than 10,000 people, where everyone knows everyone else, one has to wonder. . .

Of the Westerners who have written about Jalo, perhaps the best known of a very small and relatively obscure list is Rosita Forbes, whose *Secret of the Sahara: Kufara* documents a trek she made by air, car and camel in 1921 from the port city of Benghazi to the dangerous southern oases of Kufara (Kufra). The architect of the trip was Ahmed Hassanein Bey, a prominent Egyptian diplomat and advisor to King Farouk. In Michael Haag's introduction to *The Lost Oases*, Bey's newly republished account of a subsequent trip further south to Kufra, he notes that Forbes 'represented herself as the sole organizer and driving force behind the expedition, and described Hassanein in terms that suggested he was nothing more than her hired servant.'[49] Jalo is and has been primarily a community of merchants, who live and have lived on the transit trade linking Sudan and the Cyrenaican ports. Hassanein descibes Jalo's significance as a trading centre in the late 1800s thus:

'The Desert is a sea,' Said El Bishari, a prominent chieftain of the Majabra Tribe, and, 'Jalo is its port.' It was at the height of its importance something like thirty years ago, when El Madhi maintained the Sanussi capital at Kufra. In those days caravans of two or three hundred camels came and went between Jalo and the south each week, but when I was there the traffic had shrunk to less than a tent of that. In summer, however, it is swollen by the demands of the date harvest.

Getting There
As of early spring 2006, all my prior plans to reach Jalo had failed. My time in Libya was running out, and soon

the heat would start to become a factor – daytime temperatures in the Libyan desert could easily top 140 degrees Fahrenheit. Even if the sun and the moon had not aligned (for us, at least – thousands of visitors descended into Jalo and environs to view the solar eclipse on 29 March), it looked as though the weekend of 28 May was going to be my last chance, and, serendipitously, a date Basem might make. Preparations for his upcoming marriage were taking up more and more of his time. I very much wanted him to come, as I saw Jalo as a symbolic marker on a project we had embarked on together.

On 24 May, I caught the weekly Afriquiya flight from Tripoli to Benghazi. The next morning Basem picked me up from the Tibesti Hotel and we set out for the Southern desert in a Mercedes Vito, its seats still covered in plastic wrap. Our driver was in his mid-thirties, and was to take us on the four-and-a-half-hour drive south, through the trucking hub of Ajdabiya, which looks like any one of a thousand non-descript towns in Tripoli. Leaving Ajdabiya, the scenery immediately turns yellow. Sand and dust as far as the eye can see. Two hundred kilometres further south, a few palm trees come into view, followed by a modest depression positively thick with them. Low fences woven from dead fronds mark the boundaries of nurseries, which contain hundreds, if not thousands, of thick brownish-black palm sprigs, which seemed to resemble great, magnified stubble on a yellow cheek. This is the town of Aujela, one of the three oases that draw from the same underground aquifer. Fifteen kilometres ahead lies the town of Jalo, which, for all our fuss, arrived without making much of an impression.

'Our dreams are to work for an oil company or to get a fellowship out of here,' said the local zoning inspector.

'Are the American oil companies really coming?' asked another. The American oil company Esso (today's Exxon) took many from these villages in the late 1960s and trained them to be well operators and engineers.

Jalo only superficially resembles the place Neihoum describes in *The Sultan's Flotilla*. Of course, this isn't a port city – far from it. Presumably the plot developed from a prosaic interpretation of Jalo's sobriquet 'Port of the Desert', a reference to its role in the last centuries as a major entrepôt for goods from Darfur and Wadai. According to Hassanein Bey, in the late 1800s, two to three hundred camels came and went each week.[50]

There are palm trees, for sure. Everywhere. I asked one of our hosts about the 'parched, sandy hills' of the Sultan's flotilla.

'What? There are no hills here,' came the response. 'The nearest thing to hills are eighty kilometres away.'

In Jalo, the Libyan government set aside large plots of land for palm cultivation. Apparently, Anyone who wants a palm farm can have a plot and a loan, assuming they are willing to invest the effort to maintain it. In addition to palms, the best tomatoes in Libya are allegedly grown here.

Within a half hour, we had met arguably the most important man in town, the director of a multi-year effort to plant more than a million new palm trees in Jalo. Our guide, an architect, wasn't an expert in palms, but it seems that growing up in Jalo, everyone had more than a passing knowledge of their care and feeding. The palms are all connected to what seemed an elaborate and reasonably modern irrigation system. Our hosts, in time-honoured tradition, insisted we linger over lunch.

Ten minutes after we bade Jalo goodbye, we passed a

lone figure on the shoulder of the road. The driver slowed
and rolled down his window to speak with the man. 'Would
it be okay if we give my cousin a lift to Adjdabia?' he asked
in Arabic. Two hours on, I was lost in some thought or
other; the driver and his cousin were talking in the front
cab. Basem was completely asleep on the back of the seats
behind me. Gradually, I became aware that the front-seat
conversation was taking on urgent tones.

'What's the problem?' I asked the driver.

'Look ahead,' he said. 'Sand drifts.'

'That's a problem?' I asked.

'Could be,' the driver replied.

Salem, the driver, was from Derna, a very green place,
fanned by sea breezes. What did Salem know of sandstorms?
I thought, letting a bit of paranoia get to me.

'He's doing the right thing,' Basem said, brushing sleep
from his eyes. 'He's got himself behind a large truck.'

Had we read Hassanein's account prior to this trip, we
might have noted the chapter entitled 'Sandstorms on the
way to Jalo'. Bey notes that, according to local lore, a sandstorm at the start of a journey is a good omen. He continues
to speculate that the superstition was born from necessity
more than correlation with good luck, for sandstorms are
ubiquitous out here. Using the same phrase that guides
have undoubtedly used endless times over the ages to
comfort themselves, tourists and travellers alike, Salem told
us not to worry:

'Desert sands rise in the late afternoon, and settle in
the evening.'

'*Keep going, keep going*, no use in hanging around here.
Keep going until we can move no longer,' Basem pressed.
The driver of the truck in front of us, while he slowed

down, apparently came to the same conclusion. Soon, the number of trucks passing us in the opposite direction dwindled to nothing. Markers alongside the road counted off kilometres from Adjdabia, from 1 to 60.

'We haven't reach the sixty-kilometre mark yet,' Salem said.

Sixty kilometres from Adjdabia is sixty kilometres from a place that is only a hundred kilometres from a place we knew well. By this logic, the 60-kilometre mark seemed a good place to be.

I was mildly comforted by the fact that I'd never heard of camels being caught in sandstorms and transported miles away, à la Dorothy in *The Wizard of Oz*.[51] Then I remembered that Yasser Arafat's plane had gone down in a Libyan sandstorm, in April, 1992. That was near the town of Al-Sarra, south of Kufra. For days, it was not known if he lived or perished. It is interesting to speculate how the map of the Middle East, and the course of the Arab-Israeli relations might have been different, if fate had been less kind to Arafat, or Arafat had taken a different message from his near-death experience. For this was just before the failed negotiations known as the 'Oslo process', which nearly became a major turning point in Israeli-Palestinian relations. What the Libyans claim are the remains of Arafat's plane were, in macabre fashion, exhibited in the Palestinian pavilion at the annual Tripoli Fair.[52] Finally, we spied the sixty-kilometre mark, whereupon I abandoned concern and returned to my book. Shortly thereafter the sun poked out from the haze and we drove into town.

Ahmed Ibrahim Fagih

The Locusts

(Al-Jarad)

Translated by Ethan Chorin

In the village that follows a never-changing script, things are today exactly as they were yesterday, the day before, and last year. Over there, one of the villagers, dutifully executing his daily chores. He's drawing water from the well using a bucket raised by a beast of burden. Now he's tossing daily feed to his livestock. Now he's moving back and forth with an ox, as it cuts a furrow in the ground. From the mountains through which so many tomorrows pass floats a sweet, but unremarkable tune. It's Omran, singing as he coaxes his ox forward. He doesn't hit the animal with his stick, heavens no; he just urges it cheerfully along a path that can't be more than five metres long. Over there, you can see Mabrouk, axe in hand, sweat dripping from his broad brow. Hoeing in his small garden has made him short of breath. And there – see? Haj Salim is tilling his field, rippling with blades of wheat and barley. What's he doing, exactly? Ah, he's evicting a wayward donkey from his premises. Wait, no, he's shouting at a herd of sheep. Now he's throwing stones at a flock of sparrows that has settled in some corner of the field.

Sometimes you can find Haj Salim setting a trap where

he's found traces of fox or jackal feet, evidence of a nocturnal raid on the chicken pen.

Like clockwork, the villagers move to and fro as they go about their usual tasks. The sheep herder, poor fellow, he's lost his voice amongst the incessant bleating of his charges; baaa . . . baaa . . . Another hauls up with his forearms as he straddles one of the wells, heaving water up into stone troughs that camels drain with loud slurping noises. In short, until that very evening, everything in the village was quiet as usual.

Suddenly (of all the rare things in this village, the rarest of all was something worthy of being called 'sudden' or 'surprising') a man comes running, his voice accented with fear.

'Come, everyone, come!' he shrieks, crying out a message that makes the skin crawl: locusts are at the gates of their small village! The man's cries instantaneously transform the idyllic scene, turning the villagers into a group of mad people who dart around like chickens with their heads cut off. Faces betray the universal feeling that a monstrous creature is lurking at every corner, at every bend in the road and under the roots of every tree. Some run to their fields and their orchards and just stare, their eyes filled with longing, certain that tomorrow will bring an end to it all. Soon, all that will remain are memories. Haj Salim is among them. This is the first time he looks out over the birds landing in his field and does not throw stones at them, or spots trespassing ewes and does not bark them away in an excited voice.

The news has a paralyzing effect. Nothing is on anyone's mind but locusts. For once, the sheikhs' wagging tongues stop telling interminable stories. The women lingering in front of the village infirmary and those alongside the well filling their water jugs forget their gossip about other women, giving their targets a rest from tongue-lashing. Everyone's thoughts are caught up in the terrible ghoul branded with the name of destruction: locusts . . . locusts. Tomorrow the insects will begin their invasion of the little village. Slashing and burning, the creatures will strip the green coats from the trees, take from them luxurious shade and leave behind only dead, withered sticks. Absconding with morsels of trees and plantations, the locusts will steal food from the mouths of Haj Salim, from the members of Mabrouk's family, from the sons of Omran and everyone else in the village. No doubt about it, they would turn every green inch of land into a barren wasteland.

In the village, many events bring people together: a death, or when the village police arrest a passer-by on charges of some crime, or an old woman's bout of lunacy. Before tonight, the village in its long history had never seen a force so powerful as to graft the villagers' individual and collective fates together into a single destiny. It was plain in people's looks, and in the way they spoke, that they were distraught. As always happened when danger knocked at the village gate, the men felt the instinct to assemble. Abdul Nabi raised his voice to deliver the evening call to prayer:

'Come . . . come all you farmers . . . men of the village . . . hurry!'

They ran to the mosque, which was only crowded on two sorts of occasions: when the village faced a danger, or during the 'eid. Everyone was now assembled, huddled in a single mass. Frustrated and angry, at times groups found themselves speaking in unison. There was profound sadness in the air. Blue-vein-spotted hands flapped in anxious gestures.

A couple of the sheikhs indulged themselves, relating ancient accounts of an invasion that had transformed that village, so proud of the gentle-heartedness of its denizens, its natural beauty and bride-like freshness, into a graveyard over which the owl squawked an obituary. A third sheikh interjected with a melodramatic account of a locust-ambush on ten men camping at night in a ravine. The locusts set upon them while they were sleeping; in the morning there remained not a trace.

'O brothers, even the bones . . .' said the sheikh, pausing for emphasis, 'even the bones the locusts ate!'

At that moment, Fagih Misbah came forth to speak in his inimitable fashion. He raised his hands as if to grab a bolt of lightning from the heavens, then opened his eyes crazy-wide, as he always did when invoking Shartookh and Shabrookh and the other creatures they call 'My Friends, the Kings of the Djinn'. Creating a full-blown spectacle, he scattered drool and shook his thick white beard, invoking the will of Allah the Merciful, along with past prophecies about two great swarms of locusts sent to eat men and women and children alike. 'The locusts', the fagih shouted, 'will beset animals, trees, castles – even pieces of metal!'

All of these frightful stories about locusts; the dangers of locusts . . . locusts . . . locusts . . . With the holy men standing there with angry, bronzed faces, the crowd felt in their hearts the looming disaster. The sheikhs' talk had infused their core with a great odium. They felt now as if nothing could compare with this thing called locust: not death, not plague, not any other terrestrial catastrophe. An old man, caught up in the throes of an emotion that chilled

those around him to the bone, suddenly called out for
divine mercy: 'Your grace, O Lord! Your forgiveness!'

There followed another voice, shot through with intensity: 'What is in store for us now, my friends?'

And then another . . . 'Yes, what do we do now?'

And all of a sudden there was a torrent of voices, a
cacophony of floating question marks. Heads twisted in
confusion. A mantra of distraction.

'What to do? What to do? What to do?'

After a while, the first thing that resembled a suggestion
emerged from the lips of Fagih Misbah, who insisted there
was no other option: they must all go to the tomb of Sidi
Abu Kindil, illuminate for him candles, burn *jawa* incense,
loban and *fasukh*[53] – and entreat him to intervene with Allah
to keep this danger at bay, so that they might all return to
their houses to sleep in peace.

'Sidi Abu Kindil will not disappoint,' Misbah promised.
'He will keep the locusts from the path of the village . . .'

Once the confusion settled and the villagers could begin
to focus on the problem, Fagih Misbah's proposition was
quickly lost in a jumble of other suggestions. Among those
offering alternatives was Omran, bound to be taken seriously
for he was in his forties, meaning that he had surpassed the
age of recklessness, and hadn't yet made it to the age of
feeblemindedness. Omran's suggestion was that the villagers
make fires in different places around the village. Perhaps, he
reasoned, the locusts would change course once they saw
the smoke. Since no one could see why this wouldn't just
create a temporary diversion, many craned their necks and
traded looks, searching for better ideas. Defending his original idea, Omran waved his fist and shook his head in anger.

Mabrouk remained silent, head down, his body shaking

uncomfortably as if he were sitting on top of a village of ants. He was twenty-five. The day his father passed away, Mabrouk inherited a big family and small garden. Though he worked like a dog, he was barely able to put food on the table. For the last few minutes, a thought kept echoing against the walls of his consciousness. The idea seemed to him at alternate moments to be so laughable, so absurd, he worried that if he dared speak it, the others would erupt into laughter and seriously question his capacity for rational thought. He continued to mull this idea over in his head, when someone elbowed him. The crowd wanted to hear what he thought of the idea Haj Salim had just put forth. Was it really possible that with banging bells and drums and the hollow chiming of empty glasses they might succeed in driving the locusts from the village? The crowd had begun to settle on this idea, and were now turning to Mabrouk for his opinion. He thought it was silly, but he recoiled from addressing the assembled crowd.

'Speak, ya Mabrouk. What's in your head? You're quiet . . . why?'

'You don't like Haj Salim's idea . . . is that because you don't think it will work?'

In spite of himself, Mabrouk blurted out, 'No, I don't think it will.'

The group was shocked.

Haj Salim, the author of the idea under consideration, winced and cast a disbelieving eye at Mabrouk.

'And how is this, that my idea will not work?'

'It won't work,' Mabrouk said, 'because when we divert the locusts from our village, they will go and find other villages filled with good people, and farms, and beating hearts.'

Hearing this, Haj Salim became defensive·

'What is this, Mabrouk? What would you have us do, sign a contract with these insects the monsters that are almost upon us – not to harm other villages, where there are people and farms and beating hearts? We have not found a better suggestion . . .'

Mabrouk continued in spite of Haj Salim's interruption, and no one interrupted. He was astonished to see people were straining to hear what he had to say. Once he finished, however, many gnawed their lips and exchanged incredulous glances, marks of stifled scorn.

Mabrouk attempted to bring the temperature down a notch, methodically adding more details:

'Tonight, in the pre-dawn hours, we must assemble two groups at the southernmost edge of the village. Two groups, mind you, as otherwise each will forget their empty bags. Each person must bring with him an empty sack. A battle awaits us that even past ages have not known. In this battle, sacks will be our weapons. We will make for the place where the locusts sleep. As we know, the locust does not stir until the sun's rays rouse him. We will cram those sleeping locusts into our empty sacks and bags, then we will return and cook them in our black pots and pans. We will transfer the locusts from the dark recesses of our bags to the dark recesses of our bowels!' Here, Mabrouk concluded with delicious emphasis, '*This will be the most wonderful extirpation that has ever been known in the history of locusts!*'

At the conclusion of Mabrouk's soliloquy, sarcastic commentary could still be heard bubbling from every corner of that small hall.

'This is an army, an army of locusts. Not a single locust or two locusts.'

'An army whose queen rules its throne,' said another sarcastically. Fagih Misbah took advantage of the shifting wind to remind the crowd of his original idea, exhorting a mass pilgrimage to the tomb of Sidi Abu Kindil, Sheikh of the Saints and the Virtuous Ones.

Just then, a heaviness fell upon the crowd, as darkness had arrived. Children called their fathers to dinner, with the age-old urging, 'Mother says to tell you dinner is already cold . . .'

Mabrouk felt the crowd had not understood sufficiently what he had said, and that he must explain the idea better.

'Listen, brothers,' someone interjected, in a lull between cacophonies. 'According to my thinking, the words of Mabrouk are not devoid of some logic . . . but this army of locusts . . . if it were to be spread above us, it would cover the sky itself.'

'Mabrouk has told us that these two groups, each of which does not exceed fifty individuals, will collect the locusts and then dispose of them. If you ask me, this is impossible,' said another.

Sheikh Masoud nodded, as if to fill the void.

'And why fifty men only? Why don't we send the whole village, with its large and small, its old and middle-aged, its children and women, and all the *shabab*?[54] Everyone, absolutely everyone, should participate in this campaign.'

The silence that followed these words was deafening.

Sheikh Masoud had opened a new window on Mabrouk's suggestion. Even a fly on the wall would have noticed: The crowd was almost sold.

The first to raise his voice in clear support was Haj Salim himself:

'I want to say there is absolutely nothing wrong with Mabrouk's idea.'

'I swear by God that's true!' said another.

'Why don't we try this tonight? If it doesn't work, we'll go back to Haj Salim's idea tomorrow.'

'We will kill two birds with one stone,' said a third.

'On the one hand, we will get rid of the locusts, and on the other we will be able to feed our children for two, perhaps three days.'

Only one person remained steadfastly against the plan.

'You are all crazy,' screamed Fagih Misbah. 'There's no doubt about it now, you are all completely mad!' he muttered as he struck the ground with his stick, then stormed out of the room, wondering how these people could shun his sage advice in favour of the ravings of a young upstart like Mabrouk.

And so the plan unfolded in the early hours of the morning, as a rooster somewhere first thought about stirring, as dogs bayed at the stars and the wind carried the howling of a lone wolf from a faraway place. The southern perimeter of the village witnessed a gathering unparalleled in the history of all the village gatherings. Their numbers were great, very great. Ashur managed to capture perfectly the thoughts running through everyone's mind when he said he would never have imagined the village contained so many people. This was a motley crew of men, women, the old, whom time had bent forward, and the very young, whom the coldness of night couldn't stop from jumping this way and that. Outwardly, the only attribute these individuals shared was an empty sack slung over each shoulder.

One woman brought with her a nursing baby. Amer came riding on his donkey. Abdul Nabi had even brought with him his small wheelbarrow, in which he would put two or three sacks of locusts. Dogs nipped at the heels of those bringing up the rear. The sounds of the treading of feet over vast areas of land mixed with the barking of dogs, the braying of the donkey and the clatter of the small wheelbarrow.

So it was that the villagers set off into winds laden with the scent of citrus. It would have been apparent to anyone watching that each individual was part of a whole. The unique scent that pervaded the place, an intermingling of orange blossom essence, sheaves of wheat, and *balah*,[55] was a symbol of unity. There was no full moon to light the way as they covered the ground, but the stars compensated, pulsing as if they were heaven's very eyes, their luminescence dissolving pockets of darkness. When the group arrived at the area where the locusts slept, shafts of luminous dawn suddenly exploded from above, enabling the villagers to scoop up the nefarious insects with ease. The horizon simmered in ochre; the colour of burnt mountain-tops tapered off into a thin layer of blue, before being crushed by obsidian black. The heavenly aurora above carried within it something resembling a palpitation. One would have been forgiven for thinking that it was a great, living being.

The locusts had chosen a wide hill upon which to make their bed. Under the light of dawn, it appeared as though it were an unending field of ready-to-harvest sheaves of wheat, caramelized to a golden hue. Here was the defining moment. The troops began their attack. Men doffed their cloaks and threw them into any number of heaps. They tied their belts around their bellies and readied their sun-scarred forearms, from which grew thick mats of hair. Those wearing baggy pants rolled up the bottoms, from the feet upwards. The mother of the newborn wrapped her bundle with care, kissed it, then laid it down in a safe spot under a tree. Amer tethered his donkey's two forefeet and left the animal to eat its fill of grass. Some of the villagers had carried with them jugs of water; others, thinking ahead to the inevitable wailing of hungry children, carried with them small pails of loaves of hard bread. Food and water were distributed strategically across the battlefield. Soon all these details were forgotten. Everybody was engrossed, transfixed by the task before them, indifferent to thorns and jagged bits of rock which might cause their hands to bleed, to bugs and scorpions. All that concerned them now were the locusts before them and the need to gather them up before the sun had a chance to warm their carapaces. Children stepped out tentatively in between the feet of the advance guard only to retreat suddenly, frightened by the clamour of a copious shooing. One old woman, Saida, never stopped shouting, all the while urging them on, insisting that they find the locust queen. In places along this human phalanx, villagers started singing. Some sang the harvesting song. Some of the sheikhs raised their voices to deliver the satirical poetry they recited during the days of the war against the Italians, in so doing making plain the connection between this struggle in which they were engaged, and wars with guns and bullets. The voices rose, singing . . .

'We are fighting the enemy amongst us . . . our boys are brave . . . our boys . . .'

In another spot, others sang in unison . . . 'Moon on high . . . travel on, come here . . .'

The younger children, too young to have been exposed to these patriotic anthems, found something hidden in the nearby chasms: echoes, curious and beautiful, set off by the singing. The children strained to hear, their small black eyes open with fascination. Then they howled in unison:

'Haww, awww . . .'

And the echo responded . . .

'Hawww, hawwww . . .'

Standing astonished, they all laughed and clapped in overwhelming joy, as if they had stumbled upon the greatest discovery in the world.

Throughout all this, the locusts were calm and still, as if already dead. The human chain advanced inexorably. The mass of villagers appeared at timeslike a never-ending line of soldiers, at others like a winding snake ingesting a huge, wide carpet. Each of the members of the chain silently wished it possible to widen the line or multiply their numbers, so they might scoop up yet more locusts.

When the hand of the old farmer reached out to snatch a group of locusts in front of Omran, the zeal of the two was so great that a fight might have broken out if the old man hadn't withdrawn his hand in time. Some of the sheikhs present seemed to be off in some parallel universe, channelling rage at past injustices. It was as if they had had with these creatures something approximating a blood feud, and how sweet was the revenge! Voices cried out from everywhere, urging the group to redouble their efforts. The most insistent of them all was Sheikh Masoud:

'Faster, fellows! Push forward!'

But look, the unfolding dawn revealed his mistake: half of his group was made up of women and children! And in one of the corners of the great line, euphoria overtook seven friends, among them Ashur. They agreed to make a bet, to see which of them could be first to the top of the hillock, each collecting locusts on his way.

Ashur's six companions had exerted themselves to the point that, despite the cold weather, beads of sweat fell from their brows. Even so, Ashur took the early lead, cutting the distance in record time. Standing at the summit, he raised his hand in elation . . .

'Huyya, huyya!'

Ashur felt at this moment like a great leader in the throes of battle. After him came the others, their bags full of locusts. Before the sun could rise from behind the far-off mountain peaks, even those in parts of the line that lagged furthest behind had finished their mission. Everybody stopped to look at their catch and marvel at the miracle that had fallen into their hands. Their collective hearts were full of great pride. Each felt as if this miracle had fallen simultaneously upon him personally and the group. With that epiphany, and for the first time since the crisis began, smiles broke out all around. Under the light of early day, the sandy hill showed red. There was not a trace of the locusts that had lately covered it, save a few odd specimens jumping this way and that, trailed by hopping children. And there, look there . . . Haj Salim is surveying the scene, wondering how in heaven's name they had managed to do what they had done. In the name of Allah, what had they done!

The women anticipated the moment they would arrive back at the village and could boil the locusts in their black pans. Finally, they could quell the children's endless clamour for bread, of which there was never enough. Shortly there-after, the children would discover that when boiled, those bottomless handfuls of locusts were so tasty! As the crowd, lugging locusts on backs and shoulders, returned to its small village, joy was in their minds as well as on their faces.

Every step was a pleasure! They marched, and they danced. There ... Abdul Nabi with his small wheelbarrow containing three bags of locusts. Chasing a few children, he's making car sounds as he moves ... beep! Beep! The children burst out laughing.

Look over there at Ashur and his beloved donkey. Over that way, the mother carrying her newborn in her arms. What a beautiful sight. Oh, and over there, Ashur, winner of the bet, joking with his companions. To a soul, they loved their village, which now appeared to them a vision of green. Life-green. The sun was now at their backs, fashioning long shadows from their figures. Individual projections merged into one enormous silhouette, that of a single living creature, the largest the world had ever known.

Source: Thalath Majmua't Qissasiya, Ahmed Ibrahim Al-Fagih, Qita'a al-Kitab Wa Al-Tawzi' wa Al-I'lan Tripoli, 1981.

Mizda

Fagih's description of the besieged village matches to some extent the village of his birth, Mizda, located 180 kilometres south of Tripoli. Like Jalo and Ghadames, the history of the place is inextricably tied to the ancient caravan trade; like many of Libya's traditional cities, Mizda has both a 'modern' and an 'old' section. The Guntrar tribe built the old town, which today resembles nothing if not a series of scaled-up ant-hills. The new town, home to more than 40,000 people[56] is reasonably nondescript. As for Ghat, several hundred miles to the south, rock drawings in the vicinity suggest people lived here as far back as 12,000 years ago. During Roman times, Mizda sat on a major supply road linking Oea (modern-day Tripoli) with the Berber town of Gharyan and outposts farther south. Roman-era milestones still mark the old roads, which have since become the shoulders of a wider, paved route.

Mizda lies in an area of extremely low rainfall. Until very recently, nomadic pastoralists sowed seeds and barley in autumn, before heading south for the winter with their camels and sheep. Approximately twenty-five kilometres to the east of Mizda, across uneven and stark terrain and perched precariously on top of a steep hill, sits Chafagi Amer Church.

I first set eyes on Mizda in spring 2005, on a tour run by the Libyan Archaeological Society, an organization whose members belonged overwhelmingly to the Libyan expatriate

community, including but not limited to oilmen and diplomats. Departing Tripoli early in the morning, we arrived
in Mizda around noon. To an outsider, Mizda is a fairly
unremarkable town, one of the towns described by Fagih
in his book *Huqul al-Rimad* (Fields of Ash) as 'smelling of
poverty'. Indeed, this was the first place, outside parts of
Tripoli's Old City, where I had seen abject poverty in Libya.
While Libya is not nearly as wealthy as its now more than
USD 20 billion in annual oil revenues would suggest, and
despite the fact that higher education and medical care are
a shambles, the Libyan government can at least be said to
have managed to lift the vast majority of Libyans out of
the depths of poverty. In the late 1990s and early 2000s, a
Libyan might drive a car given to a member of his family
as 'patronage' for services rendered (particularly if that person
was a member of the Revolutionary Committees, or served
in the army or the police force or the security services).
On a USD 125 per month salary (mandated) he could fill
his car with 35c/ litre petrol, and purchase basic goods, like
flour, pasta and sugar, for a pittance. If he subsisted on a
government salary what he couldn't have was access to the
growing market for imports, or luxury goods of any kind.
He could live, simply. There were pockets of poverty in
places like Mizda, where distribution systems were not good,
and fewer villagers made it 'out' to places where work was
to be found, and thus became able to support an extended
family.

Leaving Mizda properly behind, our bus rolled down
an unpaved, rock-studded road for about half an hour,
before coasting to a stop in a clearing by a dry river bed.
The forty of us, oilmen, diplomats and family members,
aged and young, clambered out onto the escarpment, then

fanned out like bush monkeys to eat our packed lunches under crispy collections of twigs before setting out on a five-kilometre hike to Chafagi Amer. Part of the Ghadames Basin, this was one of the areas attracting the attention of the many international oil companies returning to Libya. The surface geology is as interesting as whatever is percolating beneath. The panorama resembles the rolling hills of California, save that there is barely a shred of vegetation, apart from the occasional khandel, a very odd and unlikely-looking plant to find in a place like this – something like a miniature watermelon, attached to a waif of a sprig of green. To make an analogy with the animal kingdom, it's as if a chihuahua gave birth to a baby elephant. Underfoot, friable rocks of various striking colours, purples, yellows, and reds. I started to put some of these in my pocket, when I recalled the story of a man on a walk in the desert, who picked up and kept in his clothes a piece of rock containing uranium, with rather dire consequences. Pushed by superstition, I tossed the more alien-looking of the specimens away.

As the sun began to set under an overcast sky, it was almost as if I could see that triumphant scene from *The Locusts* about to unfold, with the crumbling of the soft rock beneath my feet standing in for the cracking of carapaces. After half an hour of walking over the crests of upturns in the rock of ever-increasing altitude, we could make out a formation in the distance, on top of which sat what was obviously a man-made structure. As we got closer, the thing became clearer and more unlikely. Chafagi Amer seemed to have been built on top of a gargantuan stack of loosely-piled rocks – more than 100 metres high – all of which seemed to threaten to come tumbling down at any moment.

At the foot of the pile, those already worn out by the walk over undulating terrain let out audible squawks of protest at the thought of having to climb a very steep gradient. Looking for a foothold here, jumping up there, the younger ones in the group managed to reach the summit in about ten minutes. Of course, by then, the church was clearly a church, on the walls the remains of a couple of impressive mosaics. All of which begged the question, why here, in the middle of nowhere, in such an inhospitable spot? Clearly there was some defensive intent, but how do people live in such a place? Scampering up further, through holes in the crumbling stone walls, I popped through the roof, from which one has a brilliant view of the wadi below. The sky had by then started to clear, just enough to let in shafts of amber light, which amplified the reds of the valley below.

Chasing Ibrahim Al-Fagih

In a country with no telephone directory and few street addresses, finding the authors or agents of people who wrote last year – let alone this year – is no easy task. Aside from those authors we knew personally, I reasoned that the easiest of the authors to find would be the semi-public figures; the second set would be those who were connected to communities where we had existing literary contacts. Benghazi, despite its size, constituted such a community. Ahmed Al-Fagih, both prolific and politically connected, was rumoured to pass through Tripoli every few months. In 2004, Fagih was the Cultural Counsellor in the Libyan People's Bureau (Embassy) in Greece. By the time I got a message to the Libyan mission there, he had been appointed

Ambassador to Romania. Approaches through Romanian contacts produced nothing. It was then that Azza Maghur (as usual, it seemed) came to the rescue, producing the email address of Al- Fagih's son, then living in Cairo. Within a couple of days, I received a cheery note from the Ambassador saying he was pleased that we had found his work enjoyable, and gave his permission for us to publish the translation.

Maryam Salama

From Door to Door

(Min Bab Ila Bab)

Translated by Ethan Chorin

Fatima closed the door behind her in silence. It was as if she had been pleading to prevent all manner of catastrophes from befalling her. She remained in that place, held back by walls, behind a door that blocked all sound. Her eyes were damp with tears from a long, harsh night. As morning came, she took a moment to inhale a brisk whiff of the early air. Fatima tried to gather her strength and her broken self, so that she could begin her first steps on this road she had come to know well since the day she left her job three years earlier. Now and then she recalled that day with great pleasure, lingering on every last hour, beginning with the first refreshing breeze that hit her face. It was then the beginning of spring. Birds chirped and fluttered their wings in the trees that flanked the road. Threads of sunlight landed like kisses onto the foreheads of those just now leaving their houses, rushing about to make their appointments with predetermined fates.

Even though it was her first day as a nurse in the Ghadames Central Hospital, Fatima insisted stubbornly that this was just a normal day. Even if the day were in fact special, the inevitable process of accretion would ultimately erode all element of uniqueness, and cast it fleetingly into the realm of work and duty.

Fatima signed her name on the attendance sheet. As she opened the door to the office, she found herself face to face with the Director. No, make that eye-to-eye. He smiled and nodded. She did the same. She took leave, but the Director summoned her back.

'Fatima, I want to introduce to you Doctor Valery Tshenko, from Ukraine. You will be working with him in the cardiac ward. Doctor Tshenko is also starting today. It's pure chance that you will be together from the beginning. I hope you both find the arrangement agreeable.'

All of a sudden, Fatima could hear the sound of her own footsteps on the pavement. Today's route was the same route she took yesterday – with the same electrical pylons, the same trees, storefronts, cars and pedestrians. But without being fully conscious of it, she felt something different. Fatima caught herself looking across the street, as if she might find him there. The old city of Ghadames with its white walls and covered streets waved to her from afar. Ghadames, with its walls thrashed by a wild desert, its dust and ruins, its old houses and the scent of her mother's perfume. Fatima didn't remember much about her dear mother except that she used to work in silence, tracing out a design on the wall, and daubing it with shades of brown and blue. These threads of colour greeted everyone who entered into the place, and helped create an atmosphere of beauty and warmth. Only at night, just before bedtime, would Fatima's mother speak, repeating to her the story of Ghadames in its days of glory, when the gurgling of water-wheels, farmers rejoicing and young girls singing 'Ana benyo benyo' ('give me, give me, sir!') kept the dead of night away

. . . how they would toss chicken eggs into the nearby spring, Ein al Firas – even if they were the last they had. Everyone was overflowing with goodwill. Fatima loved how her mother always ended her stories laughing.

'Did you know, Fatima, Ein al Firas dried up the day you were born.'

'But why, mother, why did Ein al Firas dry up?'

Fatima's mother died shortly after her father decided to leave Old Ghadames. Fatima never heard the answer to her question. The next morning she forgot all about it, as she headed out to play the game that was her only indulgence. Fatima did not know or intuit the meaning of 'girl'. She was happy kicking the twine and wool-thread ball like boys and her nearest male relatives did, blissfully unaware that her abilities were those of a girl and not a boy . . . ignorant of the wide differences that made boys boys and girls girls, a difference that the ages had shaped out of social accretions called 'traditions' and 'customs'. Then, one day, Fatima's breasts began to fill out, and her features became those of a woman. From those days on, she was ensconced in the house. Its roof became her cover and its street her special world.

Valery was very keen to learn Arabic.

'What use is the language to you?' Fatima would ask him.

The eye of the messenger is the heart! Of course, Valery's goal was to understand Fatima in her own language. The demure and proper Fatima tried to speak with her beloved instructor using what limited English vocabulary she had; he did the same with what he could muster of Arabic. But

really, they were like any lovers . . . more was spoken with
a whisper and a flash of the eye than spoken words. These
were the ties that bound them in the absence of a common
language or homeland. Wasn't it true that Valery was a man
and Fatima a woman? Weren't they working together?
Were they not in love? Their hearts chose not to focus
on the unlikely prospect of love between Ukrainian and
Ghadamsiiya. How many times had Fatima scolded Valery
for suggesting that there were significant differences?
Thrown together, weren't they proof that love is bountiful,
that love is a torrential river before which everything falls?

Fatima focused her attention on the path in front of
her to the muezzin of the old mosque. She strained to find
a piece of sky from within the narrow corridor where she
found herself.

'Allah, Lord of the Heavens, deliver me from this place!'

Haj Ali was a good man. He loved Fatima as he loved
all of his children. They in turn loved him. But with this
pair? The only thing left to finalize was the marriage of
his daughter to one of his cousins. This was really the limit
of his aspiration for himself and for her.

Valery knocked on the door and entered Fatima's house
with ease, just as he tried to read the mind of Fatima's
father, with whom he broached the subject in Arabic that
was clear and to the point. Haj Ali did not believe his ears;
he traded looks with his children, who never spoke in their
father's presence except with his permission. Taken aback,
he couldn't say a word. After a while, Haj Ali made an
effort to speak, taking care not to reveal any emotion:

'Here, we do not marry our daughters to strangers . . .
Drink your tea and go tend to your business.'

Haj Ali stayed his sons with an icy look whose meaning

they understood well: *stay silent*. Valery did not stay to drink his tea. He bade them farewell, then left the house.

Fatima was her father's daughter, his progeny. She did not speak in his presence, nor did she try to defend herself. He did not wait for her to speak.

'I would never tell you that you shouldn't work, or that your place is in the home,' he said calmly. 'But what happened today was a mistake, and should not be repeated.' With a flick of the hand he showed he wanted action, not words, and cut off all response.

'Soon the road will be at an end,' was the first thing Valery said when he next saw Fatima. He had wondered how it would be. What would she do? What would she say? Would she greet him with her usual smile? Would she speak to him in her Ghadamsi accent, speaking his greeting '*seeramsa*', so that he would respond '*sabah al khayr*'?[57]

Valery was waiting for her.

'Fatima,' he said, after she was silent a short while, 'I am going back to Tripoli.'

Fatima was taken aback. The intensity of her reaction betrayed the storm brewing within her. Valery took her to his bosom . . .

'I will go, but I will return to you. Trust me. If you do not despair, I will not . . . I cannot live without you.'

To this day, Fatima waits with love and patience, her eye firmly on the path.

Source: Maryam Salama, unpublished.

Ghadames

Nestled in a border cul-de-sac separating Libya from Tunisia and Algeria, the town of Ghadames is 650 kilometres south of Tripoli by road. The town, whose sobriquets include 'the Pearl of the Desert' and 'the Gate of the Sahara' for its position literally at the edge of the sands, is one of the most picturesque in all of Libya. Major stopping points along an intermittently paved road include the granary at Qasr El Haj and the Berber village of Nalut. Despite an increasing stream of European tourists and the presence of a serviceable runway, currently there is no air service to Ghadames. The result: travelling from Tripoli by road takes up to seven hours by car. One can take comfort in the fact that this is substantially faster than the seven days it used to take to cross the 120 miles from Jebel Nafusa by camel.[58]

Ghadames figures prominently in the Libyan pantheon of prospective tourist sites, which includes of course Leptis Magna, the Berber town of Ghat further south, and Cyrene in the east. At least in part, this is due to UNESCO, which in 1985 named it one of its Sites of Human Heritage, which include old walled towns like Morocco's Fes, Sana'a in Yemen and Lamu on the Kenyan coast. Fearing the encroachment of the new town on the old (in the 1970s, Ghadames' built space exploded from 32 to 167 hectares – it has approximately doubled since), and presumably mindful of the future potential of Ghadames as a tourist attraction, the Libyans undertook a rare, coordinated and ultimately successful lobbying campaign to put Ghadames on the global cultural map.

While not much information in English is available in Libya on Ghadames, local bookstores sell a history in Arabic, *Malamih Ghadames* (*Features of Ghadames*). Azza Maghur recommended to me a novella by Joelle Soltz, wife of the former Austrian Ambassador to Libya, entitled, *Les Ombres de Ghadames* (*The Shadows of Ghadames*), which recounts a girl's transition from the freedom of adolescence to the shut-in existence of adult females, presumably familiar to the mother and grandmother of Maryam Salama's protagonist in *From Door to Door*. While Fatima resents the restrictions on her life in the early twenty-first century, the contrast between the barriers she confronts and the extreme traditionalism of just one generation before is easily overlooked. Ghadames receives other attention from the now-annual arts festival held there in early October.

On the morning of 25 December, I set out from Tripoli with two colleagues, in the company of a former Deputy Minister of Tourism, many of whose relatives were still in the business of weaving brightly coloured leather shoes, prized as wedding accoutrements. Into red and green woolen Ghadamsi sacks, which resembled feedbags for horses, we placed our own clothes and shoes and began the six-hour ride south. About two hours out, and just past the Berber city of Gharyan, known for its pottery and troglodyte dwellings, we made a short detour to take a look at an amphitheater-shaped granary, constructed some time in the twelfth century. In two hours more, the plain scrubland began to bend upwards, and we began to make out a rock face in the distance, on top of which lay the town of Nalut. The formation seemed at first impassable, but as we got closer, rappelling figures morphed into cars taking a zigzag path to the summit, behind low walls strung with green and white banners bearing revolutionary slogans.

Over Nalut and the hump, we passed through two hours of unremarkable scrub scenery dotted with groups of camels – including half a dozen albinos, which I had understood were generally quite rare. Gradually, the landscape was broken by miniature oases, irrigated by streams of slow-moving, brackish green water. At one of these clumps of palms we stopped for a picnic. Jumping over a series of rivulets, while spitting out the pips of half a dozen blood oranges, we came upon a wizened old man sitting cross-legged in front of a palm tree. Salim Chadli, he said his name was, as he sat grinding date seeds into animal fodder. We took a group picture, with which he seemed eminently pleased, as it was on a digital camera and thus instantly digestible. Setting off in the land cruiser, by sunset we reached a checkpoint, the light for which was provided by a single solar cell. A large cluster of dark green palms lurked just beyond. Just time to reach the guesthouse, as there were no hotels in Ghadames per se. No immediate signs of the old city.

Our distinctively Ghadamsi guest house, with its bi-colour ochre-white exterior and roof jambs to ward off the evil eye, had no interior heating, only a pile of velour blankets and scary space heaters. We were served a meal of Libyan soup – consisting of cubes of lamb in a light stew of pasta and vegetables – delivered with demure cheer by our Beninois caretaker Aziz, one of the literally hundreds of thousands of sub-Saharan African labourers who come via Niger and Chad to seek out informal work in Libya. Up on the roof we stood freezing, gazing in awe at the stars hanging above us in the black night. The next morning, as we waited for the Old City to open, our guides took us through the Ghadames Museum, devoted to displays of local weavings and leatherwork.

At 11 am, we entered the Old City through a southern gate, in view of a very old cemetery. Unmarked graves evoke the simple profundity of the Muslim funerary rites, devoid as they are of any attempt to stave off or deny the inevitable. The gate leads directly into a covered passageway, which itself leads eventually into a semi-enclosed area where the residents of New Ghadames still gather before weddings and funerals. Each house itself is a kind of fortress, protected by thick doors made of palm wood. An average of six or seven dead-bolt locks are embedded within. Most of the town is sheltered from the light of day. Entering through a northwest gate, one proceeds through a network of passageways, covered by the very structures they link together. While men moved throughout the town using ground-level passages, Ghadamsi women, sequestered in their homes above, jumped from house to house via connectors on the roofs. Maryam Salama describes the geographic limitations that accompanied inexorable sexual dimorphism: 'Then, one day, Fatima's breasts began to fill out, and her features became those of a woman. From those days on, she was ensconced in the house. Its roof became her cover and its street her special world.' Marks on the ceilings delimit residential areas that each were once the exclusive domain of a given tribe. Doors are marked with tiny silver, green and gold rosettes to indicate the master of the house is a 'Hajji', the honorific accorded to one who has made the pilgrimage to Mecca. In the middle of our tour, we came upon a team of UNESCO-financed masons rebuilding part of a small mosque, replacing the *hilal* (crescent) that crowns it. Further along through the maze, past square-shaped tracts filled with goats or sheep, walls are draped with fig and grape vines.

In recent years the Ghadames tourist authority has been encouraging those with property in the Old City to develop their vacant homes as small pensions catering to high-end tourists. All that's left is to set up the electrical and water connections. We headed out for a two-hour jaunt into the neighbouring dunes. From Ghadames itself, the desert is barely visible through the groves of palm and goat enclosures.

The town of Ghadames is essentially a fortification, designed to protect its inhabitants from attack by desert marauders. About a mile out in a southwesterly direction, one can begin to make out the beginnings of the Sand Sea. As the land cruiser rocked and jaunted its way through the dunes like a metal camel, patches of sand appeared on the right and the left, and the vehicle's tires found it harder and harder to gain traction. To the right was a Massada-like mesa. As I scaled the mountain face, I cast my eyes downward in a vain search for fragments of pottery – vain, because this area had undoubtedly been scoured by thousands of tourists before me. At the summit, the remains of cisterns hewn into rock were full of modern-day rubbish. Half an hour west, as the vehicle surfed a narrow path between two hills, the dunes suddenly appeared. Compared to the dunes I encountered in the Tunisian oasis of Douz, here they were massive creatures. Perhaps due to an optical illusion resulting from the blowing of sand across the dunes' prows, here one was conscious of the fact that the dunes move. A few Touareg in black and brown robes sat encamped at the foot of the nearest solid sand-wedge, waiting to offer tourists a piece of sand-baked bread and coffee, or a ride on a reasonably well-fed camel. Twenty or so kilometres in the opposite direction lay the third prong of the local tourist special, a collection of small lakes – ponds really – whose depth is, according to what the guide told us, unknown. Half-way to China, at least! A school of enormous tilapia swam lugubriously from one side of the pond to the other. A white salty crust surrounds the lakes, giving this area the appearance of a New England swimming hole emerging from a winter frost.

December, 2005

Ahmed Mohammed Lannaizy

Mill Road

(Shari'a Al-Tahouna)

Translated by Ethan Chorin

Shari'a Al-Tahouna was one of the city's oldest streets. 'Street' in this case meant two lanes facing one another, cordoning off a part of Shari'a al-Bahr, or 'Sea Street.' The southern part of Tahouna Street straddled the cemetery, while the northern part came up against the jail. Each lane contained no more than four small houses. One of the houses on the south side of the street had been converted into a mill powered the traditional way, by a camel circumambulating it blindfold. The mill had switched over from wind to camel-power after Italian shelling destroyed part of the previous structure.

The disabled lad who paused that evening at the junction of the two lanes known as Shari'a Al-Tahouna would not have known there was once a windmill in that place. The young lad's eye fell upon the southern end of the street, where there grew a large lotus tree, whose branches covered the square and extended far beyond the cemetery walls. This seemed a promising spot in which to rest, so he stopped to catch his breath. The morning had seemed an eternity. He had spent most of it roaming the streets looking for a place to rest, after a truck had dumped him and his companions into Baraka Square. They were mere children, orphans, whose parents had perished in the Italian genocide. During the occupation, the Italians had set up an orphanage in the village of Soluq. After the war, the Western Occupation forces briefly took over the orphanage, before closing it down and packing the children off to the city to meet an unknown fate.

As Younes passed through the city streets, his hunger intensified. Utterly exhausted, he threw himself upon the ground, leant his back upon the tree's thick trunk, and stretched his legs over its whorl-filled base. Haj Buhileqa, the mill's owner, noticed the lad and invited him to enter his home. Buhileqa asked his partner Saidi Ali Al Kritli if he could set him up in the mill's stone apse, until a more permanent situation could be found.

Saidi Ali Al Kritli was a tall man. His two black eyes gazed forth. A moustache hung from his face, bronzed by years of exposure to the sun. As usual, he wore a white shirt with baggy, blue pants. On his head sat a black *kalbek*.[59] His shoes came up almost to his knee. As the name suggested, Al Kritli came from the Greek island of Crete. He was one of many who had fled Greek persecution. In Libya, Al Kritli married an African girl. Her family lived in the city with the many other immigrant families in shacks known locally as the 'Aaraeb al Abeed.'[60] Together, they had a one child, a daughter.

Haj Buhileqa met Al Kritli at Café Barakat. When he learned that the young man had experience with mechanical mills, together they made a pact to get the old mill going again. From that day, Saidi Ali lived with his wife and daughter in the annex to the mill, itself adjacent to

Buhileqa's house. It took Saidi Al Kritli some time to finish assembling the electric engine that would drive the mill. No longer would wooden posts and a leather harness drag a blindfolded camel around the mill, nor would its owner whip the camel when it dallied.

The street, hitherto very peaceful, was now disturbed continually by the engine's roar. News of this innovation spread to nearby streets, and soon the mill was not wanting for customers. Aunt Fatima was offended that the mill spread the odor of naphtha everywhere, but she was the only member of the village who stayed away. Besides, she told herself, the machine-milled flour was finer than strictly necessary. For the best taste and the quickest leavening, barley bread required coarser flour.She continued using her hand grinder.

The mill operated throughout the afternoons. As the days passed, the villagers became more and more receptive to using it. Younes helped run the place. He learned how to work the engine, and how to fill it with gas. He poured the grain into the machine deftly, bending over to catch the milled products that accumulated in the scuttle. Saidi Ali Al Kritli never ceased to be impressed with Younes' dedication and skill in executing the various parts of his job.

Younes' left leg was slightly shorter than the right, but this did not slow him down. He did not venture out from the mill except for lunch or dinner – or when he heard a knock on the wall separating the mill and the attached house, his cue to rush out to take a plate of food delivered by Saidi Ali's daughter, Aziza.

Aziza would wait behind the door for him. Younes shook the flour-dust from his face and his clothes, while walking towards her. She cast a smile his way, causing him to blush as he accepted the plate from her hands. Younes rarely said anything to Aziza, and when he did it was typically a disjointed thought like 'how wonderful a cook your mother is!'. Younes always turned away from Aziza the moment he grasped the plate's edge. As he turned, her gaze followed him. She thought to herself, 'how handsome and refined you are!' Younes was not the sort to be ashamed of anything, except his stub leg, for which he tried to compensate with a charm that endeared him to everyone. In this way Younes lived in companionship with a family that loved him like a son, and had neighbours who looked out for him. He never got in trouble – except once, when Haj Buhileqa found him singing with young men who occasionally visited the mill. The lyrics went like this:

> We have forgotten our families and neighbours . . .
> Now we are soldiers in service to the Italians.

Catching some of the rhyme, Haj was furious. 'I don't want to hear this ever again, Younes. These are very bad words . . .'

'Yes sir,' Younes responded. 'Never again, sir.'

'Things are different from before, Younes. You have family and neighbours whom you'll never forget, and who won't forget you!'

Younes didn't mean to offend anyone with the song, least of all Haj Buhileqa, who was like a father to him. He'd repeated the rhyme to illustrate events he witnessed as a child under the Italian occupation – unspeakable things engraved in his memory. Haj Buhileqa left the mill in a

hurry. He regretted hurting the boy's feelings, for just as
Younes considered him a father, he considered Younes a
son.

The owners of the shops in the nearby souk (especially
Faraj, the owner of the local grocery store, and Suleiman
As-Saghir, the butcher) felt Aziza's absence. At first, it didn't
occur to them what had happened. When they learned the
reason for her seclusion – she had reached the age when,
according to tradition, her father would veil her – they
were doubly sorry. When Aziza had come to buy household
necessities, they vied with each other to approach her, to
chat her up. They showed her their best wares, to win her
favor. The beautiful young woman was a mix of Cretan
red and the darker hue of the Africans. She was elegant
and spoke with much grace.

Umm Aziza was surprised one morning to receive her
neighbour Sadina, wife of Hussain Al Shaeeb, who said she
wished to speak with her about Faraj the grocer. Faraj, it
seemed, had asked her husband to mediate in requesting
Aziza's hand in marriage, and in assuring her parents that
he would agree to all of their conditions.

Umm Aziza offered some refreshment to her guests,
and listened patiently to Sadina's ceaseless extolling of the
suitor's qualities:

'Oh God, if only every girl could have a husband like
him . . . He's a true man.'

'Tonight I'll speak to him. He's the master of the
house, you know.' So it was that Umm Aziza relayed the
message to Aziza's father. When Aziza learned of this,
however, she ran to her mother, and told her she did not
want to marry anyone. Sadina waited a number of days
on the offchance that Aziza's mother would change her

mind, but there was no further news. With that, she assumed the grocer's request had been refused. The news of grocer Faraj's proposal spread amongst the neighbours, who now also knew of the refusal. Just as Umm Aziza had been surprised when the first suitor knocked on her door, now she was faced with Ghalia, the wife of her neighbour Jama Yusef. Suleiman the butcher asked Jama, to ask her to inquire with the Al Kritli family about the possibility of his marrying their daughter Aziza. Of course, she said, Suleiman is prepared to meet all of their demands! Ghalia sat drinking the tea Umm Aziza prepared, talking about the suitor, enumerating his good qualities and his family situation.

Ghalia was taken aback by Umm Aziza's frostiness:

'The girl is still young. Her father doesn't want to give her to anyone yet.'

'But why not, ya Salima! Everyone who comes to ask for her hand is fighting over her, why not, ya Hana . . .'

'Wallah, ya Hana, everyone meets his fate.'

As Ghalia left, she regretted her failure, and muttered to herself:

'A disaster before the Prophet! We *must* rejoice in the wedding of Aziza . . .'

Saidi Juma invited all the residents of Shari'a At-Tahouna for a nighttime gathering at his house. As usual, they started to discuss events that affected the village, living under the shadow of fascism. They talked about the regulations against Libyans entering the cinema in national dress, as well as other things that touched their lives and interfered with their ability to plan for peace and stability.

The topic of the day, of course, was Saidi Ali Al Kritli's refusal of his daughter's two suitors. Saidi Al Kritli tried to change the topic, but those present pressed for the reasons for his refusal.

'Why don't you give Aziza's hand to Younes Haluled?' said someone in the crowd, '. . . Ya Saidi Ali . . . I believe that Saidi Younes Hussein Haluled is the one who will respect her . . .'

'Wallahi ya Saidi Juma,[61] I vouch for Younes. I know him well.'

Here Haj Buhileqa took a moment to speak his mind:

'She is *your* daughter, ya Saidi Al Haj. We put our trust in God and whatever He requires of us.'

Saidi Hussain and Saidi Juma spoke in unison:

'God bless you, Saidi Al Haj, we fear those who might compromise the happiness of our son and daughter.'

In the evening the neighbours lined up at the house of Saidi Hussain. To fight the oppressive heat, some sprayed the street with water. Slowly, the invitees began to coalesce into small groups. Fagih Ramadan arrived, and after greeting everyone present and exchanging the usual salams, he took a seat at the centre of the gathering, and scrutinized the faces of those sitting near him. The crowd made and animated gestures as he spoke. The children of Shari'a At-Tahouna started to serve coffee, followed by cold drinks. Fagih Ramadan cleared his throat. He pulled some papers from a small bag. To those gathered he presented the bride's father, and the groom's agent, Haj Buhileqa. Next, the witnesses. The text of the marriage contract had been settled beforehand; the assembled group watched as Fagih Ramadan signed the document. Having dispatched the formalities, Fagih invited all those present to join him in wishing the newlyweds success in life and family, and delivered a blessing for the father. Thus blessed, the marriage opened a new page in the history of that small street, between the jail and the cemetery.

Source: Hadith Al Madina,
Ahmad Mohammed Al Lannaizy,
Mu'Tammar, 2005.

Stories from the West

Tripoli

Green Square

Saraya Castle

Leptis Magna

Zwara

Zintan

Tripoli and the
Old City

Things are never quite as one imagines them. While I could have consulted the Internet before I arrived for a view of what my future lodgings and environs really looked like, I chose to assemble images from various places into a quaint collage: a 1940s' colonial structure with cockroaches, creaking walls and a strong sea breeze, flanked by pictur-esque mosques with minarets painted green. In a romantic haze, I had willed myself into a version of the Saint George Hotel in Algiers where General Eisenhower coordinated Allied resistance to the Germans. A family friend, who in the late 1970s was interviewed for a job with one of the American oil companies still operating at the time, described it as a dusty, antiseptic and very dry place (figuratively and literally). Tripoli is characterised as much as by what it is, as by what it could be and what it is not.

There are no camels in Tripoli, nor are there many palms. Indeed, Tripoli is unique for the absence of many things: there is none of the livestock that mingles with traffic in most other Middle Eastern capitals. In this respect, perhaps it is more like Tunis or Algiers. Rarely does one see a ship or a skiff on Tripoli's coast, save the occasional fishing boat at dusk. The town 'centre' consists of a group of oddly shaped high-rises, to which the Corinthia is the newest addition. The most prominent high-rises, Burj Al-Fateh and Dat Al-Imad, look like part of a Star Trek mock-up. The former's insides have been hollowed out, and the impression given is that of a rusty tanker hull that has been inverted and raised forty stories. The best view of Tripoli is to be had from the revolving restaurant on top of Burj Al-Fateh – from the creaks and groans that accompany the turning mechanism, one is afraid that the thing will unhinge and hurl one into the sea. Dat Al-Imad consists of five identical towers arranged in a loose star, each looking like an inverted soda bottle. The latter buildings were originally off-white, but with the passage of many dust storms have acquired a kind of gritty, orangish hue that makes one will a massive deluge to come and clean them up. On Revolution Day, 1 September 2005, foreign companies were conscripted to donate to a landscaping fund. Some did, and two months later there were a few new palm trees and fresh turf on the dividers. Tripoli is full of playgrounds, conveniently located in the centre of roundabouts or at the intersection of several freeways.

The Old City

The breach in the wall of the Old City nearest to the Corinthia comes about a hundred paces to the left as one exits the hotel grounds. While the main entrance to the right, a block before the start of Shari'a Rachid, is with its cafés and raucous crowds obviously the start of something, this side entrance bears no ceremony. Uneven stone slabs take you up and through the ramparts, into a series of alleys and pits of garbage, including a two-storey pile of discarded clothes, surrounded by piles of refuse, upon which teams of emaciated cats play 'king of the mountain'. The smell of human waste is pervasive.

As with the old cities of Sana'a and Fes – and contrary to the Old City of Ghadames – people actually live in Tripoli's Old City. They are perhaps not the original residents, or even descendants of original residents. Most of those who live in the Old City these days do so because they have no choice; black African refugees or the poorest of Libyan families. The original 'Tripolitanians', including those whose parents and grandparents lived behind these walls, now reside in apartment buildings in the Souk Al-Juma area. A thin alley links the West Wall entrance directly to the Arch of Marcus Aurelius, into which a restaurant, Al-Athar or 'The Ruins', has been built, behind Nadi Bab Al-Bahr, in the vicinity of the Gurgi Mosque and the imploded ruins of the 19th century American Consulate.

The unobtrusive side entrance leads in a more or less straight line to Al-Athar. Returning in the direction of Corinthia at night, one can't help but feel as though one has wandered onto the set of Aladdin, with the sparkling palace looming over a scene of deprivation:

> Beyond the glitter of the Corinthia, carefully kept separated by its high walls, African immigrants and Libya's poor were selling trinkets from plastic sheets carefully spread out amidst the garbage and rubble on Shari'a Rachid.[62]

In late 2005, a few major changes have occurred: under cover of night, many of the squatters' camps and most of the African refugees have been removed – to where, no one seems to know, or really care.

In the area around Nadi Bahr (The Sea Club), Ottoman square courtyards, mosques and hammams have been restored. Now they are museums and restaurants, catering to this new breed of visitor: tourists. Despite being a formal advocate of renewal, of economic opportunity, of cultural preservation, having been here 'before'; having spent days and days wandering alone through the most filthy of these alleyways, poking my head into the 'little shop of taxidermy horrors', with its reconstructed gila monsters and chipped tusks of elephant, I can't help but feel that these huge groups of elderly (and mostly wealthy) Europeans and Americans are interlopers.

Green Square (Formerly Martyrs' Square)

One of the most notable of Tripoli's landmarks is Green Square, bordering the entrance to Medinat Al-Qadima (Old City) and Qasr Al-Saraya (Qasr Al-Hamra', or Red Castle), which houses the National Museum. The side of the square facing Al-Saraya is chopped up by three parallel streets, including 1st of September Street and Mezran Street. If 'all roads lead to Rome', most of Tripoli's streets lead to Green Square.

On 1 September 2004, 'Revolution Day', the square sprang to life with oddities of various kinds, including a parade that featured ostriches chained to the back of flat-bed trucks, giant cardboard mock- ups of NASCO refrigerators, and ten-year-olds on motorbikes, all vaguely suggesting a new-age North African Shriners' convention.[63]

On normal days, the area is a kind of parking lot, which empties in the evening to make way for garishly decorated horse-drawn chariots, African gazelles – both live and stuffed – and Harley Davidsons. Two columns frame the fourth side of the square, which looks out onto the port.

Saraya Castle

The spot on which Saraya Castle stands has allegedly been occupied since Roman times. In 642, Amr Ibn Al 'As, one of the two mightiest of the Arab conquerors, is said to have besieged an earlier version of Saraya for over a month. The Spanish occupiers and Knights of St John added yet other parts.[64] In 1551, the Ottoman Turks added high walls and colonnades, features we would recognize today. In the eighteenth century Ahmed Pasha Karamanli (1711–1745) made the castle his personal headquarters. At the time, a moat surrounded three sides of the structure and connected it to the sea. When the Italians invaded in 1911, the Governor made it his office. In 1952 the castle became the centre for the Libyan Department of Antiquities. In 2006, the castle is separated from the sea by a four-lane highway, built upon landfill in the mid-1980s. On the other side of the highway sits a long line of food concessions and a floating restaurant in very sorry condition called Lebda Al-A'im, or Floating Leptis (Magna), all of which make any clear view of the sea from Green Square and its environs impossible. At night entire families, including ageing mothers and toddlers, play a dangerous game of leap-frog, leaping from one lane to the next in their efforts to cross from one side to the other. An interesting feature of Libyan planning is the placement of children's parks in between highways and next to busy intersections. In any case, gone is the picturesque corniche of the 1960s. The government has reversed Ziad Ali's fable about bringing the sea to Saraya, and put it back in its place.

View from Café Saraya

On the north-east corner of the square is a boxy, quasi-modern structure sporting a multitude of smoky, large-paned windows. Two illuminated red signs read 'Matam wa Maqha Assaraya' ('Restaurant and Café Saraya'). The café sprang up here in the last couple of years. It was built on the site of one of the Banco D'Italia, a branch of the Italian Central Bank, reputedly the most beautiful of the old Italian colonial buildings. The building was converted after the Revolution into the hall of the General People's Congress and razed with the transfer of the GPC to the coastal town of Sirte in the late 1970s. As if anticipating what I was going to say, Basem moved to counter it: 'Everything that exists now could be said to have been once in another place. We were sitting somewhere else, yesterday, just as someone was sitting in the seats we are occupying today.'

Sitting with one's back to those windows and the frigid interior of the café, through a smattering of leafy palms, one has a clear view of the fort, which today houses the Tripoli Museum. On one corner of the square stands a clock tower, recently renovated, its face ringed with strips of neon, bright green and blue. Continuing the panoramic sweep, to the left and slightly down, is a colonnade, its arches painted Libyan green. Many taxi drivers have told me that the mast that tops the real Saraya, the castle, is none other than that of the USS *Philadelphia*. The Philadelphia, her captain, and her crew of 307 ran aground on an uncharted reef near Tripoli harbor in 1803, while trying to enforce a naval blockade against the Barbary pirate Yusuf Karamanli. To prevent the Philadelphia from falling into enemy hands, the Americans set out to burn it, launching a commando raid that has been referred to as one of the 'great military operations of the age.' Closer inspection of Saraya's mast reveals an enormous metal – not wood – pole, clearly of more recent vintage.

Maidan Al-Gazala

Some way up the street, along the quasi-corniche, there is a roundabout. Here stands the fountain of the 'Girl with the Gazelle', much as Genaw describes it. With the recent Revolution Day celebrations (September 2005), the statue got a polishing and the fountain sprang to life, adding an element of modesty to an otherwise erotic sight. It is certainly tempting to ask why, when all the other free-standing vestiges of Italian aesthetic have been razed or removed, this one stayed. Perhaps the answer is obvious.

The Girl with the Gazelle: Stolen

Within a year of the 2011 Revolution many sites and shrines across Libya became targets for vandalism or destruction by those who claimed they were 'un-Islamic'. Over the following years, the Sha'ab mosque in Tripoli, which contained Sufi graves and shrines,

Sufi shrines elsewhere in the country, and Roman ruins at the Western coastal sites of Sabratha and Leptis Magna, were all hit. The Girl With the Gazelle was an obvious and early 'offender'. On September 4, 2014, Tripoli residents were startled to find that the girl and her gazelle were gone – presumably for good. Social media lit up with Libyans railing against this attack, and those who would dictate their narrow moral code to the Muslim majority[65]

Maidan Asa'a

Not far from the derelict site of the old American Consulate, on the other side of Green Square from Café Saraya, is Clock Tower Square. Maidan Asa'a is a small open area in the shadow of, predictably, a large clock tower. Facing the eponymous restaurant is the oblique backside of the imposing orange Saraya Castle. The square has undergone a bit of a facelift over the past two years. Perhaps it is not too presumptuous to guess its custodians have realized the value of its picturesque setting. Half of the ratty sets of tables and chairs in the courtyard have been replaced by new, sparkling aluminium models shaded by the type of Cinzano umbrellas ubiquitous in Europe (adhering to proscriptions against alcohol, these read 'Pepsi').

After a year of frequenting the Assaraya Café almost exclusively, I got tired of the place, and moved over to one of two metal chairs at the entrance to Asa'a Café. The outside area is minded by its laconic, rail-thin owner and a waiter who claims to know the whole of the foreign diplomatic community. As I sit, my head stuck into one book or other, within the narrow hallway linking the square to the restaurant inside, a waiter who called himself Maurice propels himself with glee and a skid off a runway of polished tile onto the square outside. His record rests at a full two seconds airborne.

A House on Gargaresh Street

A year and some months into my Libya tour, the Embassy moved me into a single-storey villa a couple of blocks off Gargaresh Road, mentioned in *Tripoli Story* as an upmarket shopping district. The turn-off to my place was marked by a miniature replica of the Eiffel Tower, which rested on top of a former assembly point for the local Basic People's Congress, now a police station.[66] I found it strange suddenly to be out of the hotel, into a three-bedroom villa. Ample as the place was, it was tiny compared with many of the surrounding houses. It was still winter, and the nights were cold. The combi heater- air-conditioners were engineered more to keep one cold than hot. At night, anonymous figures sat in cars, their presence betrayed only by lit cigarette butts. During the day, the neighbourhood was alive with children – one day I counted ten in the house across the way. The neighbours were polite but reserved. As I waited for my ride, a copy of the Hans Wehr Arabic dictionary in hand, they'd cast me alternating wary glances and polite smiles as they backed their cars into the street. I smiled back. Over time, the atmosphere lightened. Kids would come up to me in groups and ask, defiantly, 'How are you?'. Whatever answer one gave was greeted with a hefty dose of skepticism. The girls were much softer. For weeks one of them spied on me from behind the fold of a curtain on the third story.

When she realized I had noticed, she tried to engage me in a conversation across the way; 'Where are you from? Are you from America?'

In the garden lived two turtles, one of which I named Nimrod. One day, a second dared to emerge from the undergrowth. I saw the two of them kissing one morning, so I called the mate 'His Lover'. I had not a clue how to sex a turtle, but figured the details of their relationship should remain a private affair. At the height of the sanctions, Libyan turtles fetched in Malta five dollars a head, a fair profit in those days.

After a week or two I began to be awakened at dawn by a horrific screeching, which sounded like the mating call of a peacock, but louder and gruffer. For weeks, this bird caused me no end of grief. I had fantasies of paying a local kid to kidnap it, whatever it was. I told my colleagues about the ostrich next door – an executive with the oil services company, Halliburton, kept one chained in his back yard as a pet. I described the noise to many of my Libyan friends. Their best guess was that it was not an ostrich, but a black and red rooster, whose crowing is completely disproportionate to its size. The creature tortured me for two months, before the neighbourhood fell silent. I hope he tasted good.

In the evenings, I often rejected any responsibility for cooking and headed two streets down and one block up, past a one-room hairdresser and a rug seller, to restaurant Al-Sahra, or 'The Rock', where I'd often eat lasagna and a plate of olives. The owner was yet another of that cohort of Libyans educated in the States. A bit further down the road was a small bookstore, over which a blind older man in a spot-stained ghalabiya presided. Every time I poked in his store, I always bought something, whether I wanted it or not. He always wished me a great day.

The 'Italian' grocery store was half a mile in the other direction, much of the way bordered on the far side by the twenty-foot perimeter wall of Gargaresh Mental Hospital. I wondered how many people spent their days behind those walls, and what they thought about. One day I pretended to be blind, counting the number of times I had to change my path in order to avoid being hit by a car, motorcycle or running person. Twenty times in a fifteen-minute walk.

For most of the time I lived in the house on Gargaresh, the main street and its tributaries were being dug up so as to lay fiber optic cables. The result was a veritable obstacle course and epic traffic jams. One night, a young man on a motorcycle tried to jump a line of cars and wound up flattened at the bottom of a trench. 'Libyans don't drive into puddles,' a friend told me, 'because one never knows whether it's really a puddle or a major excavation.' I often wished I'd been able to take a picture of Gargaresh every week for the previous five years, to see how drastically things had changed. The place, along Bin Ashur neighbourhood on the other side of town, constitutes the epicentre of familial commercial activity. Five straight miles of store after store, random permutations of identical products, from watermelons and oranges to stationery to grilled chickens and plumbing parts. Mixed into these 'staples', one increasingly found showrooms filled with pricey furniture, Vespas, children's toys, Belgian chocolates and French perfumes.

Mottah Genaw

Caesar's Return

('Awdat Caesar)

Translated by Ethan Chorin

After being been carted back to his birthplace in Leptis
Magna, Caesar took for himself a high pedestal overlooking
the main street leading into the market area of the monu-
mental city. When he thought about days of old, and the
state of the city in which he was born so many centuries
ago, the contrast instilled in him a profound sense of sadness.
In Caesar's time, Leptis was at the height of its glory. People
called it the Jewel of North Africa. From its ports sailed to
the markets of the southern Mediterranean all the marvels
of the Continent, from esparto to ivory, wheat and the
hides of ferocious animals. All that was left now to Caesar
was to pass out his lackluster days, to wait for something
– anything – that might permit him to discover life anew.

During these hopeless, modern-day evenings Caesar
made a habit of climbing down from his perch and
wandering the alleys of the ruined city, devoid of tourists
so many years after its inhabitants had themselves disappeared. Caesar passed through the rubble of the old market,
where dancing shadows conjured up games of his youth.
He savored memories of the monuments he had commis-
sioned; he recalled with great fondness how splendid the

marble baths used to be. Now they were bone dry. He wanted to jump into the water and scrub away the layers of dusty stickiness, cemented in place by the summer heat and years of neglect.

Finished with contemplating the distant past, Caesar moved to more recent times, unearthing memories of the period during which he was 'Commander of Tripoli'. Then, he presided over the comings and goings of people in Green Square. There was an odious period during which a gallows had been erected there. Thereafter they called it Martyrs' Square, over which kiosks were erected, in an environment of remarkable cleanliness. Behind these kiosks lingered horse-drawn carts, dolled up like brides in their wedding finery, waiting for someone to take them for a quick whirl around the city.

Driven to distraction, Caesar climbed down from his lonely perch at Leptis and plotted his return to the dais at Green Square, to a spot that haunted him even now. Creeping out beneath the eyes of the neglectful guard, Caesar made it out of the gate before sunrise. The fact that Caesar had no cash was not a problem, as the taxi driver wouldn't dream of refusing the man of bronze he found on the curb. He recognized Caesar instantly, and made it a point to flaunt his passenger before his fellow taxi drivers who would later have to concede it was he who returned Caesar to his rightful place, while everyone else dozed. The taxi driver deviated from his usual route so as to bring Caesar to the dais, before the city awoke from its sleep-induced doldrums.

Tripoli was not as it once was; in the spot where Caesar's dais once stood, dozens of hawkers were now sprawled on the ground next to plates filled with filth of various kinds,

chattering in all the tongues of Babel. There were no
decorated horse-drawn carts, no kiosks. Caesar was at a loss.
How would he now regain his old seat? These strangers
clearly knew nothing of the fact that this area was once
his, his alone. Nor was there any indication – not the
slightest sign, mind you, written or otherwise – that this
place was Caesar's. The old register had been burned, and
with it collective memory. No one knew him other than
those who had pledged their eternal love and fealty. Indeed,
this number had been reduced to nothing, nil, zero.

'There is nothing here,' Caesar thought to himself.
Nothing to attest to the fact that Caesar is a part of this
city's heritage, that Caesar was once considered one of
Tripoli's finest landmarks!

Caesar lingered in the midst of a bemused and gathering
crowd. Thinking from his clothing that Caesar belonged to
one of the official agencies that periodically came to kick
people out of the square, the people of Tripoli cast him
wary looks.

Caesar looked around him. Everything was different.
Chaos and destruction sopped up memories wherever they
might be. He remembered friends from another time, and
wondered in silence as he crossed the square: perhaps 'the
Girl with the Gazelle' would still be in her beautiful fountain, arching her back towards her companion as she cradled
his neck gently in her arms. Caesar remembered how, during
the blazing hot days of summer, he had envied the girl her
spot, bathed by a continuous stream of water and a soft
breeze from the opposite shore. He, on the other hand, was
forced to stand atop his perch in the square, perspiring in
his heavy costume.

Caesar continued on to the roundabout where he used

to find the Girl with the Gazelle. At the sight of him, the girl's features formed a weak smile, which she struggled to broaden. Over the years, her faded smile had lost its former allure, her lips cracked by an intense thirst. It seemed to Caesar that dirt had practically gobbled her up, such was the extent of the dust and grime that adhered to the plates of the waterless fountain. Just then Caesar experienced a kind of epiphany: by God, all this dirt and neglect was not something that had just 'happened' to him and those he knew. Somehow it had become a distinguishing mark of life in this place. Caesar tried to comfort the girl with his words, but to no avail. Just as he was impotent to save himself, there was little if anything he could do for her. The Girl with the Gazelle knew this. Neither dwelled on the matter. Simultaneously, an idea occurred to both of them. On the morning of the next day, Tripolitanians were astonished to see the two metal figures standing at the head of a long line before the offices of the Libyan Maritime Transport Company, waiting to buy tickets to Malta.

Source: 'Awdat Caesar, Qisas Qasira Majlis Tanmiyya Al-Ibda'a Ath-Thaqafi, Libya, 2004

Septimius Severus and Leptis Magna

Septimius Severus, a.k.a. 'the African Emperor' and 'the Grim African', is the protagonist of Meftah Genaw's story, *Caesar's Return*. The story's premise is derived from the fact that at some point during the Italian occupation (1911–51) the colonial authority moved an impressive bronze statue of Septimius Severus from the place it was discovered in Leptis Magna to Green Square.

At the time of Severus's birth in 145 ad, Leptis was a Roman colony and one of the three sister cities of Leptis, Oea (present-day Tripoli) and Sabratha. Severus's name is indelibly associated with the town and current-day ruins of Leptis Magna, whose inhabitants were largely traders and farmers.

Who was Severus? Greek historian Claudius Cassius Dio (155-235 AD) describes Severus as 'small but physically powerful, a man of few words but with an active and original mind'.[67] Septimius Severus altered the shape of the empire, weighting it towards the East. He was a 'remarkable phenomenon, the first truly provincial emperor, and a full product of Africa'.[68] Noted for his courage in battle and the ability to grasp the bigger picture, Severus began his career at a time when demographic and political forces favored the aspirations of provincial Roman officers, and the Roman Empire was at the apogee of its geographical and political influence. Severus served in Sicily, then commanded a garrison in Syria under Pertinax, who was involved in the Parthian Wars and the struggles against the barbarian invasions from his base in Gaul. Septimius's political legacy is mixed. Gibbon lays the blame for the subsequent disintegration of the Roman Empire at his feet. Others attribute the fall to forces long underway. Whatever his virtues as a leader, Severus was not known for being particularly kind; he had residents of Leptis flogged for inappropriate displays of affection, and allegedly engaged in mass executions.[69]

Present-day tourists owe much to Severus's vanity, for the ruins of the magnificent structures to be seen are a product of his vast building program. Leptis is known for its magnificent public baths. The aqueduct dates to the year 120 ad. Cobblestone streets were full of flying phallic symbols, warding off the evil eye.[70] *Caesar's Return* is notable for its strong implicit criticism of the physical degeneration of Tripoli during the 1980s and 1990s. Genaw puts the message in the mouth not of a citizen of modern Libya, but of the builder of monuments and hero of Ancient Tripolitania, Septimius Severus. The pedestal remains, but the statue has been returned to Leptis, where it stands guard outside the site's museum.

Conversation with Meftah Genaw

I met Mr Genaw in his second-floor office on Abdel Nasser Street in Tripoli on a very hot, humid day in late June 2006. This would have been precisely the sort of day his character Severus encountered while communing with the Girl with the Gazelle – a day on which one would prefer altogether to remain indoors with the air conditioning on full throttle. Genaw is a large-framed man who speaks in

a soft, measured tone. He seemed a bit bemused by my
interest in the story, and the fact that we spoke in Arabic.
While he speaks little English, Genaw is a talented linguist,
having mastered Czech and a bit of Italian. 'In speaking
and reading other languages,' he says, quoting a well-known
proverb, 'one develops different personalities.'

I asked Genaw about his work, how he came to write
short stories. A somewhat unlikely literary figure, Genaw
was trained in the former Czechoslovakia as an aeroplane
mechanic. From his description of the work he practiced
during the subsequent years, he was bored. 'Everything is
according to notecards, you never see the bigger picture.
This is not a creative activity,' he said. Genaw's propensity
for the verbal is more obvious in his choice of second
career, that of lawyer. 'You're right, I changed 180 degrees.'

Ironically, perhaps, it was a mandatory year-long
program in Czech, paid for by the Libyan government, that
first afforded Genaw the opportunity to write. Thereafter
he wrote a number of short pieces. Genaw professes a love
of Czech literature and is quick to point out that Milan
Kundera, one of a long list of talented Czech writers, is
completely unknown in the Arab world. Genaw says he
was particularly influenced by the writings of Yaroslav Hasek,
a Bohemian satirist who gained posthumous fame with
Good Soldier Svejk, which some call the first novel about
World War I. The targets of Svejk's satire are bureaucracies
and 'all ideologies', wherever they may be found. Genaw
said the inspiration for *Awdat Caesar* came from many places,
foremost a feeling of wounded pride: in the 1960s and
1970s, Tripoli was full of buildings and hotels on a par with
those in the European capitals – Al-Kabir, Al-Mehari and
Al-Waddan, one of the gems of 1960s-era Tripoli.

Why Septimius Severus? 'He was a kind of hero for the older generation,' Genaw said, 'a Libyan who took Leptis from being Leptis Minor to being Leptis Magna,' and brought prosperity to the region now known as Libya. To care for Tripoli and Libya's archaeological sites, he says, is to care for all of Libya. The Italians, for all their flaws, educated the older generation about a period they held to be Italian history, but which in fact is Libyan history.

Ziad Ali

The Castle and the Water

(Al Qala't Wa Al-Ma')

Translated by Ethan Chorin

They say 'Saraya Al–Hamra' (the Red Castle), an enormous fort in western Tripoli, was built a fair distance from the sea. A Turkish *wali*[71] converted it into a grand castle, which later governors inherited. That very day, an old woman approached the castle and called out to a sentry. She begged him to let her see her condemned son, and for the wali to commute his sentence, which it was in his power to do. With a cold heart, the sentry tossed the old woman out. The wretched woman sat wailing in pain and bitterness, when she heard a disembodied voice speaking to her:

'What's wrong with you, old woman?'

The old woman told the voice about the catastrophe that had befallen her son, and it responded:

'I advise you to go to a certain place, where there is someone who can help your son.'

And as a drowning person grasps at a straw, the old woman gathered herself up, and entrusted herself to Allah on her way to the place where she hoped she might find a sheikh to help her.

Arriving at a distant mountain, she found a sheikh lighting a fire, then placing above it an earthenware pot.

She greeted him and told him her story.

'Rest a while,' he said to her: 'After we've had a meal together, we will go to the *wali*, Allah willing.'

The old woman didn't want food or anything else, so concerned was she with not wasting time. The sheikh calmed her. After she had eaten a little, he said to her:

'Try now to close your eyes . . .'

She did so, and heard his incantation:

'With your permission, O Lord, we are now in the vicinity of the castle.'

The sheikh motioned for her to climb a ladder now before them. They entered the room of the *wali*, who laughed at this limping Bedu with his antiquated clothes and talk of releasing some old woman's son. The wali said, scornfully:

'Bring the sea to me and I'll release the son.'

The sheikh went down the ladder and out to the edge of the sea, a fair distance from the castle. When he got to the water, he tapped it with his cane and said to it:

'By God's command, follow me.' As he turned in the opposite direction, the waters of the sea followed behind his cane.

The sentry was frightened by this sheikh with his power to command the sea. He hurried back to the wali, who came outside. The wali shouted out:

'Verily, I command you to release the son of the old woman . . . if the sea comes any closer it will drown the castle!'

To which the sheikh replied:

'My son, I wanted to bring the sea to you as you ordered. My task is done.'

Fearing for the castle, the wali asked the sheikh kindly

to take the sea away and put it back in its place. The Sheikh replied.

'Do not worry, it is God's will that the sea will not harm the castle, nor the castle the sea.'

And this is how the castle survived to this day, even as the water crashes against its ramparts.

Sana'a, Yemen, 7 July 1981

Source: Al-Teer Alethi Nasi Rishahu,
Dar Al-Arabiya Lil-Kitab, Libya, 1991

Kamel Maghur

The Old Hotel

or Miloud and Rubina's Story

(Al-Funduq Al-Qadim)

Translated by Basem Tulti and Ethan Chorin

The city of Tripoli is saturated with old hotels. Single men constitute the bulk of tenants of most of those characteristically small, windowless rooms that look out over alleys full of grazing animals. Where windows might otherwise be, some walls are covered with posters of Ali Ibn Abu Talib, fighting the infidels with his sword, or Antra es-Shaddad, splitting his opponents' heads in two. Most of the images, however, are of half-naked women. Those coming in from the market leave their belongings in the yard and lie on the floor without bothering to remove their hats. They cover their faces with pieces of clothing as they wait for daybreak and whatever new business it may bring. Lugging around with them flasks of various suspect liquids, guests drink and drink until they can no longer utter a tune, or until they can no longer resist sleep. On Mamoun Street stands one of these relic pensions, built ages ago. While the surrounding streets change, the Old Hotel does not. Souk Al-Hout, the nearby fish market, was

built in the 1930s by the Italians. In the market square –
also built by the Italians – one used to be able to buy bread
and animal feed.

Just adjacent to the Old Hotel was a spot that had
been home to many different establishments, none of which
seemed to last longer than a month. There were perfume
shops and different types of grocery stores, a pharmacy
that sold traditional medicines. Different types of wild
plants covered the sidewalks. The specimens came from
faraway places and smelled awful. Even though the street-
cleaners collected the floral cuttings, they couldn't take the
stench with them. The faces of the people working in the
area were far less constant than the surroundings. Along
the sidewalks there were stationed carriages – some were
pulled by animals, others by people. Like all the other aged
lodgings in Tripoli, the Old Hotel resembled a large, shape-
less slab.

The front doors of the Old Hotel were always open.
An unlit entrance led into a covered yard. Most of the
rooms were gloomy; a few scant rays of light made it into
the premises through the entrance; fewer still made it up
the stone stairway to the second floor. The rooms on the
ground floor were mainly workspaces; those upstairs served
as guestrooms and living spaces for bachelors. The upstairs
shutters were closed until sunset; the lower rooms were
more fortunate and breathed from dawn till dusk. When
women stayed in the Old Hotel, they took lower floor
rooms next to Fagih Yusuf, who would recite from the
Holy Qur'an and create modest talismans, some of which
he promised would cure untreatable illnesses. Every once
in a while a woman would sneak into the Old Hotel,
covering her face to conceal her identity. Climbing the

stairs silently, she might have a bottle with her. These would listen to the songs of their male companions, then slip out with the approach of dawn.

No one could remember when Miloud Ben Suleiman moved in to his first floor room. He was like all the others, a single man dragging his bare feet behind him, searching for shelter and food. Miloud had just left behind the hopeless town of Zwara, where fishermen display nets full of puny fish, and seawater courses through narrow roads. Miloud didn't miss the vacant stares of men in the markets or the furtive glances of women, capable of breaking through closed doors. He didn't miss those eyes, staring and full of contempt, as his glance passed through openings in cotton dresses. The eyes followed him as he wandered, homeless, passing in and out of the shops where he performed odd jobs, whether unpacking goods or grinding date seeds. When darkness fell, Miloud would make his bed on the beach.

Newly arrived to Tripoli, Miloud found himself in Shalom Algazelle's workroom. The place was dark and smelled of a mixture of homemade wine, stale sweat, and garlic – mixed with fish skins. Whenever a woman, chasing her own road to heaven, entered Fagih Yusuf's room, a crack in the door sill allowed heavy smoke to seep in. Miloud didn't need a bed, or a pillow. A smooth rock served well enough. Most days he didn't even need a blanket. The room was spacious, and Algazelle's wares were all over the place. Miloud didn't know what this stuff was, but he noticed that many of Algazelle's evening clients left carrying what seemed to be large quantities of it.

The first time Shalom saw Miloud, he was leaning against the wall of Souk Al-Hout, scratching his crotch.

One hand on the hip of his waistcoat, Shalom asked, 'Are you looking for work?'

Miloud nodded, then picked up Shalom's straw shopping bag, from which the smell of fish and garlic percolated to fill the narrow road. With Miloud's assent, Shalom emitted a sigh of relief, then invited Ben Suleiman to follow him. A bit later, a cry rang out: 'Oh, God! He is an Arab! What am I going to do with him?!' Rubina's hand instantly shielded her pale breast, which she had just finished wiping clean with a bit of her own spit. She spoke flirtingly, in a manner not quite befitting her age. Shalom smiled and whispered in her ear. Taken somewhat aback by the enthusiastic reaction, Rubina fanned her eyelashes, motioning for Miloud to bring the bag into the kitchen. The house in the small hara[72] was small, and the air was stale. All the rooms were closed except for one with a straw mat and two mattresses and pillows in front of it. With each visit to Rubina, Miloud's stomach filled with beans, and his nostrils with the smell of garlic. If he happened to burp, he'd taste the homemade wine over again.

This first time, Miloud settled himself in the corner of the room and studied Shalom Algazelle and his client. Whereas Shalom was short, Rubina was full-bodied and rather tall. Her red hair divided her head in two parts, and the whole she covered with a translucent yellow headscarf. A wisp of hair brushed against her forehead; traces of saffron coloured her lips dark red. She wore a sleeveless dress that revealed patches of her porcelain appendages. Miloud noticed as Rubina inched ever closer to him.

From then on, she'd darn his shirts and pants, and pass on to him some of Algazelle's clothes. She insisted Miloud grow his hair out and shave his moustache. She would come to visit Algazelle and Miloud in Miloud's room, then accompany Miloud to Souk Al-Hout, where he would watch as she shopped and haggled. He sated himself with the vision of her body, her hips especially, as she moved back and forth in the foreground. 'You will have a home and learn the taste of sweetness,' Rubina once said to him.

Miloud looked into her eyes, wondering why she would bother to occupy her mind with someone like him. Miloud had long grown accustomed to observing the movements of the Old Hotel's residents and transients, as Algazelle unloaded upon him one bit of advice after another. To tell the truth, now he was much more interested in watching the soft gyrations of Rubina's hips and the patch of white skin at the nape of her neck, upon which rested a Star of David. The smell of garlic seemed to stick to her, the way puddles hugged the street after a rainstorm. At Rubina's request, Miloud stomped these puddles away, splattering passers-by, who shot back a volley of insults. 'Don't you even think of becoming a *morcante*,'[73] Shalom said to Miloud, fixing him with a steely gaze. 'Too much work. You can sweep, carry things . . . but never become a morcante. That's not a life!'

Neither Haj Saleh, who stood two meters outside the hotel, nor Haj Meftah, whose shop faced the old school and the trees surrounding it, nor Mukhtar the butcher over in Souk Al-Hout, or Fagih Yusuf, who never left his room, were traders. They'd sell what they could, while the master merchants lay in wait for Jews and Christians, whose money they kept in their shops, wrapped in all manner of bags and boxes. Those were the bigger fish, men who borrowed

from banks owned by men who wore white suits and
knee-high trousers. On Mamoun Street, Rashid Street, and
in Souk Al-Hout the only people you found were Arabs,
Maltese and Italians. Their accents differed from those of
the men in white suits. Their language was different from
those in knee-high trousers.

'I suppose I can't be a *morcante* then,' Miloud reflected,
as he shadowed Shalom on his rounds of the hotel,
responding to the needs of its occupants, whether for food,
water or simply conversation.

Algazelle told Miloud he thought he should buy a tea
set, and Rubina volunteered to pay for it. Miloud repaid
her bit by bit every week, adding in something for the
kettle. Thereafter, the residents and guests of the hotel were
accustomed to the smell of freshly brewed tea, fragrant and
tempting, wafting from Algazelle's room out into the yard.
The smell of tea floated out to neighbouring shops and
street peddlers. They heard about it at the old school too.
Even covered women stopped by Ben Suleiman's door; a
few of them plucked up the courage to ask him for a cup
of that translucent tea. As they sipped the tea and the froth
that covered it, they began to show their satisfied, smiling
faces.

By this point, there were no outward traces of Zwara
left in Miloud. On his legs were trousers he'd bought from
the market. He wore a white hat. Gone were the traditional
clothes, traded for a blue coat with red buttons and two
pockets on either side. The coat even had a breast pocket,
in which he kept his room key. He started to wear shoes
to protect his calloused feet.

As Miloud sat before the tea set, with his right hand
he raised the kettle high. It produced a soothing, sputtering

sound. He collected the yellow froth in a cup. He would later add it back to the tea, which he poured into smaller glasses. This way he served hundreds of people, including Fagih Yusuf's female guests. After receiving good news from Heaven, they'd sit and drink some tea.

So this is what happened to Miloud Ben Suleiman. He forgot Zwara; he forgot its pain, the men, women, and stares of contempt from women on the street and behind closed doors. As he rested his head on Rubina's supple thighs, the memories returned: how he first came to Tripoli. Their first meeting. The beans. How frightened Rubina was at first by the Muslim man whose head now rested on her thigh. Just now, she reminded him of Shalom Algazelle's unfortunate demise.

One day, a group of men broke through the entrance and banged on Algazelle's door. The men weren't masked, and weren't wearing traditional clothes. Their faces betrayed an incredible anger. One of them pulled on Algazelle's neck and cut it from ear to ear. Fearing what might come next, Rubina swore she was Muslim:

'I say the shahada.[74] I fast and sometimes even pray.'

Sitting in shock in a corner of the yard, Rubina mumbled to herself, oblivious to the blood gushing from Algazelle's veins. She didn't notice how it clotted on the clean floor of the yard, or the fact that there were puddles all around that Ben Suleiman hadn't brushed out onto the street.

'I swear by Sidi Almarghani and my grandfather Ben Suleiman . . . she's a Muslim now,' Miloud repeated, over and over.

Miloud's eyes bulged out; the veins in his neck were visible. With his right hand he stayed the knife of a man making for Rubina, his intention obviously to inflict upon her the same fate as that of Algazelle.

'I swear . . .', he pleaded. 'She even named herself Sliema.'

When the men left, Rubina threw herself into Miloud's arms and held him tight. She couldn't see that Algazelle's clotted blood had turned black, that he looked like a dead and diseased animal.

Thereafter, Rubina took to staring at the low ceiling of the covered yard. Occasionally, she'd beat upon Miloud's chest. It was as if Shalom's ghost were standing right there before her. At times her gasps were so loud they could be heard beyond the hotel's walls. 'Shame be on the Jews of the neighbourhood. The one who doesn't die here leaves on a boat!' Miloud grumbled.

Miloud responded to the sight of Rubina by closing his eyes. He told himself, 'Whoever said to be a trader is difficult! Whoever said this is only work for those who wear short trousers and white suits! Whoever said that Miloud Ben Suleiman can never be a morcante, that the best he can do is to sweep dirt!'

Feeling Rubina's knee, he savored the fact that this room was his own, and that he had the key to another. That he had men who worked for him, one to make the tea and another to carry his packages. He even had an accountant who visited shopkeepers to settle their accounts – money that was added to that left by Shalom, plus a trace of Rubina's savings. Rubina spent her money throughout the city, in the streets and all the cinemas. Miloud walked by her side without carrying a quffa.[75] In front of others, Miloud called her Sliema the Muslim. She'd laugh and say, with a hint of sarcasm:

'I swear I even say the fajri prayers.'[76]

With the change in circumstances, Miloud began to find the atmosphere of the Old Hotel suffocating. As he stood in front of the entrance, hawkers were selling wild plants and cans. They envied his white trousers, silk jacket and blue shirt, all left by Shalom. The veins on Miloud's neck were visible. He played with his keychain while he waited for one of his men to arrive with a package.

Everything about the neighbourhood changed but the Old Hotel and Souk Al-Hout. Mamoun Street was different, and so was Sharia Al-Rashid. Some of the landmarks had moved a bit – at least, so it seemed. Men in suits and short trousers, as well as women in short skirts, were no longer welcome. Women continued to visit Fagih Yusuf, whose beard was now dyed red with henna. A large number didn't cover up as they used to. The fagih chanted incantations, while invoking heavenly revelations and demons alike. It didn't matter whether he was in the presence of a veiled woman or one who was uncovered.

Despite the fact that it looked the same from the outside, there were changes inside the Old Hotel. Noise forced the single men to leave and the yard became a repository for old boxes and bags – Miloud kept them there until he could distribute them among the trader-tenants. Soon, of the guests, all that remained were Fagih Yusuf and Miloud's men. One carried the goods, another made tea in the room on the right. Customers waited outside to get their tea, ten piasters per cup. One by one, Miloud repossessed the rooms. Not long after, the only residents were Miloud and Fagih Yusuf, whose presence Miloud found somewhat calming. Miloud no longer wore a hat. Untrimmed, his hair became black and curly; each morning Rubina combed it with Vaseline. Before he went out, she'd burn incense and recite protective mantras. Every morning she taught him a new chant: 'Shambarookh and the Ten Words . . . Kubbara in the eyes of the Arabs and Christians,' she repeated.

Rubina was beginning to suspect that one of these days Miloud might not return. Indeed, after meeting Oreida, Miloud Ben Suleiman felt the same way. While his outward appearance had changed, inside, Miloud was the same old Miloud. He had begun to miss Zwara and his old food, and longed to sleep on the beach, to spy on women as they sunned themselves in cotton dresses showing much of what at other times they hid. Miloud craved those blue eyes and pink cheeks, women with green-hued tattoos on their soft bodies, sparkling as they splashed water on one another. Rubina's porcelain flesh didn't appeal to him anymore. Rubina . . . Sliema . . . whoever she was.

Resting his head on her thigh, Miloud couldn't feel anything below him now but an old rock. It was as if Rubina had fossilized. He no longer savoured those evenings the two of them feasted on beans and haraymi,[77] and drank homemade liquor on a straw mattress laid out in the yard. He couldn't stand giving her money. He longed to escape Mamoun and Rashid Streets.

One day, Miloud awoke to a decision. The neighbourhood shopkeepers and street peddlers were surprised to see him place his hand on the front door of the Old Hotel, walk into the main corridor and count the rooms, all as if he were seeing them for the first time. Again he fixed his gaze on the staircase and felt the sides of the doors. He tapped at the dead floor with his feet, and in so doing felt the effects of the wood-eating black stains fed by moisture produced by daily washings of the tea set.

'Shambarookh and the Ten Words . . . what nonsense!'
Miloud muttered to himself. He shook his head vigorously,
but his curly hair didn't budge.

'You might really consider Oreida,' he heard Fagih Yusuf
whisper from some dark corner.

The shopkeepers and the street peddlers took note of
the tall woman who began to frequent the Old Hotel.
Oreida arrived always in a multi-coloured carriage, drawn
by a white horse wearing a bell and two jasmine necklaces
around its neck. She wore a pure white farashiya)[78] that
only partially covered her face. When she smiled, a single
gold tooth sparkled in the sunlight.

Her face was lit like a star at night; her eyes were the
colour of honey. Carefully-pencilled eyebrows crowned her
long lashes. She held the end of her farashiya with her left
hand. Extending her hand to raise a cup of tea, the thin
bangles that covered her arm from hand to elbow jingled
and sparkled, illuminating her arm. Heels made her taller
than she already was – so tall she literally looked down
upon people. Those who saw her found they couldn't move,
even blink, until she was out of sight. Once she finished
her tea, Oreida would stroll down to the fagih's room. She
wasn't like the previous visitors. Oreida strutted around the
garden affectedly, then paused at the entrance. She drank
in the stares of those she'd distracted from their shopping.
She didn't haggle, nor did she buy.

The 'Arsa'[79] as the fagih used to call her, entered the
room and sat before him on the floor. He lit incense and
chanted hymns. They spoke. Finally, she would place a small
bag of money in his lap. From the moment he saw her,
Miloud wished she would come to him, so that he might
serve her his trademark frothy brown tea, then observe as

she drank through her teeth. But Miloud knew Oreida was not thinking of him. Today she arrived in her carriage with white horse adorned with bells and jasmine necklaces. She flitted by, ignoring everyone and everything until it was time for her appointment with the fagih.

Sipping the tea which Miloud brought, the fagih broached the subject of Arsa. She was old. She lived on Baz Street, but was free to move where she pleased. Not the morals police, nor a madam, nor the health inspector could stop her. She had so many acquaintances she might be considered a landmark. Arsa! She stayed at home when she wanted and wandered the city at will. Despite all that freedom, her appointments with Fagih Yusuf were fixed. She consulted him and she financed him. He supplied her with the talismans and amulets that drew men to her.

Despite all her suitors, there was nothing permanent in Arsa's life. Maybe it was because she didn't find anyone she could trust with her money. Perhaps she didn't find one deserving of her home-grown nectar, a quaff from the cane of Moses: delicious, but doled out sparingly. As the fagih savored his words, his left hand pulled the small hairs in his moustache and beard. Miloud had no access to Oreida.

It was then that Fagih Yusuf said to the Zwarian, as he swallowed what was stuck to his throat of the bitter tea, 'What Arsa craves is money.'

Miloud was beginning to like the idea that he might not return home to the small hara; that Rubina's chants weren't going to keep him long. Perhaps he would only give her a small share of what Algazelle had left him.'What do you think, fagih?'

'Money can build you a road through the sea.'

'Oh, no. God save me from the evil of that Zwarian. A magician, he is. He practiced magic on that Muslim-Jewish woman.'

That was Oreida's reply to the fagih's contrived statements about Miloud, how much money and real estate he owned.

'If I follow him I will lose everything that I have. Look at what he did to Rubina.' For the story of Ben Suleiman and Rubina was well known, even to those who lived on Baz Street.

Without dwindling support from Miloud, Rubina rented a sewing machine, to which she was tied from the minute Miloud left the house until he came back at night. The women of the hara hired her to sew clothes – mostly for weddings, but also funerals. As news of her skill reached Dahra and Benashur Streets, women from Fernaj and Souk Al- Juma knocked on her door.

Sliema took solace in these visits. She sat with the women and listened to their stories about their husbands, their lives, altercations with neighbours; the roads they took, what they saw during the day. They repeated the gossip they heard, at times in a state of near-ecstasy. Miloud found excuses to leave her alone. Rubina's clients and friends bothered him, as they filled their home with stories and arguments. He couldn't move around, with all the cloth in the house and yard.

Miloud found his way to the small hara and Bab Al-Jadeed. Occasionally he passed through Baz Street and Sidi Omran, hoping to see Oreida without her farashiya. Then he'd return to Mamoun Street to consult Fagih, who could usually calm his nerves. Invariably Fagih would tell him that the heavens had answered his prayers. An opportunity was near! The good news came at a cost, of course.

Miloud was generous with Fagih Yusuf, beyond the teacups filled with almonds and plates of good food; the rewards were commensurate with the quality of the news that flowed through the Fagih's thick beard and moustache. Fagih Yusuf mediated between Miloud and Oreida. He took Miloud to Souk Almusheer, where he helped him pick out various bracelets, gold coins and necklaces for the 'Arsa'. If Ben Suleiman never actually saw them adorning her chest or around her arms, he could be sure she wore them at weddings.

The more good news Fagih Yusuf found for Miloud in the heavens and the more promises he elicited from Oreida, the more generous Miloud became – and the less he gave to Rubina, who had grown tired of sewing night and day. The house was crowded with all manner of women, to the point that Miloud lost his patience, and stopped using it as refuge. Indeed, he had decided not to come back.

In the same way that the hotel visitors were surprised to see Ben Suleiman buy the Old Hotel and use it as residence, they were surprised to learn that he had begun to use only two rooms on the top floor. He bought a desk and a bed from Mezran Street and put one piece in each room. He hung pictures of women, some striking indecent poses, some covered, as if to remind him of Oreida or to warn him that she might at any instant come into either or both rooms. He imagined her, gold tooth sparkling, sitting on a chair or the bed drinking the tea he made for her. Fagih Yusuf's seances with Oreida got longer and longer.

At the end of each, he would hurry to the office where Ben Suleiman sat anxiously waiting for news of Arsa's demands.

'She's accepted,' Fagih announced one day, 'but she wants her dowry in advance – preferably today or tomorrow.'

Oreida wanted cash to buy a place and suitable furniture. She wanted Ben Suleiman to pay off her debts to her madam. She wanted to be with Miloud, sweet as honey, pure like the Hinsheer stream, redolent like the jasmine of Almanshiya, warm and refreshing as the white sandy beaches of Zwara. Ben Suleiman wouldn't need his office or bedroom. The garlic smell that used to penetrate his veins would stay with Rubina and her clothes. He would no longer need to tramp over her customers' clothes; nor would he see the shadows of the houses of the hara, or be subjected to the noise of Mamoun and Rashid Streets. The fagih promised him special incense and talismans to make time pass quickly, as if an hour or part of an hour. He even offered the possibility that he ultimately he might not have any need for him to mediate, that Miloud would speak with Orieda directly, without need of amulet or incense.

The shorter and shorter were Ben Suleiman's visits, the more upset Rubina became. He'd leave the house in the mornings and return in the middle of the night. Some nights he didn't return at all. Her talismans didn't help, nor did her insomnia or listening for the door's creaking. She had little of his money, and even less of him.

'What's happening to Miloud? How awful, how awful,' she would repeat to herself. Indeed, Ben Suleiman's feelings for Rubina seemed to fade with each new day. It began to dawn on Rubina that he wasn't coming back. The last time, Ben Suleiman was absent for more than three days. Rubina poured all her energy into sewing. Waiting was by now an old friend. She didn't enter the bedroom, but slept instead on a straw mat. Her eyes studied the ceiling, looking for a ghost. There were no more fires in her kitchen.

Oreida too disappeared for three days, and Fagih Yusuf was nowhere to be seen. The women waiting at his doorstep returned, some in tears, afraid that the pious saint had died or an illness had befallen him. Ben Suleiman opened the door of the office, leaning on the balustrade of the top floor most of the time, planting his gaze on the entrance, awaiting the return of Arsa or Fagih.

Ben Suleiman knocked on the door of the brothel on Baz Street. The Madam told him that Oreida had left, that she had gone and gotten herself married.

Somewhere Rubina found the courage to abandon her sewing machine and her customers' clothes and drag herself to the Old Hotel. Miloud received her with tousled hair. There were blue rings around his eyes and he was leaning against the balustrade that faced the entrance. His body bent and weak, Miloud was incapable of standing up or indeed moving. First propping him up, Rubina then took Miloud in her arms. He paused for a moment in front of Fagih Yusuf's room. It was clear the magician wouldn't return. The door was left ajar, and the room was empty except for a few books stacked in haphazard piles, an ashtray covered in grey dust, pens and papers prepared for folding into talismans or soaking in water. The air reeked of incense.

In the end, Miloud Ben Suleiman made good his promise never to return to the Old Hotel. It was enough that his men returned. Rubina abandoned sewing and turned away those women who came to her door. She didn't even bother to ask who was knocking. She filled Miloud's stomach with beans and haraymi and poured him homemade liquor. With his head resting on her thigh she chanted, 'Kubbara in the eyes of Arabs and Christians.'

Ottawa, 4 May 2001
Source: Kamel Maghur, Qisas Qasira,
Dar Al-Ruwad, Libya, 200

Zwara

Thirty-nine kilometres past Sabratha (west of Tripoli) lies the former customs post and camel-breeding centre of Zwara, which Ward, c. 1967, describes as a 'picturesque line of small shops well worth a photograph . . . wonderful beaches.'[80] One of my Libyan colleagues responded to my casual inquiry about the place with an excess of enthusiasm.

'But I am *Zwaran*,' Ahmed exclaimed, with a mixture of disbelief and pride that showed he felt somehow I should have known this. One weekend in early January I took him up on his longstanding offer to show me the town of about 70,000 inhabitants. Apart from Maghur's characterizations in *Miloud and Rubina's Story*, all I knew about Zwara was that it was a Berber stronghold not far from the Libyan–Tunisian border, and home to one of the largest fishing fleets in Libya – a mere fifty or so boats. Zwara is also infamous for being the primary staging point for the illegal transit trade in African refugees, who pay up to 2,000 Libyan Dinar each for passage to either Sicily or Lampedusa. It takes the average worker more than two years to save this amount. Locals say the trips have a 95 per cent success rate, despite – or because of – half-hearted attempts by local authorities to intercept the boats before they reach international waters. What happens to these hapless people once they reach the other side is another story.

Ahmed and Adel, a senior geologist with one of the Western oil companies, picked me up at home late in the afternoon and we headed west by car, via the towns of

Sabratha and Zawiya, the terminus for a major oil pipeline from the Libyan interior.

My first impressions of Zwara were of a city not unlike many other medium-sized towns in Libya. With a light late afternoon rain, the dirt roads had already turned to mud, while massive puddles, mini-lakes, remained from the previous deluge. The road into Zwara is dotted with 1970s model two-storey concrete structures, many of them unfinished. One difference from Tripoli is the presence of endless fruit stalls, filled with much fresher produce than I had been used to seeing in Tripoli. The stalls cater to those Tunisians who come across the border for good buys in clothes and toiletries, and the Libyans travelling to Tunis, many for medical care.

Dinner consisted of a Zwaran specialty: fish of all kinds – sepia, squid, trillia, murjan, shola, in various tomato-based sauces, ready to be spread over plates of couscous. The evening conversation – males only – touched the history of the Berbers in Libya, their origins, language and tastes. While the authorities permit the sale of the odd CD imported from Algeria or Morocco, books written in Amazigh, one of the three main North African Berber languages, are banned. At the time of the Arab conquest of North Africa under Amr Ibn Al-As, all Libya was either Berber or Roman. My host made the point that, even though the 200,000-strong Berber community is tightly knit, most Libyans have some Berber blood in them.

During my stay in Libya, I had been invited into people's homes but a handful of times, and in the majority of cases these were families that had already crossed the Rubicon by marriage with a foreigner. My guests offered to put me up, but it was clear to me that the most comfortable solution was for me to go to a hotel run by (of course) a cousin or friend of the family. I was escorted by five members of the extended family to Zwara's newest hotel, the Dolphin.

I was chatting with a Tunisian waiter in a baby blue breakfast nook the next morning when Ahmed and Adel arrived to take me to Farwa Island. We drove back through a collection of huge puddles out onto the main road, into 'downtown' Zwara, renamed *Khamsat Nuqut*, or 'Five Points' after a speech Colonel Gaddafi gave here on 16 April 1973, outlining his plans for the Popular Revolution which created the political and economic landscape that is present-day Libya.

Here in plain view are Miloud's narrow streets, and shops with façades illustrated by drawings of fish in various stages of dismemberment. We left the centre and headed towards the Tunisian border, past a stretch of gorgeous sea, whose beach – what one could see of it – was littered with plastic bags and cans. In the middle, a newish-looking kiosk bearing an even newer advertisement for 'Bitter Soda'. Further on, garbage faded out and there unfolded a sandy seafront, carpeted by waves of small blue and yellow flowers – fig trees, their branches bare of foliage, olives, and the occasional grapevine. Kamel Maghur's characterization of Zwara in *Miloud and Rubina's Story* as a 'hopeless city' is rather unkind and not completely accurate – at least not today, as a visitor's first thought is probably 'what a nice place for a resort'.

At the end of a thoroughly enjoyable day, Ahmed drove me back to Tripoli in his old Peugeot, all the while reminiscing about his three years at the University of Oklahoma, which he clearly considered one of the highlights of his life thus far. So there we were, on that evening, sitting next to each other in a car manufactured before I was born, talking about Oklahoma and laughing over the awkward and catchy lyrics to Dolly Parton's 1970s' song, 'My Potential Boyfriend' and 'Two Doors Down', the meanings of which would be lost on most Libyans – save perhaps those who had spent three years in Oklahoma.

The Old Hotel, Rashid Street

In recent years any number of European prime ministers, African presidents and their entourages have rolled up the incline and drop bar manned by seemingly insouciant guards, to the Corinthia Bab Hotel, with its inset-glass façade and symbolic sandy-orange 'door' to Africa. Go in the reverse direction by foot – people rarely do – and thirty paces below you'll hit the busy street, where taxis are cheap and life is real. Just ahead, the newly re-plastered walls of the Old City. A little to the right, crowds of men mingle around derelict coaches and shared taxis bound for Egypt, or south to desert spots like Sebha and Kufra. There are no pavements, and in the early afternoon, the traffic is murder. To the left is Shari'a Rashid – Rashid Street – which intersects with Shari'a Omar Al-Mokhtar three blocks down. Home to the Old Hotel, this area is still filled with old, grubby rooms for rent, most of which lie in the upper reaches of apartment buildings built on top of a colonnade that stretches most of the length of the street. The vast majority of shops sell clothing, fake Rolex watches and pirated CDs. If you're in the market for a 'Gaddafi watch', the most prized form of tourist memorabilia, here's where you get the best deals and the most interesting specimens, sold by young men with wheelbarrows full of appliances. In 2005 I found a Gaddafi watch with the Leader's profile emblazoned over an American flag. Manufactured in China, of course.

Souk Al-Hout, the fish market, was a landmark in pre-Revolutionary Tripoli. Halfway down Al-Rashid, the painted green colonnade opens out into a warren of indoor shops. Follow the smell further north, into the belly of the covered market, and suddenly you're in the middle of a fishy operating theatre tiled dirty white. Men with oversize yellow gloves manage a triage of sorts, tossing fins, fillets and heads into piles for sale or rubbish, when they're not poking taught carcasses with ballpoint pens to demonstrate their resilience. On a bit more, past spice sellers and bins of random toiletries, a store sells hand soap in bulk. When I first read The Old Hotel, in my mind's eye I placed it right around here, in one of the alleys behind Shari'a Al-Rashid, within a stone's throw of Souk Al-Hout.

Maghur & Partners

Azza Maghur's single-storey office sits on the corner of a narrow street in the Dahra neighbourhood of Tripoli, not far from the Italian Embassy. I met Azza on the referral of a contact in London. Basem's prior connections to her sealed the deal. A prominent, Sorbonne-educated commercial lawyer, Azza gave us wonderful perspective on Libyan commercial law, delivered with infectious enthusiasm over small cups of mint tea.

Having discovered early on that Azza's father, a Libyan

diplomat and ex-Foreign Minister, had also been a writer, I asked if she'd be willing to let us look through a few of his books, as well as those of any other Libyan writers with which she was familiar. Loading us with copies of *Medinat Al-Beida,* The White City, one of Tripoli's nicknames), she made a plea for us to 'go out and find those young Libyan writers'. While she cautioned that much of this work remained unpublished and was difficult to find, she thought that there was material worth the search.

It does not take long in conversations with Azza – on any topic – to see that she absolutely adored her father. Black and white pictures of the elder, broad-shouldered, bespectacled Maghur, adorn the walls of the offices' ante-room: Maghur as Libyan representative to the UN; Maghur in Scotland, flanked by Azza and other members of the legal team (including Basem). Azza's personal study is filled with glass cases, behind which stand leather-bound legal books in French and Arabic, each carefully arranged under Arabic tabs, 'Civil Law', 'International Treaties', etc. The walls of the secretary's office are covered with detailed maps of Chad and Tunisia, with lines marking Libya's claimed borders in disputes over oil-rich real estate, and etchings and paintings illustrating 'working Libyans' in various poses. Over her desk hangs an enlarged, framed cover from her father's last book, entitled simply *Qisas*, or 'Stories'. The drawing is of Maghur in his later years, bearded and dressed in a suit, looking as though he were just about to set to work. I have no doubt this was just the impression Azza was looking for.

In early March 2005, Azza tells us how her father, who developed his literary reputation over the course of the early 1960s and 1970s, found himself drawn again to writing.

It was, she said, as if he felt compelled to expel the last of
the ideas and observations accumulated over the previous
decades, during which he had been a direct participant in
many of the most tumultuous political struggles of post-
Revolutionary Libya. During the two years before he died,
the elder Maghur stole time to write wherever he could,
jotting down bits of dialogue and plotlines on scraps of
paper. He scribbled in the cafés of European capitals, hotel
lobbies, in his office, on anything he could find – match-
boxes and receipts, even. One imagines that amidst the
chaos of his professional responsibilities, Kamel Maghur
found it comforting to return to the 'professional hobby'
of his early years.

Over the half-decade before his death in 2000, Maghur
produced an enormous amount of work, some of it in draft
form. The piece included here, *Miloud and Rubina's Story*,
was written in the late 1990s. Today Azza shows us, with
great pride, a brand-new plaque, just delivered, on which
is written in English and Arabic 'Maghur & Partners'.

Lamia El-Makki

Tripoli Story

(Hekaya Trabulsia)

Translated by Ethan Chorin

It was the night of *Eid As-Saghir*. From Khalifa's perspective, this was not like the Ramadan nights of years past. He was now in his forties, accustomed to nights like these. Full of delight and joy for Ramadan and Eid, this was the time he would scoop up his wife and boys and drive them in his rust-covered, tattered car to bargain shops spread throughout Tripoli's shabby banlieu: the Bu Sleim public market, shops along Shari'a Rashid, and the tents tradition-ally erected during Eid al Fitr to sell clothes and cheap, Chinese-made toys. On *Eid Al-Adha* the same tents would spring up in front of *Souk Al-Noflieen*,[81] and along Ras Hasan Street. There one could find everything one would need for Eid Al-Kebir, for the slaughter and quartering of meat, including knives, floor tiles and chopping blocks.[82]

This night, *this night*, Khalifa is at the wheel of a brand-new luxury car – the latest model, of course – holding in his hand a cell phone in blatant violation of a law that prohibits the use of *naqaalat* while driving.[83] Today he is taking his family to shop at Al-Jaraba Street and Gargaresh. At his side, his wife Aisha is lost in anticipation. She is imagining herself shopping for clothes and household goods in places frequented by the middle and upper class, people who one would expect would buy their holiday sweets from the trendiest spots in Tripoli. No longer would she bother tiring herself out, preparing holiday treats at home with her mother-in-law and her daughters.

Khalifa's circumstances changed at last after he decided to say goodbye to his administrative job. How long ago now that seemed! He had his doubts, but finally took the plunge, imitating colleagues who ditched their positions as functionaries to open businesses, businesses of the sort he hoped might make it possible for him to trade in his junk-heap of a car, toss out his ratty shoes and buy the things his wife and kids needed. Ah, and to subscribe to a cell-phone service, the one that didn't disconnect whenever you left Tripoli!

Khalifa's venture began as a modest proposition, arranged between him and two business partners. Soon it blossomed, and they were hiring others. Now he could afford to trade in his life of bankruptcy for creature comforts. In a short time he went from scrounging and want to relative opulence. Khalifa wore now a suit and Italian-made shoes; Aisha strung her neck with jewels and gold. Khalifa quickly replaced the furnishings in their modest traditional-style house in Fashloum, and helped renovate his parents' house in Sidi Khalifa. He expected soon to be able to move the family into a two or three-storey villa in one of the upmarket neighbourhoods.

Amazing. Simply amazing, Khalifa thought to himself. He was meeting friends and partners in fancy restaurants and five-star hotels. His chest puffed out a bit with the thought that he could send his eldest son to the United Kingdom to pursue a course in English, something only his former bosses had previously been able to do! As for Aisha, she began to go out more often, attending occasions for friends and family, each time clad in a new evening dress of the most 'in' cut, with jewelry to match. She started receiving invitations from people she never dreamed would pay her any attention.

Khalifa certainly wasn't stingy with her. He bought her a cell phone. Naturally, she was no less than the other women of the family. To each special occasion she went out carrying this custom-made cell phone, on which she could read text messages from her husband or their driver, who could now tell her that he was waiting outside the door, instead of having a friend announce her name over the hall speakers. The rest of the time, those interruptions would be one of her sisters calling to discuss food, or plans for lunch, or the way to make such and such . . . Do you add cumin to the kefta or not?! Will she go to the 'sbou' with someone from her new social circle, or not, and if she does, what will she wear, an evening dress in European style, or a traditional outfit and an Arabic suit? Of course, this would all depend on whether the party had zimzamaat, or a DJ!!![84]

Aisha encouraged her husband to work constantly. If she gave it any thought, perhaps she assuaged suppressed guilt with the knowledge that he also had all the creature comforts he could ever want. She did not actively make his life miserable as she used to, of course, for he was now the goose that laid the golden eggs. For Aisha, Khalifa now served no function apart from the work he undertook. The important thing was that the opportunities (and the money) kept on coming.

'There's no avoiding it,' she'd tell him. 'No better time to make "business."'

It didn't matter that no one — not she, nor anyone else in the family — knew exactly what Khalifa's 'business' was, nor anything about his longer-term plans. The important thing: this was that he earn yet more from his new occupation. Only this was enough to gain the respect of those around him and to make the neighbours horribly jealous; also Aisha's relatives, those who weren't so lucky as to have husbands like him.

Khalifa was finally basking in the pleasures of the refined life of which he had long dreamt. Even travel abroad had become possible. The price of the ticket, lodging and the visa — all had become matters easily settled (though even this he wasn't really prepared to enjoy, for he didn't speak any foreign languages). Something was missing, a bit of the *joie de vivre* he had experienced occasionally in the past.

One day a crazy idea hit him. Perhaps he could change the routine of a life which had now become routine. What if he married another woman, someone more youthful and beautiful than Aisha, someone who knew nothing of his past. He had no doubt that the young girls would find him attractive just for the fact that he was wealthy and could provide them with a comfortable life. The sad bit of it was, he was pretty sure that Aisha would not mind, not as long as she could keep her clothes and finery, not as long as she could eat well and carry a cell phone wherever she went.

Source: Lamia El-Makki, unpublished.

Lamia El-Makki, Aspiring Writer

Lamia El-Makki is a paradox and, at the same time, a model for what many Arab intellectuals would like to claim they have inspired or influenced in some way. A devout Muslim, she is adamant that family obligations are paramount, and brooks no compromise to conservative attire. At the same time, she believes women should hold professional appointments, and that they should be men's equals at jobs for which they are equally qualified. Lamia's piece *Tripoli Story* has a fresh, unselfconscious style and – in addition to being full of Libyan place-markers – is an attractive piece of cultural anthropology.

Ali Mustapha Misrati

Special Edition

Translated by Basem Tulti and Ethan Chorin

The phone rang in the office of the Associate Editor for
Political and Financial Affairs at an unnamed newspaper in
a neighbouring country. The Editor fixed his tie (the one
he'd bought in Paris). Massaging his Parker pen with its
golden nib, a gift from an oil prince from the Arab south,
he extinguished his fancy cigar in an elegant crystal ashtray.
He prepared himself to meet with 'His Excellency' the
Editor-in-Chief, who wanted him in his office immediately.

'This must be some important matter!' he thought to
himself. With his fingers he rapped cautiously on the glass
door. In a moment, he was standing before the boss.

'We need to do a special edition. Show us what you've
got.' The Editor bowed like a question mark drawn by a
trembling hand. He smiled as a professional waiter might.

'We've done special editions on Kuwait, Qatar, Bahrain,
Saudi Arabia and Shakboot.[85] Sir was happy with what we
managed to do there, no?'

The boss swayed on his revolving chair and said, as if
he were chewing his words, 'Yes, yes, but there's still North
Africa.'

'True, we need to do something on those places. Special

issues on glossy paper. Which country are you thinking about?'

'A special edition on . . . Libya.'

The Editor scratched his gel-coated head. He had just returned from the barbershop where he had spent an hour having his hair ironed and combed.

'Libya. Libya,' he muttered to himself quizzically, lifting an eyebrow as if trying mentally to locate the place.

'Don't you know that they've discovered oil in Libya?' the Editor-in-Chief pressed. 'Didn't you read the story in *Life*, and those in the other flashy magazines published in Paris and London? This is the stuff of headlines. Libya is now swimming in oil!'

'Seems Libya is an Arab country. They must be generous, as all Arabs are,' the Associate Editor mused.

The Editor-in-Chief took out a map and pored over it.

'Make a tour. Visit Tunisia, Algeria and Morocco, the whole set. Do everything you can to sell subscriptions and advertisements. Take some pictures of leaders, businessmen and the wealthy cats. This must be a scoop. Give it a good go.'

The Editor-in-Chief rang for his secretary, then turned to face his colleague.

'Get your passport and photos, and pack your things. The paper is going to do a special edition on Libya.'

The Associate Editor scratched his head.

'So, where is the Libyan embassy?'

'They must have an embassy here,' said the Editor-in-Chief. 'I met one of their staff at a cocktail party, but I forget his name. Anyway, we have an embassy directory somewhere. Look it up and get that approval for a special edition.'

The Editor-in-Chief continued absently, 'Oh, and don't forget to ask about the weather. What do you need, thick coat or shorts? Take a camera, of course. And pass by the advertising and subscriptions department. They'll supply you with notebooks and receipts.'

The Editor-in-Chief gripped his fist. A special edition! It must be thick, with a lot of colour pictures. It had to be full of advertisements and pictures of important people. The Associate Editor was making to leave, when the boss interjected.

'Fifteen days. you've got fifteen days. All the material, the photos and the reports must be ready. Don't leave out a single official or minister or VIP – especially company directors. In an oil country there are lots of companies, both foreign and local. You know the drill . . . advertising and promotions pay our salaries. Now go!'

The next morning the energetic Associate Editor was on his way to Libya, land of oil. He hadn't read a thing about the place and consequently knew nothing about its people or their concerns. All he saw were dollar signs.

Upon arrival, he took a suite in the most luxurious hotel in the city. A car and guide were on call. According to the standard arrangements, he was a guest of the authority in charge of such matters.

With a camera slung around his neck, the Associate Editor began his rounds, paying his respects to ministers, rulers, corporate presidents, company managers, and all manner of generic wealthy people, clutching their fat, thick, wealthy bellies.

The Associate Editor met with His Honour, His Excellence and various people of influence. Thank God this country didn't value titles and honorifics. All the same, there was no harm for an ambitious journalist to be liberal with diplomatic niceties, nothing to be lost through hyperbole and a sprinkling of titles. Quite the contrary. The Editor showered his interlocutors with references to their fame and wit. He took lots of photos. All of the people he met were very busy – God knows with what. He used his pen to fill blank pages with remarks about self-titled geniuses, examples of piety and generosity, philanthropists and miracles of the twentieth century (every wealthy man he met was of course a self-made, self-sacrificing genius).

The Associate Editor ate in handsome villas and stayed up late regaling his hosts with entertaining stories. He collected checks of magical proportions, which encouraged him to write yet more about virtuous and generous men, described one important person he met as 'a reformer, a pillar of society', then proceeded to take pictures of the man's horses, chickens, ducks, fish and dogs. He visited companies named for people who ate other people for breakfast. They all sat at their desks like faded pictures, their fingers waiting for the end of the month's paycheck. He wrote about them all, about their understanding of economics and differential equations. Einstein would have been ashamed to see them; Darwin would have used them as examples to support his theory.

The Associate Editor visited all of the exploitative corporations. He concocted gibberish, developed photos and shot colour film. Some departments he visited only long enough to peek in the door and feel the check with his forefingers. All in the name of the Special Edition. At that point, the Associate Editor telexed the Boss: 'I'm still working on this special edition on Libya. Could you see clear to extending the deadline another week? Do you mind changing the date of publication? We've got a bonanza here. Accounts receivable will dance with joy.'

The Associate Editor received a reply almost as soon as he sent it. 'Continue your work. We'll increase the number of prints. Take more photos of officials and company owners. Good job and good luck!'

The journalist continued his rounds, taking photos of all kinds. He captured the minister talking on the phone, the minister signing papers, the minister smiling, the minister sitting, the minister standing. He did the same with the deputy minister, whom he captured on film standing, sitting and pointing with his finger. Following his discovery of how things worked here, the amount of money he collected increased exponentially. He wrote about prosperity and the comfortable lives people lived in Libya.

The Associate Editor didn't visit any hospitals. Disease was definitely not his business. He was a highly sensitive man and didn't want his sensibilities offended. He didn't visit the hovels of which he caught an accidental glimpse from his car. He pretended not to notice. He didn't visit any villages, so he couldn't recount their daily struggles. The Associate Editor wanted nothing to do with any of that. If he wanted, he could see that in his own country. He was here to prepare a special edition, full of photos of Their Excellencies, Their Highnesses. He would write only about prosperity and progress. Why talk about hovels, misery and the fight for survival?! Simply put, he didn't have the time.

The Associate Editor spent nights in cabarets drinking champagne and whisky with Greek and Italian dancers, toasting the profession of journalism, special reports and Arab hospitality. During the day he took photos of the faces and behinds of the powerful men who were doubling his money. Then he went to sleep. A private car was always at his disposal if he wanted to visit Leptis Magna, Sabrata or Cyrene. A special companion was his when he wanted. The hotel bill, the drinks, the meals and the special nights were all billed to the Account of Arab Generosity. As the saying goes, he was eating cake in heaven.

The Associate Editor had heard recently that one of his colleagues had collected £70,000 for a special edition. It was an astronomical sum, never before given to a journalist in Qatar, Bahrain or Kuwait. Would his take approach that figure? The prospect of a professional coup tempted the energetic journalist to ham it up with fake histories and biographies making it seem that the *noveaux riches* were geniuses when they were still in nappies. He wrote about battles bigger than Waterloo. He nattered on about personal sacrifices made on account of principle. He wrote whatever he thought might get him that astronomical sum. He would hold himself accountable: nothing was more important than publishing the Special Edition and collecting that unheard-of amount of money. In his photos and words would be clothed in beauty and genius. This was a country without problems, God's Eden on Earth.

At last, the Special Edition saw the light of day. A Tripoli-bound plane was loaded with thousands of copies, distributed through official circles. Huge billboards were erected advertising the Special Edition. The ordinary Libyan citizen threw it away in disgust, for he knew the truth and what was behind the truth.

After a couple of days, the Associate Editor's phone rang. Shortly thereafter, the Editor-in-Chief was once again standing before him.

'Did you hear? The Libyan government has fallen. We want you to prepare another special edition. You know the drill: photos and important people. Good luck.' The Associate Editor winked, leaned forward and whispered to his boss, 'I knew this would happen. I will take tomorrow's flight.'

The two men smiled at each other, then set about preparing another Special Edition.

The Olive Tree

Shajarat Al-Zeitoun

By Azza Kamel Maghur

*For the Martyr Sheikh Mohammad Al Madani
and the heroes of Zintan*

On the edge of the town square an olive tree stood obstinately. It displayed dried, entangled limbs and the green and black of its dark, serrated leaves, as the earth hurtled through space on its yearly ellipse. The olive tree was sturdier than any other tree: Its thick trunk resembled hewn rock, and it was pure, like the oil extracted from its smooth fruit.

Sheikh Mohammed had been a soldier. Over the years he had seen with his own eyes comrades dissolving into the bogs of Africa, and being eaten by crocodiles in the jungles of Uganda. He went through the perfunctory month-long training given to new recruits, and heard the stories of conscripts sent off to work as indentured labourers on farms and summerhouses of commanding officers. He had seen soldiers prepare to implement imaginary plans for building missiles and other instruments of war, and camps stocked with shoddy equipment that no one knew how to use. He saw pieces of unassembled fighter jets on the tarmac, and equipment laid out along the shore, even as the government continued to import more spare parts. When the Eminent Colonel[86] decided to reduce the size of his army, he used the term 'liberation' to describe the casting off of the weak.

The day Sheikh Mohammed took off his military clothing, he swore that they would never touch his body again. He left the place where he was then, and returned to his birthplace of Zintan, where he donned a pair of white trousers, a long *sooriya* and summer *farmala*, and covered up in a *hooli* made of winter wool.[87] He entered the mosque in the centre of the town in a state of equanimity, led the prayers, and took charge of his congregation. His life was missing many things, but he felt lucky nonetheless. He took a moment to fill his lungs and their narrowing capillaries with the high-oxygen desert air that enveloped Zintan.

Most Libyans didn't know much about Zintan, which erupted in rebellion immediately following the first cries from the wounded East. The Zintanis exited their houses, shouting, 'We will avenge you with our breath . . . and our blood, ya Benghazi.'

The monotony of life in Zintan was rarely punctuated, except by the racket of off-road vehicles loaded with tourists headed towards the Southern desert. The town is located on the red plateau of *Al Hamada*, a part of the vast Sahara, where the sand had been effused and eroded, between the Atlantic Ocean and Calm Coral Sea.[88] Al Hamada was mostly barren land, blanketed with small bits of iron-infused gravel, which gave the dust a red hue. These geological formations held, in addition to black gold,[89] a plant known in Europe as the 'truffle.' Rich in protein, the creature's roots are fed by rare drops of rain, until they swell up in the ruddy sand, splitting up the earth around them.

During the winter months an indolent mist sat on Zintan. This is when Zintani *shabab*[90] went out to collect truffles. They went out in groups to Al Khamada, where they sifted through sand and rocky pebbles, and groped under the earth's surface. Once found, the truffles were encased in clumps of red earth and tied into plastic boxes, which the youth took to the shoulder of the main road, and sold to passers by. They saved some pieces to flavour the *macarona ambakba*,[91] cooked on charcoal in the dry, desert air. But even the truffles prized by citizens of neighbouring countries couldn't save the Zintani youth. The rope holding Zintan's neck tightened. Oppression sat so heavily upon its people, and upon those residing just beyond the Western Mountains, that their faces turned blue and began to resemble ghosts.

Zintan did not have much to worry about, except its young men, the scarcity of water and the constant battle against a creeping desert. No one on the outside cared about the place. It had been ages since any high-level government official had set foot there. Some of the town's buildings had been built in the 1960's and '70s. These were the only things that distinguished the town from the barrenness of Al Hamada. Even eagerly anticipated tourists evaporated like a mirage, despite the knowledge and experience of Zintan's youth. No one could compete with Zintanis in desert skills, in the ability to sidestep danger, and to track both men and animals. Desert tourists require skilled guides, and equipment and amenities – yet these Zintani desert foxes had barely a 4x4 truck between them. Those vehicles were reserved for those with connections to the state security services. When the East lit up in revolt, the people were terrified, as they knew in their bones what would come next. The news lit the wick of a white candle without fragrance or colour. Instinctively, the people grouped together. Sheikh Mohammed went to mosque and picked up a microphone. This is how the Zintan revolution was born.

Sheikh Mohammed doffed his tunic, and searched in his chest of drawers for the uniform that he had sworn he would never wear again. He was surprised that it fit after all these years. Smiling, he moved out to address the youth, whose throats were hoarse from all their shouting.

Zintan sits on the edge of the Sahara, and lacks natural fortifications. The regime had sent mercenaries to infiltrate an area near the town centre called the Forest of the Scouts. A convoy of armored cars and missile carriers moved slowly, inexorably toward Zintan. The people had no defenses but themeselves and their courage. The enemy surrounded them and cut off their electricity and water. Because Zintan had lived on virtually nothing for many years, the people were able to hold on just long enough to break the siege. They staged a counter-attack, pushing the aggressors to the outskirts of the town, even though shelling continued for months.

After they cleansed their own area from infiltrators, the Zintanis went out to help the neighbouring towns, until they were able to liberate most of the Western Mountains, at a cost of its best men. Martyrs had fallen like ripe olives in the shadow of the tree, and just outside its canopy. Residents constructed coffins and shrouds in bulk, and buried their dead with great lamentation, and cries of *Allahu*

Akbar,[92] lowering the fallen into crypts, whose surfaces they smoothed and watered. They settled the martyrs into their last resting places, aligned with the *qibla*.[93] They sprinkled earth over them with their hands, and recited the *Fatiha*.[94] They wiped away their tears and hugged one another, while others took up the fight on multiple fronts, joining the ranks of young fighters whose names were called by Death.

When the fighting ended, the Zintanis turned their attention to mines – instruments of death lain by a cowardly enemy, containers of plastic explosives were ready to explode at the slightest tread or touch. Isolating and disarming the mines required some of the same skills as truffle hunting. But while defusing mines could easily result in death, the truffle is a small gift from heaven.

Zintan, a place even Libyans knew little about, was having its moment of fame. International newspapers were writing about it, whilst satellite channels broadcasted images of Zintani heroes and warriors. During periods of respite from killing, Zintanis shed tears for their beloved, and said goodbye to their martyrs. The sheikhs eulogized those covered in white from their heads to their feet. These were men who refused bribes, and withstood years of neglect. The Libyans' blood is not bought! They offered their lives for their country!

Sheikh Mohammed had become the master of the *meidan*, or public square. He spoke to his people through a megaphone. He inflamed their passions and put their plans to work. He directed the same fingers that had dug for truffles to the hammers of rifles, to old guns inherited from grandfathers, and used to hunt gazelles. He taught the youth the morals of Islam: Do not cut a tree. Do not kill a Sheikh, or a child, or a prisoner, or a runaway. He helped them realize the courage within themselves, and affixed in them a deeper faith, which they began to taste. Accompanied by his sons and other members of his family, he led the congregation.

As with other great leaders, Sheikh Mohammed did his best to avert bloodshed, despite the horror of what was happening around him, and despite the fact that these were mercenaries who had come to kill his own countrymen, and to violate all that they held dear, and for what, for money? He called out to the offenders, and invited them to safety. He called them to remove the fuse of death and killing, and replace it with inner peace.

Until was that last day the Sheikh stood tall, his chest resembling the trunk of an olive tree. He was wearing the military outfit of the *Sa'iqa*[95] carrying in his hand a megaphone instead of a rifle. He read from the *Qur'an* and prayed to God's Messenger. He called out to the besieged oppressors, holed up in one of the bombed-out buildings. He asked them to come out without their weapons, and to give themselves to safe hands. But there was no surrender. A volley of treasonous bullets shot from the rubble of one building, striking the Olive Tree. It did not topple over, but shed its green coat, and dropped its pits on the ground. The Sheikh moved on, traversing rocky groundcover as he moved slowly North, planting olive seeds as he went.

Sheikh Mohammed Al Madani, A Leader of the Revolution, Martyred in Zintan
Speaking for the Zintani Revolutionaries, a military source confirmed that Sheikh Mohammed Al Madani, leader of the city's rebels, was martyred last night, May 1, 2011. The

anonymous source told *Bereniq* that Al Madani was nego-
tiating with a number of captured security forces for the
release of civilians. The source said that a traitorous bullet,
fired by a member of the security forces, hit Colonel Al
Madani from behind, killing him. The source noted that Al
Madani was unarmed, and had come only to negotiate.
NATO forces yesterday bombed Gaddafi's forces near
Zintan, after the rebels announced that they were attacking
the area and attempting to enter the town.

Al Bereniq, May 2, 2011

PART THREE
Interpreting the Stories

On the Libyan Short Story

The first truly 'Libyan' short stories appeared in the second decade of the twentieth century, along with the earliest stirrings of national sentiment. The genre grew in popularity in the later years of World War II and the early 1960s, tracking the major fault-lines in Libya's modern history: transition to an independent state and the sudden growth of an oil economy. Most of Libya's early literature was written in the east, in the cities of Benghazi and Derna: particularly Benghazi, because it was an early capital of independent Libya and home to the best universities. Benghazi and Derna were also the urban areas closest to Cairo and Alexandria, then uncontested centres of Arab culture and writing. While the physical distribution of writers within the country is broader today than it was in the early years of the twentieth century, many of those writing still trace their inspiration to eastern, rather than western, Libya.

First Appearances: 1897–1948

The turn of the twentieth century saw the birth of a flurry of publications, including *Al-Tara'gim* (*The Translations*, 1897), which lasted but a year before the Ottoman authorities shut it down. In 1910 a more radical weekly, *Al-Asr Al-Jadid* (*The New Age*), modelled after the Egyptian *Al-Liwa'* (*The Banner*) appeared under the motto 'for the people, by the people'. Transplanted from the relatively oppressive environment of turn-of-the-century French Tunisia, a satirical journal under the name *Abu Qishsha* debuted in Libya in 1908. Prior to the outbreak of World War II, the Jewish community had its own publication, *Al-Dardanelle*.

As the titles of the above journals suggest, Libyan literary production prior to the Italian invasion of 1911 was both discursive and infused with politics – we do not see many Libyan short stories per se until the end of the 1920s. Ahmed Fagih, whose *Al-Jarad* (The Locusts) appears in this book, refers to the years 1908–11 as the 'golden age of Libyan . . . intellectual and cultural development'. Libya was at the time, in Fagih's words, a country 'seething with ideas, debates, political discussions and arguments, in an atmosphere of tolerance and social peace'.[96] From 1911–51, the inhabitants of Tripolitania, Cyrenaica and Fezzan experienced the brutal occupation and heavy fighting of World War II, all in an atmosphere of extreme poverty. In the introduction to *Al-Bawakir* (The Vanguard), a collection of stories he wrote from 1930 to 1960, Wahbi Bouri argues that the Libyan short story, heavily influenced by the growth of the form in neighbouring Egypt, was born in reaction to the Italian assault on Libyan culture. Indeed, distributed through underground networks, copies of poems such as 'Benghazi the Eternal' sustained the Libyan resistance.

Ahmed Fagih takes quite a different view, refusing to credit the Italian occupation with any creative force whatsoever. He insists the colonizers destroyed what would likely have been a very fruitful literary movement, and dates what he calls a 'literary recovery' to the period between World War II and Libyan Independence. The difference may be semantic: it was Italian policy to suppress indigenous Libyan cultural aspirations, not least by limiting education in Arabic to Qur'anic schools, mosques and special Arab-only schools. This oppression created a resistance movement that inspired many creative acts. During this dark time, perhaps the sole public indigenous literary influence was *Libya Al-Mussawar* (Illustrated Libya). Despite the fact that the magazine began as an instrument of Italian propaganda, it became a repository for substantive articles and poetry by Libyan authors. Many consider Wahbi Bouri, the author of 'Hotel Vienna', a translation of which is included in this volume, the father of the Libyan short story. A consistent theme in Bouri's work is the fight between good and evil.[97]

The 1950s: Independence and Tempered Optimism

With the defeat of the Bevin-Sforza plan in the UN General Assembly, an independent political entity was born.[98] With the withdrawal of Italian, French and British forces, a number of educated Libyans returned from exile in Egypt, Syria and Lebanon to help build the new state. Among the 1950s' generation were Kamel Maghur, Ibrahim Fagih and Bashir Hashimi. While bringing Libya to life as one of the poorest countries in the world, the writing of this period reflected a certain optimism, a desire to create new lives and to generate new opportunities.

The Anarchic 1960s: Wealth, Anxiety and Dislocation

The Libyan short story gained momentum in the 1960s through the work of twenty or so writers, focused on the clash between modernity and traditionalism. With the discovery of oil in commercially viable quantities in the late 1950s, Libyan society began to experience new pressures, including massive migration to the coastal cities and resulting unemployment, feelings of alienation, and a widening divergence between excited ambitions and hard realities. The aggressive entry of American oil companies engendered positive feelings among those with connections, who could parlay the new resource into a first-class education and good jobs. It produced resentment on the part of those who saw the foreign companies as oppressors, the new face of Western imperialism. In this environment, the short story once again presented itself as a suitable form of protest. Fagih again explains why: the short story is a 'vehicle for expressing outrage and frustration', far superior to the novel, for the latter 'demands prolonged labour and loses the immediacy of [the author's] passion.'[99] For the Libyan at this time, the American and the Jew were simultaneously 'outsiders' and 'facilitators'. The quality of Libyan short stories during this period was uneven, and while a few of the examples were well done, most were relatively crude 'snapshots'.

Revolutionary Years: 1969–86

The literary boom of the mid-sixties fizzled in the 1970s and 1980s, as all public manifestations of zeal were channelled to serve the Revolution. Authors like Kamel Maghur and Ahmed Fagih – the same creative figures that had dominated the 1950s and 1960s – remained the source of most of the literary output. While Fagih points out that writers benefited from the creation of state-subsidized publishing houses, the dearth of new literature suggested the country's creative energies were either repressed, or channelled elsewhere. Writers currently in their thirties and forties, many of whom were already experimenting during the late 1980s, complain that there was simply no formal outlet for, or encouragement of, their work during these years. A few committed writers with means fled the country. The ones who stayed nursed their hobbies more or less in private, all of which is underscored by writer and literary critic Mohammed Fagih Salih, who called the 1970s in Libya 'the age in which people before it wrote, and people after it wrote'.[100] Some of the work that 'wasn't written' during this period is just now starting to see the light of day, more than twenty years after it was put to paper.

The New Libyan Writers, c.2006

One anonymous Libyan wit said recently 'there are more Libyan short story writers than Libyan short story readers.' It is true, consistent with a trend apparent elsewhere in the Middle East (and the world, perhaps), Libyans are not avid readers. There are signs that with the recent economic and cultural opening, more people are reading, and short stories in particular. The short story remains an accessible channel of expression, especially as it is compatible with new media, i.e. the Internet, which is increasingly widespread in Libya. With the recent lifting of restrictions on certain forms of expression, and a new press law, it will be interesting to see who will be among the next generation of Libyan writers, and from where they will draw inspiration. A reasonably large percentage of the young writers today appear to be women in their late twenties and early thirties – this in contrast to the overwhelmingly older, overwhelmingly male writers of the previous two decades. Some write under male pen-names, as they say they do not feel the act of writing is yet a socially acceptable activity for women. 'New age' female writers and poets gaining serious literary acclaim include Laila Nayhoum, Najwa Ben Shetwan and Maryam Salama.

Three Generations of Economic Shock

Reading stories that span fifty years of Libyan history, certain economic and social conditions seem either not to change, or to repeat themselves. Some of these 'pockets of familiarity' are due to Libya's unique social and cultural make-up, and some arise from independent geopolitical forces. The fact that one can recognize so much of Libya in the last years of the Monarchy in Libya of 2004 is in part attributable to the 'anti-dynamic' nature of the Gaddafi regime, which draws both strength and weakness from its ability to check the development of political and social forces that might produce rapid change.

Wahbi Bouri's descriptions of Benghazi in *Hotel Vienna* give a good taste of conditions in the early 1950s. World War II inflicted deep physical and emotional damage on Libya. After Tobruk, Benghazi was the city that experienced the most damage from the Desert War: Hotel Vienna is one of the most beautiful edifices of post-war Benghazi, converted into a ghost town after most of its buildings had been bombed beyond recognition.'[101] With the discovery of oil in 1959, Libya swiftly went from being one of the world's very poorest states to a contender for outright prosperity. In Libya's favour then, as now, were a valuable resource and a relatively small population. With oil came money, the promise of jobs and a slew of new ideas, many of which posed direct challenges to what was (and remains) an extremely traditional society.

Males fled their rural homes to the cities in great numbers, hoping and expecting to find good jobs. By the end of the decade, some did get rich; a few women in Benghazi could be seen wearing miniskirts and dressing in the latest Italian fashions. The vast majority of Libyans, however, were both disappointed and disillusioned. To this, add the element of Arab nationalism, and anti-Western sentiment fanned by the 1956 defeat at Suez, and conditions in the 1960s were ripe for revolution. Ramadan Bukheit gives a very visceral portrayal of the effect of the first oil-boom on Libyan society in his story *The Quay and the Rain*, which deals not with the 'bene-ficiaries' (those of King Idris' clan and their clients) but the rural poor like Khalifa, who left their homes for a life of toil in the 'new economy'. Indeed, interior migration in the second half of the 1960s led to the creation of 'bidonvilles', whose inhabitants were both poor and diseased.[102] Bukheit's protagonist describes in a flashback laced with both awe and fear, a period when he worked as a day-worker for an oil company. The images Khalifa draws from the experiences are those of the 'foreigner' who acts in his own interest, and is wholly ignorant of the local language and custom.

Khalifa recounts one incident in which he comes to the aid of a drill-worker impaled in the process of drilling a successful test well:

How awful! They found him on the ground, impaled
upon a metal rod. He remembered how the sigh shook
him. He ran up to the body, lying in what looked like a
puddle of black water. He could smell the tar coming from
the pipe extending underground. As he carried the injured
worker to the tent, the black liquid gushed out. That
disgusting smell was everywhere . . .

Is this 'black liquid' blood or oil? At first, it isn't clear.
Oil becomes the symbol of lifeblood, which the foreign
countries are draining from the ground, as they are from
the people. Khalifa ultimately decides he must return to
his village, as unemployment is slowly robbing him of his
dignity. Symbolic of Khalifa's perceived need to regain
control is his insistence on washing before he enters his
old home:

Rain began to fall. As his family went into the house,
Khalifa stayed outside. He extended his hand to collect the
falling drops of rain, as if they were welcoming him. As
she called out for him, he spoke firmly: 'Let me wash. I
want to enter my house a clean man.'

Khalifa derives value from his connection with the past.
In *Special Edition*, Ali Mistrati lampoons regime cronies –
and underscores the perception of the ordinary man that
the outside world does not care. An unscrupulous newspaper
reporter is assigned to cover the dizzying pace of progress
in a new oil state. The editor is not concerned with the
'story behind the story', only with what he himself can get
out of it, by way of fame and material gain. When he
returns to his neighbouring country 'to learn that the regime

has fallen' (a clear reference to Gaddafi's 1 September Revolution), he happily returns to report anew. Misrati's heavy-handed satire was written in the 1960s. And yet, look at the headlines in 2005: 'big international papers' are telling a variation of the same story. As the US and UN sanctions were eased, members of the international press – those who could get visas – tried desperately to get in. Over the course of six months in 2005 and 2006, representatives of *Time*, *Newsweek*, *The New Yorker*, *The New York Times* and *The Financial Times* checked into the five-star Corinthia to write 'special editions' of their own, assured that Libya's mysteries and eccentricities, built on top of a mound of riches, would offer up a good story. Now, as then, Libya is an oil economy, full of promise.

The Sanctions Period, 1986–2004

As mentioned in the introductory essay, the 1970s and 1980s were not a fertile period for Libyan writing. One story in our collection dates from this time: Genaw's *Caesar's Return*. Genaw reanimates his protagonist, a bronze statue of the Roman Emperor Septimius Severus, for a jaunt around the square over which the statue presided in the early 1970s. The story is one of the few in our collection whose markers ground it firmly in the sanctions era, a time when Libyans were concerned more with making ends meet, than with the state of the environment.

The New Economy

Flash forward thirty-odd years to Tripoli in 2006, where the protagonists of *Tripoli Story* have emerged from a lengthy period of deprivation and despair into a new world, where their wildest material aspirations suddenly become possible. The underlying message, as always: change, yes, but at what cost? In *Tripoli Story*, Lamia El-Makki catalogues a similar sort of reaction, but from within the circle of the capital's nouveaux riches. In the dialogue there are hints that the money is being obtained in a not completely above-board way, and that greed is overtaking people who were once deprived and are suddenly in a position to spend freely.

The author exhibits cynicism regarding the durability of close relationships in the presence of temptation. This in contrast to the character of Khalifa in *The Quay and the Rain*, who, rebuffed, looks to his family and familiar surroundings for comfort. El-Makki's characters, while in a better social position, fall into a kind of moral sinkhole where money and status are the dominant values, and love is in danger of being left by the wayside. The focus is on preserving the 'goose that lays the golden eggs'. In 1970, Sheikh Amir Bin Zayed of the United Arab Emirates came to Benghazi for treatment at what was then a state-of-the-art clinic. He was said to have remarked: 'One day, Dubai will be like Benghazi.' Given the latter's current state, many Libyans wonder if the reverse will ever be possible. What will Libya look like ten or twenty years from now?

Migration

Historically, Libya has been a crossroads. If asked, many Libyans will say they are ultimately descended from Arabians of the Bani Hilal and Bani Selim. In 1051 members of these two tribes arrived in Libya, following on the heels of North Africa's Arab conqueror, Ibn Al 'As. At that time, Berbers, themselves descended from Semitic tribes that migrated to North Africa more than 3,000 years ago, made up the bulk of the indigenous population. They were the genetic substrate onto which successive waves of invaders, from the Byzantines to the Ottomans and Italians, grafted themselves. The stories in this book touch many of the migratory phenomena of the past millennium – the Arab conquests, trans-Saharan trade, African economic migration, and inter-Libyan economic migration.

Trade and Migration from the Middle Ages to the Twentieth Century

At the time of Christ, the camel was not yet a fixture of Saharan desert life. By the fifteenth and sixteenth centuries, however, the Libyan sands were alive, as goods, gold and slaves worked their way up into the Fezzan from the Sahel in camel trains, turning villages like Timbuktu, Agadez, Zinder and Kano into bustling commercial centres. As the trade moved north, part split off to Egypt or the western Maghreb, while the rest continued straight up to Benghazi and the ports of Tripolitania. Crudely, there were two main paths to the north, tracing out roughly the eastern and western borders of present-day Libya. Goods from Kano and Timbuktu found their way through to Ghat and Ghadames; in the east, goods from what is present-day Sudan moved through Kufra to Jalo and Aujela and Ajdabia. Sadiq Neihoum's 'The Good-Hearted Salt Seller' is full of echoes of this past, both in the eponymous black protagonist, referred to only as 'Zanj' (see 'Religious and racial minorities', below) and by his profession:

> A long time ago there lived in Benghazi a well-built Zanj who roamed the city's narrow streets loaded with bags of salt. Every day he moved through the ancient neighbourhoods behind his laden donkey, his finger to his ear, and called out in his stentorian voice: 'Salt . . . salt.'

Although the slave trade was theoretically abolished in 1833, the practice continued in force until the beginning of the twentieth century. One historian estimated the number of slaves crossing the Libyan Sahara between the years 750 and 1800 ad at nearly three million.[103] At the village of Jalo, some fraction of the northbound caravans took a right turn and headed for the oasis at Siwa, in present-day Egypt, most famous for its female oracle, whom Alexander the Great consulted on his way to conquer Persia. Jalo and the

north/south caravan trade is the backdrop to Sadiq
Nelhoum's *The Sultan's Flotilla*:

> In ages of old, Jalo was a port city. People called it the
> 'jewel of the seas'. Its waters teemed with the ships of
> pirates and traders. Caravans arrived at Jalo laden with
> elephant tusk; its markets were replete with spices, slaves,
> sandal – even Chinese porcelain. All of the people of Jalo
> lived like Sultans, except the Sultan himself.'

Internal Migration in the Age of Cars, Ships and Black Gold

With the advent of mechanized transport, much of the
caravan trade moved to other places and other conveyances,
such as boat and train. Technical progress created poles of
attraction further north; it was powerless to prevent the
cycle of famine, unemployment and political violence that
powers most modern migration.[104] As discussed in 'Three
generations of economic shock', above, the discovery of oil
and related activities in the 1950s and 1960s drew large
numbers of rural Libyans to the cities. Kamel Maghur's
Miloud and Rubina's Story illustrates another case of internal
migration, this time in the west, from Tripoli's hinterlands
into the city. Miloud moves back to Zwara, not because
he cannot make some sort of living in Tripoli (as parasitic
as his is), but because he misses the place, and feels his
quality of life in Tripoli is not as high as it was in Zwara.

In the years following Libyan Independence, Tripoli
and Benghazi were the places to be. The pace of migration
increased in the 1970s and 1980s. Tripoli grew dramatically,

eventually outstripping Benghazi, which was the source of much of the inflow.[105] Libya's urban population jumped from 22 per cent in 1954 to 27 per cent in 1964, and 35 per cent in 1972. The trend has continued relentlessly, to the point where now approximately 50 per cent of all Libyans live in the six main *shaabiyat* of Tripoli, Benghazi, Misrata, Marqab, Tarhouna and Maslata.[106] Tripoli has been an overwhelming pole of attraction for people from western coastal cities like Tarhouna, and the Berber strongholds of Gharyan and Yefren. Misrata, long a trading centre, has witnessed a revival in the last few years with government efforts to create a new port and free zone there. In the early 1990s, Syrte (Sirte)'s and Ajdabia's growth was aided by the growth of the petrochemical industry, and the 'Great Man-made River'. Farther south, the desert towns of Sebha and Ghat were swollen with returnees and African immigrants. Some of these were attracted by Gaddafi's open-door policy, others were pushed by crisis – man and nature-made – in their home countries. Despite these trends, in terms of absolute numbers, the desert is still quite empty.

Migration from the North

Mill Road hints at two different migrations, the first being the emigration of Muslims from the island of Crete, approximately 500 miles north of Benghazi: Al-Lannaizy's protagonist Al-Kritli comes (as one might guess) from Crete, 'with those families who fled Greek persecution and settled in the Libyan cities'. The majority of Greek immigrants to Libya in the last 200 years were wealthy Muslims, pushed out of Greece by an increasingly restive Christian majority,

who resented the Turks' 'fiscal oppression and the denial of
judicial equality and educational opportunity'.[107] The largest
groups of Muslims left Crete for Libya in two separate
waves in the 1860s and 1890s. Originally Greek Orthodox,
many of those who fled had converted to Islam for the
material privileges it accorded them in an Ottoman world.[108]

As a group, they became extremely successful traders,
a stereotype supported by Al-Kritli's obvious industriousness.
The second strand is 'African' immigration, of which his
wife Aziza is representative: 'When he became a man, he
married a girl from Africa. Her family lived in the city
with the many other immigrant families in "slave shacks".'

Present-day sub-Saharan Migration

In 2005, natural disasters like drought in the Sahel, locust
plagues in Mauritania and Mali and war in Congo and the
Ivory Coast pushed Africans to leave their homes. Gaddafi's
Open Door Policy vis-à-vis sub-Saharan Africa, announced
with much fanfare in the mid-1990s, has helped create or
expand several transcontinental migratory routes that have
Libya as their terminus. The combined result has been a
massive influx of Africans across Libya's southern border.
Libyan government officials put the number of legal foreign
workers in 2004 at about 600,000, and the number of illegal
workers at between 750,000 and 1.2 million.[109] These movements have created both opportunities and grave problems.
Large groupings of indigent Africans coalesce into bidonvilles and camps, which Libyans believed led to an increase
in drug addition and street crime, which had not until
relatively recently been visible social problems in Libya.

While, it is true, the Africans, like the Eastern Europeans, tend to do jobs that no Libyan would hold – anything requiring manual labour – their perceived burden on state resources angers many Libyans, at a time when the unemployment rate is well over 30 per cent.

As with the internal migrants of the 1960s, most sub-Saharan immigrants arrive to a reality much different than – and far worse from – what they imagined. The southern desert is said to be littered with the bodies of those attempting to escape poverty and political oppression in their home countries. These hapless souls who survive the journey find work as day-labourers, cooks and housemaids. In the morning, Tripoli roundabouts are crammed with Africans carrying squeegees and paint rollers. Early in 2005, many Africans had set up camp in Tripoli's Old City; by early 2006, the squatters had been cleared out. Libya pursued a policy of blind neglect for several years, but more recently, and as domestic gripes got louder, there has been an active policy of deportation, and rumours of summary executions of those accused of crimes. Significant numbers of Nigerians, Moroccans, Malians, Eritreans and Somalis find themselves in Libyan limbo for long periods of time.

The inability of Libyans to take care of their own needs, whether infrastructural or services, has led to a massive influx of Tunisians and Egyptians to fill these jobs. Indeed, today Africans come to Libya from all corners of the continent. One route begins in Somalia and passes through Eritrea and Al-Jawf (Kufra), where it links with one that begins in Cameroon. Yet another originates in Ghana and wends its way through Nigeria and Niger before hitting Ghadames, where Ghanaians mingle with Nigerians and indigenous Libyans. The main collection points for this flow are Agadez in Niger and Abeche in Chad. Those moving north often make extended stops along the way to finance their passage. Fare from Dirkou, not so far from the Libyan border, to Ghat or Sebha might be had for three months of hard labour in the mines of Bilma.[110] When in the 1980s Niger–Libya relations were at a low point, and during the Tuareg Revolt, transit routes shifted west to Algeria, particularly the towns of Tamanrasset and Djanet, which is three days through open desert to Ghat.[111] The most infamous of the present-day immigrants – and a kind of arch-symbol of the problems faced in Libya by the 'placeless' and dispossessed – are those who hurl themselves at Lampedusa and Sicily, in traditional fishing boats launched from staging points along the Libyan coast. The capital of this activity is the town of Zwara, mentioned in Kamel Maghur's *Miloud and Rubina's Story*. Anywhere between 1,500 and 2,500 dollars will buy a space in a fishing boat with an estimated *ex ante* probability of 95 per cent of making it to Lampedusa or Sicily without being intercepted – or capsizing.

Minorities

Berbers

If one puts stock in anthropologists and the like, Bedouin Berbers are the original Libyans. Racially distinct from the Arabian Arabs, there are approximately 200,000 of them in Libya today, out of a total North African Berber population of perhaps one million.[112] In Libya the Berber spots include Ghadames, Gharyan, Ghat, Zwara, Garyan, and Aujela.

Most Berbers converted to Islam in the late seventh and eighth centuries, and in the following years of contact simply 'blended in' to the population at large. According to recent studies, the Berbers at the time of the Conquests were ethnically closer to Sicilians and Greeks than to Middle Eastern Arabs or sub-Saharan Africans, thus Brett calls them 'typically Mediterranean'. In modern times, pockets of Berbers have steadfastly maintained their cultural and ethnic independence, connections enforced by a unique set of mutually-intelligible languages and a relatively rare Islamic sect. A particular group of Berbers known as the Tuareg have for hundreds of years resisted temptations to settle – Gaddafi himself has spent much money in inducements to try to assimilate them, with limited success. In the Middle Ages, Berbers were the ones who directed the caravan trade and, within it, slave-driving. The Roman and Arab Conquests and Southern Berber migrations put the Berbers in a position as natural matchmakers between the northern demand for slaves and the sub-Saharan supply. One result was the implantation of Berber communities throughout West Africa. In Timbuktu, until recently the largest expatriate community was of Ghadamsis.[123]

For most of the twentieth century, and in most of North Africa, public displays of Berber culture were banned. The early twenty-first century has brought a loosening of restrictions on expressions of Berber culture, particularly in Morocco, where in 2001, a Moroccan Royal Institute for the Preservation of Berber Language and Culture was established. Building on this initaitive, in 2005, the Moroccan government introduced the Berber language into the national curriculum.[114]

Berbers in the Stories

There are three references to Berbers in the stories, and all are indirect, or implicit. The towns of Ghadames, Zwara and Ajdabia are all Berber strongholds, and we can reasonably assume that the protagonists of From Door to Door and Miloud and Rubina's Story, as well as of The Spontaneous Journey are Berbers. Berber culture is less concerned with adherence to a strict Islamic legal writ than the mainstream Sunni Arabs of North Africa: one should not be surprised to see Libyan Berbers drinking wine, for example. This is paradoxical, as the flavour of Islam adopted by many Berbers after the Muslim conquest of North Africa was the puritanical Kharijite movement known as Ibadism.

The major Ibadi communities in the Islamic world today are located in Libya, Morocco, Iraq and Oman. Ibadism grew in North Africa in the aftermath of the Berber Revolt of 740, with the resulting breakdown in Islamic ideological unity. In the words of Brett, it was the local/ Berber discontent with abuses of the Umayyad caliphate that drove those in North Africa and elsewhere in the Islamic world to sectarian Islam, embodying the idea that the unjust ruler is subject to punishment or death, and rule by the 'best Muslim'.[115]

The character of the marabout, or murabit, which forms the centrepiece of *The Yellow Rock*, figures large in Berber religious life. Muslim–Berber holy warriors were called marabouts; this creature morphed in the tenth century into something approaching a mystic, a hermit-like darwish or hereditary saint possessed of powers of prognostication and magic:

> [A marabout was] . . . associated with miraculous power, and especially with the gift of second sight, and was held in awe despite the vein of scepticism which regarded many of its manifestations as sha'udha or trickery. Many indeed feared it as wizardry . . .[116]

Within North African, and particularly Berber culture, the marabout mediated between the urban, traditional (and Sunni) regions and the pastoralist Berber communities. Ernest Gellner, in his *Saints of the Atlas*, notes that:

> Communities of saints, established at the points of inter-section between the mountains and the plains, mitigate and stabilize the potential disorder of the pre-desert world . . .

they are not themselves political leaders, but their prestige
affects political decisions.[117]

The word itself comes from the Arabic root R'B'T, to
attach or connect, in the sense of Irtibat Bil-Makan, or
'attached to the place'.

The Sheikh shouted: 'This rock is a marabet. What befell
this town was the result of a violation of its sanctity . . . the
dry spell . . . the sickness . . . unexplained deaths . . . the visions!'

While the Sheikh refers to the yellow rock as the
marabet, it is he himself who assumes characteristics of the
marabout – supposedly a leader and counsellor, but in fact
someone leading the flock in a questionable direction.

Another characteristic of Berbers becomes clear in the
way a Tripolitanian speaks of Kamel Maghur's character
Miloud:

'Oh, no. God save me from the evil of that Zwarian. A
magician, he is. He practised magic on that Muslim-Jewish
woman.'

Here we find another reference to the Marabout culture
mentioned above and the widespread belief that Berbers
(and Jews) possessed magical powers, which they sometimes
put to not altogether positive use. Berber traditions – and
language – are revealed in Fatima's reminiscences of her
Ghadamsi childhood, in *From Door To Door*:

Only at night just before bedtime would Fatima's mother
speak, repeating to her the story of Ghadames in its days

of glory, when the gurgling of waterwheels, farmers rejoicing and young girls singing 'Ana benyo benyo' ('give me, give me, sir!') kept the dead of night away . . . how they would toss chicken eggs into Ain Al-Firas – even if they were the last they had.

The mother – and grandmother – figures in *The Spontaneous Journey* perform all manner of talismanic rites to ward off the evil eye, all of which are more prevalent in Berber societies than not:

Wise women are tolerated, if they are discreet and not perceived as having the evil eye. They concoct philters and potions – typically, love potions, brews to make a travelling husband return or to maintain his affections, or else to bring harm to an enemy.

Sub-Saharan Africans

There are two instances of references to black Africans in the stories, the first of which occurs in *Mill Road*:

When he reached a marriageable age, Al-Kritli wed an African girl. Her family lived in the city with the many other immigrant families in shacks known locally as the Aaraeb al Abeed.

Aaraeb al Abeed means, literally, the 'pens for slaves' (araeb, additionally, is a word typically used in connection with animals). The second mention of black Africans comes in *The Good-Hearted Salt Seller*. The inhabitants of Benghazi

called him 'Abdel Milh'. Abdel Milh means 'Salt Slave', and
the physical descriptions of the Zanj are far from nuanced
or complementary:

> While frightened by the zanj's appearance, the children
> followed his elongated frame with their eyes as he staggered
> through the alleys behind his hapless donkey. Resembling
> a looming palm tree, the zanj flapped his bright red tongue
> at the local children affectionately. They nearly died with
> laughter each time they heard his throaty voice, resembling
> the croaking of a frog.

It is perhaps worth asking whether or not the authors
share the views of their protagonists, or placing a mirror
to the face of Libyan attitudes towards 'the other'. It could,
of course, be both.

In modern Libya, minorities are commonly associated with
magic and the disruption of social mores, and are even seen
as carriers of evil. Jews and Berbers both enjoyed periods
of relative prosperity, but Black Africans have never had it
good in Libya – or in the rest of the Middle East for that
matter. One thing is clear: if looked at from north to south,
Libya is a gradually darkening strip of humanity, a mix of
African, Mediterranean and Arab.

Jews

When an author includes a reference to something Jewish
in these stories, he uses the word 'Jew'. This would not be
significant other than for the fact that mention of Berbers

in the same collection of stories is purely implicit, conveyed through context or diction. Africans, for their part, have the benefit in these works of no nuanced identity other than that attributed to them by the colour of their skin. As there are no Jews in Libya today, most of the references occur in stories written before 1967. Berbers, while culturally different from the urban Arabs, at least share the same religion and many of the same traditional cultural attitudes, and are not seen as members of the 'other' tribe. Africans are a different story – references to them tend to be (whether consciously or not) both racist and dismissive. It is fair to say that the attitudes of Libyans to minorities – as revealed in these stories – are not particularly positive.

Muslim–Jewish Relations

Well before the nineteenth century, Libyan Jews were traders and financiers, furnishing capital that sustained the caravans that linked Sudan and Chad with Benghazi. Jews were the principal intermediaries between Libyan Arabs and European buyers in luxury items like ivory, precious metals and slaves. At the time, there were thriving Jewish communities along the coast, as well as in Kufra, Sudan and Mali. Throughout North Africa, Jews lived segregated from Muslims in packed city quarters near the casba known as *hara*, an Arabic word for 'quarter'.[118] Hara have been described as labyrinths 'of dark and dirty alleys', marked by a 'nauseating smell, misery common to all social prisons'.[119] The hara of Tripoli and Benghazi, however, were somewhat less squalid, and the Libyan Jews were not bound to them as they were elsewhere in North Africa.

While many claim the Libyan Jews, like the Greeks in Cyrenaica, had lived in relative harmony with their Muslim neighbours for centuries, this notion is belied by travellers' accounts, such as that of Jean-Raimond Pacho, who asked a Jewish resident of Derna why he voluntarily lived in conditions of wretchedness and ignominy. The response, which Pacho says was delivered 'with an intense coldness', is significant, as it shows the degree to which the Libyan Jews truly felt Libya was their home: [We stay] 'because [we] were born [here], and [will] remain [here]'. Pacho says he realized then that 'love of country could transform sands into a habitable abode.'[120]

The Italian occupation of Libya in 1911 stirred up whatever latent and not-so-latent confessional tensions existed between Jews and Muslims and created a quandary for the Jews: on one hand, it opened up new professional opportunities; on the other, it produced a situation where the Arabs were more likely to see the Jews as exploiters and collaborators, going as far as to accuse them of providing logistical support to landing Italian forces. The Italians attempted to bring the Jews to their side by showcasing the success of Jews in Italy.[121] They stacked the Banco di Roma and its Libyan branches with Jews. Arabs complained that the Jews were their last resort for loans, and that it was on the small, presumably unsecured loans that the Jews made obscene profit – up to 90 per cent interest. In the first three decades of the twentieth century, three distinct quarters emerged in Benghazi: Arab, Italian and Jewish. As the Italians filled the Western area, the Arabs started to move out, into what was thenceforth solidly the 'Arab' quarter. Arabs continued to practise traditional crafts and trades, including the buying and selling of precious commodities, gold, silk and jewellery; Jews became expert printers and traders.[122]

If the Jews thought they had friends in the Italians, the incoming Facist regime disabused them of this notion. By 1922, the Italians had turned from their early favouritist policy to 'demoting' the Libyan Jews to the 'level of the Arabs'. The Jews were divided in their views of the Italians. Some believed they were civilising saviours; others could only see direct descendants of the Romans, who had obliterated the Jews in Barqa. The early twentieth century brought further developments that impacted upon the Jewish–Arab relationship negatively: the rise of Jewish nationalism, the creation of the State of Israel in 1948, and the Six Day War of 1967. The local Arab population resented the Jews' relative prosperity, and blamed them for many of the hardships of the 1950s and 1960s. The crowning blow to Jewish confidence were acts of violence that occurred in 1945. On 4 November a raging mob killed 120 Jews, in the process desecrating homes and synagogues. Three years later, in the summer of 1948, gangs ran through hara of Tripoli killing and pillaging. There were 35,000 Jews in Tripoli at this time, 5,000 in Cyrenaica, and 8,000 in small enclaves across the country. By the end of 1949 almost all the Libyan Jews had left.

Jews in the Stories

In Bukheit's *The Quay and the Rain*, Khalifa attributes price-gauging to the Jews: 'Khalifa muttered excuses (for his inability to provide for the family's needs) . . . the shop-keepers were raising their prices. Some, he said, blamed the

Jewish traders.' Chouraqui argues that the French, with their blatant pro-Jewish discrimination, reinforced social divisions and created conditions that ultimately required the Jews to leave North Africa after their colonial masters were gone: 'the Jews were faced with economic ruin and anxiety.'[123] Chouraqui argues that this favouritism was more of a factor in acts of violence against Jews in the 1940s and 1950s than were events in Palestine, which many still felt was a distant problem. Kamel Maghur's treatment of Jews in *Miloud and Rubina's Story* is kinder, perhaps, but illustrates the fact that Tripoli's Jewish population was more cut off from their Muslim counterparts than they were in Benghazi, where both communities lived together, and were indistinguishable from one another in dress and speech. References to Jews in Maghur's *The Old Hotel* indicate a separation, both physical and attitudinal, between the Jews and the Arabs in Tripoli. (There is no exact date on the story, but presumably it takes place in the late 30s and 40s, while there was still a significant Jewish population in Libya.

Some of them keep the money of Jews and Christians in their shops, wrapped up in all manner of bags and cases. They'd sell what they could, while others – the master merchants – angled for the eyes of suit-wearing Jews and Christians. These were the bigger fish, who borrowed from banks, which in turn were owned by those who wore white suits and knee-high trousers.

The line attributed obliquely to a frustrated Miloud, 'Shame be upon the Jews of the neighbourhood. He who doesn't die leaves on a boat', must reflect a strong undercurrent of anti-Jewish feeling in the general population.

It was daring of Maghur to write a piece openly exploring the relationship of a Muslim Arab and a Jewish woman (though more scandalous would have been the opposite, a relationship between a Muslim woman and a non-Muslim man, which we have in Maryam Salama's *From Door to Door*). True to his 'realistic' style, the relationship does not end well. *Miloud and Rubina's Story* is a tale of mutual desperation and curiosity; two people trying to escape the confines of the roles their respective societies. In Rubina the Zwaran initially finds freedom, sexual and otherwise. Whether or not Rubina is a prostitute is left unsaid, but it is clear the relationship between the two is genuine. The Zwaran ultimately loses interest in Rubina, and longs for the very aspects of tradition and familiarity that he fled. Abandoned by Miloud, Rubina is forced to return to the hara, where she works as a seamstress.

Between Depression
and Elation

By Western standards, much of Libyan literature is horribly depressing. The main criterion for including stories in this collection was 'connection to place'. There is nothing (at least nothing obvious) in our rules that would predispose us to having amassed a collection of downers. Yet most have some tragic or profoundly twisted plot. The most cheerful story in this collection is about a struggle against an invasion of locusts; other themes include loves lost, things 'alien', injustice and poverty, and the desperate search for meaning in small things. The choice of subject matter is no surprise to Ahmed Fagih, who views the short story as a tool which writers choose as a surgeon might a surgical knife, for its ability to respond to the need to express a specific emotion, a collection of thoughts that might exist for a short period of time or which lie dormant, only to flare up when circumstances provoke them.

While the tendency might be to see Libyan literature as somehow special for its lack of overt humour, this trait is not unique. Arab writing in the 1930s and 1940s was generally more upbeat, incorporating wit, irony and sarcasm as a matter of course. From the late 1950s, however, the

Arab writers seemed to have become gripped by despair, which flowed into literature: as Salma Jayyusi says:

> The atmosphere of gloom and consternation, or at least of regret, which has overshadowed life in the Arab world since the early fifties, seemed to seep into the fiction of most authors, both novelists and short-story writers, with little involvement in comical representations.[124]

Jayyusi goes on to say that much of post-1950s Arab literature is characterised by a 'nostalgia for normalcy, a deep longing for normal happiness, for a normal capacity to plan one's life, to build one's future with some sort of confidence and forward vision.'[125] Longing for normalcy is a key element in Libyan short stories, whether overt or not.

Humour

Unless one is inhuman, like the marabout in *The Yellow Rock* who 'never, ever laughed', one cannot escape humour. In the traditional Libyan culture of twenty to thirty years ago, while it was considered *'aib* (shameful) to laugh in public, Libyans were not known to be a depressing or depressed people.[126] Sadiq Neihoum was offended by what he saw as a prevailing negative attitude towards life and place in Libyan literature, and tried to fight against these stereotypes, as with his essay defending Benghazi from written characterizations as a dull and depressing city. 'Certainly, Tripoli is not Oslo or Stockholm,' Mufti points out in conversation, and he is right – recent visitors to

Tripoli come away with the impression that Libyans are a positive and extremely expressive lot, seemingly not given to extended periods of brooding.

The stories in this collection, if read carefully, would seem to support Neyhoum and Mufti's claims. None of the stories are 'comic', per se, but a large number write in ways that indicate the authors are far from humourless. Stories that fall into the category of obtuse satire are *Special Edition*, *Caesar's Return* and, to some extent, *The Yellow Rock*, all of which constitute rather biting attacks on 'bureaucracies', albeit un-named bureaucracies. Misrati portrays the Associate Editor in *Special Edition* as a man without conscience, the ultimate ingratiating personality:

> The Associate Editor spent nights in cabarets drinking champagne and whisky with Greek and Italian dancers, toasting the profession of journalism, special reports and Arab hospitality. During the day he took photos of the faces and behinds of the powerful men who were doubling his money. He described one important person he met as 'a reformer, a pillar of society', then proceeded to take pictures of the man's horses, chickens, ducks, fish and dogs.

Misrati, like Fagih, uses hyperbole to make his point, as with the greedy, venal Associate Editor in *Special Edition*:

> The Associate Editor didn't visit any hospitals. Disease was definitely not his business. He was a highly sensitive man and didn't want his sensibilities offended. He didn't visit the hovels of which he caught an accidental glimpse from his car.

The villagers in *The Yellow Rock* debate what sort of sacrifice may satisfy this Marabout. When the sorcerer suggests specific body parts, obviously connected to live bodies and souls, they are cast into indecision (upon which bureaucracy preys). In one part of the same story, villagers seem not to understand that the Marabout intends to kill two of them: 'No . . . the sacrifice is a piece of both of your livers.'

In *Caesar's Return*, Septimius Severus cannot disguise his disgust at the decay of Tripoli town. The straight-man protagonist turns comic at the end:

> Simultaneously, an idea occurred to both of them. On the morning of the next day, Tripolitanians were astonished to see the two metal figures standing at the head of a long line before the offices of the Libyan Maritime Transport Company, waiting to buy tickets to Malta.

The artistic device is in all cases the same, a form of hyperbole, in which the author juxtaposes a lengthy discourse with a thought or idea that at first reading seems completely out of place. The suggestions produce discomfort, which seeks an outlet in a stifled laugh.

Tragedy and Despair

As love is the opposite of hate, the flip side of humour is often anger, sorrow and despair. In *The Quay and the Rain*, the poor dockworker gradually loses everything, and witnesses some horrible events on the way. *From Door to Door* isn't much happier, but at least one of the doors remains open to an eventual positive denouement. By contrast, *My Dead Friends* leaves no room for redemption: A., the man with no name, seeks to regain his identity. A morbid reckoning accompanies the funeral of a friend he hasn't bothered to see in five years, which leads A. to obsess about his own mortality and imperfect legacy. The fact that he uses money he has set aside for the education of his sons to pay for the house on the square is a sign to the reader that he has perhaps truly given up – not only on himself, but on his flesh and blood too. The *funeral* will be his legacy. A. is a learned man, reduced to naught.

While *Hotel Vienna* is rather maudlin, the end is somewhat unexpected in this genre: despite overcoming (at least temporarily) his family's prejudices, Nouri does *not* ultimately win the girl. Despair precipitates mental illness in *The Mute*, where the only way the central character (note she is also nameless) can deal with the brutality of her day-to-day life is to will herself into a world of half-realities or outright fabrication. Ultimately, she cannot maintain this division between 'reality' and 'imagination' and commits suicide.

Sometimes, when describing despair, an element of humour creeps in: the absurd premise of *The Locusts* is a case in point. A village saves itself from a disaster by 'eating the eaters'. Neihoum, by contrast, has a dark side to his writing, and uses humour as an anarchist prick, to shock his readers into questioning which way is up. It is almost in spite of ourselves that we chuckle at the discord between the downtrodden zanj (a kind of anti-hero) and his nagging wife, and the travails of the anxious and despotic Sultan, whose nervous energies are calmed by a professional nail-biter.

Superstition

What is superstition, other than a human psychological mechanism for managing unknown and unmanageable forces? Writing in the 1950s, the Protestant theologist Paul Tillich emphasized the degree to which the modern soul is prone to anxiety. Advances in science had revealed a limitless universe, and exposed the depths of non-being:

> The courage of the modern period was not a simple optimism. It had to take into itself the deep anxiety of non-being in a universe without limits and without a humanly understandable meaning. This anxiety could be taken into the courage but it could not be removed, and it came to the surface any time when the courage was weakened.[127]

A society that has put superstitions to rest may revert to these thought patterns in times of stress. In the North African context, it is difficult to separate traditional magical thinking from individual and collective manifestations of anxiety. It is safe to assume that such attitudes, deeply ingrained, come to the surface more readily in times of stress. In *My Dead Friends*, A.'s obsession with buying a house on a square takes on elements of fetishism: the only decision left for him to make in life is one that shapes how those (supposedly close) in life will feel about him when he is gone.

Women in the Stories

Women in Libya enjoy rights and freedoms that are denied women in many other Arab societies: they can drive, vote, hold high office and initiate divorce. In Al-Jazeera-hosted panel discussions on women's rights in the Arab world, male Libyan callers typically call in to proclaim that for years, Libyan women have had more rights than they have in any other Arab country – and they're right. At the same time, 'liberated' Libyan women, as the West understands the term, are rare. Superficially at least, 'traditionalism' appears to be on the rise, as reflected in a dramatic increase in the number of women wearing the veil. The trend can be seen across the Muslim world, but particularly in neighbouring Egypt, where women actively choose to turn towards 'traditionalism' at the expense of the imported Western model. But what do these symbols mean, really? Are the women driving themselves backwards, or moving towards a different vision of equality?

Libyan Women: Then and Now

Dr Muhammad Mufti describes the situation of Libyan women in the 1940s as 'a kind of hell'. Foreign and Jewish – he makes the distinction – women would drive around in Western-style dress, while 'Libyan women weren't even allowed to visit the market.'[128] Indeed, during the Monarchy, women had few legal rights of which to speak. During the latter years of King Idris's rule, women acquired some guarantees, particularly with respect to employment. These were insignificant compared with what took place after the Revolution, when women had (on paper at least) the right to maternity leave without fear of dismissal, and employer-provided day-care centres for the children of working mothers. Article 91 of the Law on Work states specifically that there should be no discrimination between men and women in salary, if both are qualified for same job.[129] Mu'ammar Gaddafi's role in pushing for a more progressive family code is indisputable: Gaddafi intervened personally and directly with the Libyan ulema', or religious elite, to pass the 1984 Family Law, drafts of which had been rejected twice before.[130] Its significance lay in introducing an element of male–female reciprocity into the legal code. It effectively abolished the notion of repudiation of the female spouse by the male, and 'cast the marriage contract as an agreement between two quasi-autonomous agents'. Women whose father or guardian refused their choice of husband could now appeal to the courts, which could make a desired marriage a reality.[131]

Women in the Stories

The gender issue is prevalent in the stories, perhaps more so than any other outside the economic problem, to which it is linked. Collectively, the stories treat the marital dynamics of Libyan couples, male sexual repression and restriction in a patriarchal society (in one case, embedded in commentary on female sexuality), and the role of women as mothers and workers. In *From Door to Door*, which its author, Maryam Salama, insists is a 'true story, continuing to play itself out', a young nurse from Ghadames excites her father's ire when she expresses a wish to marry a foreign doctor with whom she works. 'Our people don't marry foreigners,' the father tells his daughter's Ukrainian suitor. While implicitly acknowledging he must accept change (he points to the fact that he's already gone so far as to allow his daughter to work), Fatima's father makes it clear there are limits. Salama's character retreats into imagining a physical age when the distinction between male and female doesn't exist. She seems to place the blame with tradition, which she describes as 'accretions'.

Hotel Vienna, which takes place some sixty years previously, presents the reverse scenario, a relationship between a Libyan male and a foreign woman. The focus of tension falls more overtly on the religious differences, as opposed to tradition. In *The Spontaneous Journey*, Najwa Ben Shetwan uses the meeting of sea and sand as a metaphor for the strength of repressed sexual and romantic emotions. In a note to the editor, Ben Shetwan says the essay is an indirect commentary on the state of love in the Arab world, where women are not permitted to have relationships outside marriage: 'the heroine knows no love except for that which makes her explode (with passion) in front of every living creature that does (not) control her accounts or keep her from (them):

> Despite the amazing quantity of dust that swirled around us, I was able to love you there; to house you in the expanse of my thoughts. I did this despite what obstacles arose before me, including warnings from the head of our household, whom the State charged with overseeing this dusty baladiya. You linked the bloodlines of our two families, and penetrated me as the sea would infuse parched earth.

Abdullah Ali Al-Gazal broaches the question of sexuality and independence in an even more direct fashion in *The Mute*, which contains scenes that are much more explicit: compare the image of a young girl disrobing in slow motion under a waterfall to Ben Shetwan's more cautious reliance on double entendre.

El-Makki's *Tripoli Story* is contemporary to Salama's *From Door To Door*, but takes place in the well-to-do suburbs of Tripoli, the front line of the Libyan battle of the sexes. The story is unusual in the author's perspective, a female attempt to understand the effect of 'tradition vs. modernity' tension on the male. In her microcosm of the 'nouveaux riches', she reveals a certain hypocrisy, as tradition is often used as a fig leaf to cover individual sins. Indeed, no one cares 'where the money comes from'. The female characters objectify their husbands, prodding the 'geese that lay golden eggs' to produce ever more. The male character contemplates taking another wife, not because he feels entitled, but because he feels unloved and underappreciated. Al-Gazal, like El-Makki, imagines what it would be like to be the 'other son', and in so doing presumably tries to draw awareness to the social pressures experienced by women. Here we have a male Libyan talking about – of all odd things for an Arab writer! – the pain of a woman's menstrual cycle, and the (both female and male-imposed) pressure to marry and procreate.

Stereotypes and Caricatures

Sadiq Neihoum presents a particularly scathing caricature of women in *The Good-Hearted Salt Seller*, which has been criticized along with many of the other stories in *Qisas Atfal*, for contributing to a distortion of moral norms. Neihoum's defenders say that the critics miss the element of satire, i.e., that Neihoum was simply holding up a mirror to attitudes common in Benghazi during the 1970s. The image of the woman as 'shrew', or 'self-serving', is reflected in many of the other stories. The 'arsa' in *Miloud and Rubina's Story* is a calculating prostitute, duping Miloud into a relationship through the lure of money. It is quite possible that she is a manifestation of the Libyan man's worst fear: the arrival of women who act like men. In his book *Al Hadith 'An Al-Mar's Way Al-Diana* (Meditations on Women and Religion) Sadiq Neihoum decries the state of Libyan women, which he links to the backwardness of the Libyan educational system. The contemporary Libyan woman, he says, is caught in a bind, between the 'unwavering traditionalism of an older, benighted generation, and ideas imported from the West.' In a foreshadowing of *The Green Book*, Neihoum argues against this wholesale import, the result of which is a mishmash of conflicts within the family: 'The daughter insists upon liberty, which she learns in the books, and her father insists on his right to control, which he gained through the previous ages. The son views the father as backward, and refuses to marry the woman he chooses for him. He wants to choose his own, and refuses to live in the father's household. The daughter goes to school but sees the mother as ignorant.'[132] Neihoum advocates a new ideology: 'When one builds a house, one doesn't borrow bricks from others . . . we must pursue our unique way.'

Many of the stories in this collection involve double-dealing of various kinds – Miloud pays for gifts for the 'arsa' by short-changing Rubina, the kind-hearted Jewess. The wife in *The Good-Hearted Salt Seller* is the supreme paradigm of the nagging hag, constantly berating (when not beating) her husband for not providing her adequate comforts. The wife in *The Quay and the Rain* also presents an image far from that of the stereotypical female 'nurturer'. She too is the voice of want, of need, reproaching her hard-working husband for failing to provide for the family's needs. In *Tripoli Story*, the female character, in a similar vein, is never satisfied with her husband's efforts, even though he has become successful beyond her dreams, and provides well for her.

Women to the Rescue?

Susan Faludi claims that her recent book, *Stiffed: The Betrayal of the American Man*, was the result of a failed attempt to verify the stereotype of the 'aggressive and misogynistic' American male. To Faludi's surprise, she finds that the majority of the men she interviews are less misogynistic, than depressed and disillusioned. It wasn't what they wanted to do to women, or what women did to them that was at issue, but rather what society had done to them:

> There was something almost absurd about these men struggling, week after week, to recognize themselves as dominators when they were so clearly dominated, done in by the world . . . the men had probably felt in control when they beat their wives, but their everyday experience was of feeling controlled – a feeling they had no way of expressing because to reveal it was less than masculine.[133]

Just like his American counterpart, the Libyan male is struggling to retain a collective sense of place in the face of an onslaught of changes that have occurred in the years since the discovery of oil. Just as the American male expresses rage at his economic impotence, so does the Arab man. As the Moroccan Arab feminist writer Fatima Mernissi puts it:

> To define masculinity as the capacity to earn a salary is to condemn those men suffering from unemployment (or the threat of it) to perceive economic problems as castration threats.[134]

Faludi argues that, in the case of America, the sustained movement of women into the workplace is a kind of symptom of a pervasive materialistic culture that men themselves created.

> Truly, men and women have arrived at their ornamental imprisonment by different routes. Women were elevated there as a sop for their exclusion from the realm of power-striving men. Men arrived there as a result of their

power-striving, which led to a society drained of context, saturated with a competitive individualism that has been robbed of craft or utility, and ruined by commercial values that revolved around who has the most, the best, the biggest, the fastest. The destination of both roads was an enslavement to glamour.[135]

Both Mernissi and Faludi speak the vocabulary of modern feminism. Faludi seems to feel that relations between the sexes in American society, while imperfect, have evolved to the point where some lessons may be learned: 'Men and women are at a historically opportune moment where they hold the keys to each other's liberation.'[136] Sadiq Neihoum, were he alive today, would probably feel Libya still has a long way to go. As Saba Mahmood argues in *Politics of Piety*, the vast majority of Arab women, particularly those in traditional societies such as Libya, simply don't think in this vocabulary, laden with terms like 'oppression' and 'resistance':

> While these studies have made important contributions, it is surprising that their authors have paid so little attention to Islamic virtues of female modesty or piety, especially given that many of the women who have taken up the veil frame their decision precisely in these terms. Instead, analysts often explain the motivations of veiled women in terms of standard models of sociological causality . . . while terms like morality, divinity, and virtue are accorded the status of the phantom imaginings of the hegemonized.[137]

In creating characters such as the shrewish and unappreciative wives in *The Good-Hearted Salt Seller* and *Tripoli*

Story, Neihoum and El-Makki, à la Faludi and Mernissi, underscore how materialism and greed work to pervert gender relationships and tear families apart. Many Libyan women say what they want is not necessarily 'full equality' with men – whatever that means – but dignity, and the ability to pursue their dreams in a manner consistent with Islamic mores. These views are consistent with the views expressed by Neihoum and Mahmood. All that said, one has to wonder what real hope there is for a 'third way' as long as Libyan women writers still feel more comfortable writing under male pen names, and highly educated women are deemed poor marriage material.

The Revolutionary Context:

The story *Ashajarat Az-Zeitoun* (The Olive Tree) is taken from Azza Maghur's collection of short stories about the 2011 Libyan Revolution entitled *Fashloum*, after one of the poorer neighbourhoods of Tripoli. The NATO and U.S.-backed Revolution deposed Libya's leader Muammar Gaddafi and, after a period of relative calm, ushered in a protracted period of intense civil conflict. Maghur's stories, *The Olive Tree* in particular, are significant, as some of the best-formed examples of 'revolutionary literature', i.e., written either during or immediately after the 2011 Revolution, and which talk about the revolution itself. They represent both continuity with the genre and structure of stories that came before it, as well as a clear break from the pre-Gaddafi and Gaddafi-era literature.

Maghur is certainly not evasive about time, place and personalities- indeed that is her point, to be very specific about both. The hero of the story is Mohammed Madani, a Zintani commander, former member of Gaddafi's army, and one of the Revolution's charismatic figures. A Sky News report on Madani's death captured the tone of Zintanis' grief, noting that it was tinged as much with sadness for Madani, as with fear for what would become of them, if the city fell to Gaddafi's forces.[138]

The Olive Tree evinces a national pride that still connects the majority of Libyans, despite the internecine struggles. It also illustrates the degree to which Western Libyan communities were involved in the Revolution from the start. And the courage that was required for Libyans to face the regime, in its immediate backyard.

Benghazi, not Tripoli, was the epicentre of Libya's Feburary 17th Revolution, which followed those in Tunisia (December, 2010) and Egypt (January, 2011). The fact that Libya's populous Eastern city was able to break free of the regime's grasp relatively quickly, was due to a number of factors – rooted in its long-time status as an 'occupied city.' Benghazi's tradition of defiance of authority was fed by regime atrocities, military support from the West, and a good deal of luck.

When NATO forces struck at the miles-long line of armaments at Benghazi's gates, Zintan hoped for similar relief. When loyalist forces arrived in Zintan to press-gang locals into national military service, Zintan's leaders refused, provoking a showdown that lasted until May, when NATO strikes checked Gaddafi forces, one day after Mohammed Madani's death. Zintan then served as a re-supply and training centre for other rebel groups the region, and paved the way for the rebel push on Tripoli, which fell in late August of 2011.

Maghur's *Fashloum* is song or paean to the Revolution and a memorial to the fallen. It reflects both the pride of region, with references to the fabled prowess of Zintani fighters, but also evokes the idea of loyalty to a greater Libya, and common cause. It refers to Islam in the manner to which most Libyans would be accustomed – socially conservative but stubbornly moderate, and espousing a strong moral code. The story's hero, Mohammed Madani, is potrayed as someone who would '*avert bloodshed, wherever possible – even the blood of an enemy mercenary who had come to kill his own countrymen.*' This stands in contrast to the 'perfidy' of the regime's security services, who would shoot an unarmed man in the back. The text is mocking of Gaddafi, in use of words intimately associated with the regime, such as *zahf,* that Gaddafi used to described his 'continuous revolution'. *Al Zahf Al Akhdar* (The Green March), was the title of the Revolutionary Committees' newspaper. While Zintan would come in for its share of criticism in the chaos of competing militias and fears of old-regime resurgence, on the whole the town, made up of a mixture of largely old Arab families in a heavily Berber region, is seen as moderate.

In addition to the above, *The Olive Tree* also marks the passing of the baton to a new literary generation – quite literally, in this case, it is one of first pieces of short fiction published by the daughter of one of Libya's great short story writers, Kamel Maghur.

The Graffiti of Benghazi

Originally published in Words Without Borders, Aug 17, 2011

Six months after the February uprising, there are several major differences in the physical appearance of Benghazi,

Libya's rebel capital. The city is unmistakably cleaner, the result of a few pre-uprising civic works (including the cleaning of Benghazi's putrid central lake) as well as the newfound civic pride that has compelled citizens to sweep up in front of apartment buildings and storefronts. The streets are festooned with the ubiquitous red, black, and green of the Monarchy flag. Many of the burned-out, Italian colonial-era buildings, such as the Cinema Qureena on Maidan Al Shajara (Tree Square), have been either boarded up or cordoned off.

The flavour of the transformation is clearly set by graffiti, from crude black scrawls on walls and old billboards, to elaborate, intricate illustrations and caricatures, heavily focused on Muammar Gaddafi and a few recognizable figures of the Tripoli regime. Some of the messages are angry, others urgent; others are just plain creepy, or humorous, or both. Many of these efforts are interactive in a decidedly low-tech way, as new hands add to (or poke fun at, or laugh with) another's work.

One wall painting shows a mod Gaddafi wearing rectangular-framed glasses, his hair parted into a massive black, two-part afro, from which bombs are falling. Another depicts The Leader and his second-eldest son, Saif Al Islam, erstwhile symbol of reform, a smiling, miniature devil resting on Saif's shoulder, appearing to offer him a gun (a clear allusion to the 'good Saif'/'bad Saif' dichotomy that grew with the latter's February 21 'last bullet' speech, warning that Libya would dissolve into civil war). One drawing portrays Gaddafi as half man, half water buffalo, with crossbones interwoven into his facial hair. One of my favourites is a Janus-like conglomeration of Omar Al Mukhtar, the hero of the Libyan resistance to Italian fascist occupation, and a lion (Omar Al

Mukhtar's moniker was 'Lion of the Desert'), next to which another hand, far more glib, has drawn a laughing Gaddafi and a 'V' for Victory (or perhaps 'peace') sign. At times the words give an indication of when the graffiti was written: 'No foreign intervention', reads one, 'We will not beg, and we will not budge'. Another reads: 'This way to Qatar Street', clearly a reference to the leading role played by Qatar in rallying other Arab states to the rebels' cause. Note the prevalence of the (dissonant, of course) Nazi swastika and stars of David, the latter presumably referring to 'street' talk that imputes some personal and/or institutional connection between Gaddafi and Israel.

Benghazi Blues

Originally published in Foreign Policy, August 5, 2011

Travelling to and from Benghazi is a bit like reading a graphic novel or a postmodern comic book, with the shifting emotions of the residents of the Libyan rebels' de facto capital plastered on billboards and splashed across graffiti-covered walls. The book's introduction is grateful, embracing, and polished: 'Freedom Is Our Destination' reads a newly erected billboard by the airport's arrival terminal, astride a line of flags from countries that have formally recognized the rebels' Transitional National Council (TNC).

Another placard along the main road leading into town shows a smiling, elderly man in traditional dress and red fez, his hand outstretched, offering the visitor a yellow daisy, a flower that grows in abundance in the neighbouring Green Mountains.

In the centre of town, another chapter opens in the book of Benghazi, altogether more raw and gritty: 'Topple Gaddafi and his hangers-on' reads one piece of black scrawl, not far from 'Game Over' and 'Fuck Gaddafi!' (the latter two, presumably for the benefit of Westerners, in English). Emblazoned on buildings near the port are elaborate drawings, both skilled and creepy: One popular set, presumably sketched by the same hand, shows Muammar al-Gaddafi as the devil, swastikas emblazoned on each side of an exaggerated afro. Another depicts Gaddafi's second-oldest son, Saif al-Islam, not long ago the regime's most visible symbol of reform, as a small, smiling devil perched on his left shoulder.

But it's not just the Gaddafi clan that bedevils the rebel capital. At 5 a.m. on July 29, two hours before my planned departure to Benghazi, my colleague and I were alerted to the assassination of Abdul Fatah Younis, commander of Libya's rebel forces, with two of his lieutenants. A week later, the circumstances of the assassination remain murky: The TNC has confirmed that it had issued an arrest warrant for Younis (a fact it had previously denied), but continues to blame infiltrators loyal to Gaddafi for the assassination. Meanwhile, one rebel minister (and many locals) said the army chief was killed by an Islamic faction within the rebel movement.

The conflicting reports, many of which have a false ring to them, have increased observers' doubts about the TNC's capabilities, while casting a pall of intrigue and anxiety over rebel-controlled areas.

I was travelling to Benghazi with my colleague, a Libyan–American who had left Benghazi some 30 years ago. We had created an NGO to help set up a series of clinics to address physical and psychological trauma among eastern Libya's residents. It had been more than five years since I had last been in Libya, as a commercial/economic attaché in what was then the U.S. Liaison Office, prior to the opening of the full-fledged embassy in 2006. During that period, I travelled to Benghazi many times to report on various aspects of the local economy and, on the side, to collect material for a book of translations of Libyan short stories.

There's a certain rough charm to Benghazi. Despite crumbling colonial facades and a fetid lake, fed for years by the effluent from an abattoir (a hallmark Gaddafi maneuver), one could imagine how beautiful Benghazi must have been in the pre-Gaddafi years. The city allegedly maintained some of its appeal through the early years of Gaddafi's rule, but by the early 1990s, a well-established reputation for Islamist-fed opposition provoked a systematic and brutal crackdown and a cessation of outside investment – all of which took a further toll on the city's physical appearance, if not its spirit.

In 2005, in the midst of Libya's reintegration into the international community, a range of loyalist bureaucrats and trade-promoters described to me their grand plans for the development of Benghazi's waterfront and prime tourist locations farther east. Today, that same seaside property has been taken over by an impromptu, carnival-like spectacle, with souvenir hawkers standing next to photos of those who have lost their lives in the struggle, martyrs to the cause.

The notion that east Libya could become a nest of jihadists remains, for the moment, somewhat far-fetched – but in the current environment, anything is theoretically possible. Many of the older residents with whom we spoke thought that extremism could still be controlled, but that order was key. 'Within a prolonged uncertainty or a power vacuum, these elements will grow, certainly,' said one. Just as Benghazi inherited Cairo and Alexandria's learning and culture in the 1940s, 1950s, and 1960s, the growth of Islamist influences in western Egypt and elsewhere could aggravate existing pockets of religious extremist ideologies, as will wartime indoctrination of unemployed youth.

Contacts spoke of escalating conspiracy theories. Some thought Younis's assassination was a vigilante killing by an 'Islamist' faction; others thought it was an inside job, perhaps the result of a power play within the TNC. Nobody with whom we spoke gave much credence to a so-called Gaddafi 'fifth column', as the Western media was quick to report.

On one of our forays downtown, a young man, perhaps 18 years old, approached us listlessly: 'There are snipers around,' he said. 'Watch out! Bang, bang!'

We hailed a cab back to the Tibesti Hotel, site of a shootout the day before we arrived, and were quizzed incessantly by the driver about our reasons for being in Benghazi. It seemed that he, like the youth before him, was intent on provoking unease – quite the opposite impression given by soldiers in uniform and older residents, all of whom were pointedly respectful.

Later, I stepped out of the car to take a picture of a particularly interesting piece of graffiti, when an enraged young man approached us, yelling in Arabic: 'What are you doing? Who are you? You cannot take pictures; this is illegal.'

'Illegal by whose orders, and who are you? Did we make revolution to be told what to do by random people acting on their own whim?' shot back a Libyan friend, incautiously. A few other young men, also not in uniform, approached, automatic weapons drawn and ready to fire.

There is a sunnier side to the new freedom in Benghazi. Residents are openly questioning everything, not least of all their leadership. The July 26 edition of al Libii (The Libyan) poses a series of hardball questions to TNC chief Abdul Jalil: 'Why is Mahmoud Jibril, who has alternated between 'prime' and 'foreign' minister, never in the country?' 'Why are you staffing the ministry of finance with academics and not experienced businessmen?' 'What are you doing about inclusiveness on the council of opposition groups outside of Libya?' The questions go on, and Jalil treats each respectfully.

As the TNC is discovering a free press and a politically motivated population can be the new leadership's best friend and its worst enemy. Much of the latest criticism comes from the TNC's handling of the news of Younis's death. Even many of those wholly unsympathetic to the man faulted the way information was being disseminated – or not. 'Younis was a military man – there should be a military investigation, by a military tribunal. Everything according to a process,' said one engineer from the Libyan diaspora who had returned to assist the TNC with technical issues. 'Even if the TNC had problems with Younis, it should have been dealt with straight on, according to a process, not the shadows.'

A highlight of our trip was a two-hour visit to the office of a mutual acquaintance, 'S.', who is well over 70 years old. By dint of his age, education, and family background, he carried significant respect within the community – a fact evident by an almost incessant procession of well-wishers who, if S. didn't know them personally, made every effort to appear as if he did.

After about 20 minutes of conversation, the editor of

one of the dozen new newspapers in Benghazi entered with a stack of broadsheets. Today's headline: 'A Strong, Unified Libya.' His optimism buoyed the conversation, which had turned slightly dour.

'Look at what we have accomplished. There are 25,000 guns loose in Benghazi, and we've got 10 or 12 shooting deaths a month,' he gushed. 'What would happen if law and order were suspended in any European or American city for even 24 hours? You'd have chaos!'

In a key televised address the afternoon of July 30, Jalil called for the armed militias in rebel-controlled territory to submit to the TNC's authority – or face the consequences. The TNC leader, whose mien is hard to read, looked more exhausted and worried than usual. Behind the scenes, the TNC named one of Younis's cousins as his successor – clearly a gesture to Younis's tribe – which also provoked criticism in some corners from those who saw it as a sop to a long-outdated notion that somehow tribalism rules modern Libya.

The TNC made good on its promises within hours: On the night of July 30, the leadership attacked one unit, alternately described as 'Islamist', pro-Gaddafi', or euphemistically, 'independent', after it defied the order to consolidate. The result was a nightlong firefight at the city's perimeter that allegedly left scores dead and plumes of smoke rising into the dawn sky.

We awoke on July 31 to an extremely tense atmosphere within the Tibesti. Hotel staff furtively passed around printouts taken from an opposition website. A few calls later, we learned that the U.S. envoy's office and the U.N. compound were both under lockdown. The Internet seemed to be failing, and there were few Westerners in evidence.

Benghazi was gripped by a pervasive feeling that order could break down at any minute – an eventuality that our small NGO was ill-equipped to handle. I managed to hold a Skype connection just long enough to ask a third member of our group, who was to arrive later that week, to contact the U.N. office in Cairo to ask its indulgence in getting us out that day. Our driver tried to assuage our fears, saying, 'I've crossed the city this morning; everything is quiet.' It was a reassurance that we would hear many times, whether we asked for it or not.

Forty minutes later, we were back where we started a few short days before, facing the kindly old man with the red fez and yellow daisy. The plane, thankfully, was an hour late in from Cairo, but we still had no seat confirmation. 'We've been authorized to take you as far as Heraklion,' the capital of Crete, came the eventual reply from a U.N. staff aide. If we had any doubts that we had made the right call to leave, they were dispelled once we saw the assembled passengers: hardened aid workers, many of whom were with us on our inbound flight, insisting they'd be in Benghazi 'indefinitely.'

As the plane began its ascent over the Green Mountains, I reflected on the chaos of the last few days. A particular piece of graffiti along the outbound airport road stuck in my head. Roughly translated, it read: 'We will not beg, and we will not budge.'

That's fine when facing a common enemy, but not particularly helpful when trying to communicate with one's own: Resolving the question of who killed Younis and bringing those parties to justice – wherever they may be found – will be key to the TNC's efforts to maintain popular trust.

After all that the people of Benghazi and the rest of Libya have been through, the worst of all outcomes would be a return to the past, or a fractious future. If Libya's rebels are able to accomplish this feat, the story of what has happened here may yet prove one of the most inspirational of the Arab Spring.

Author Biographies

Ziad Ali (1949–) was born in Tripoli. His publications include a collection of short stories (*The Savage Trun, Don't Embarrass the Beautiful Death*) critical essays on Arab poetry (*Words Live Longer*), popular tales (*The Bird Who Forgot its Feathers*) and legal and literary commentary (*Culture and Crime, The Legal and Political Thought of Mohammad Ali Shukani*). Ali is a member of the Libyan Novel and Short Story Association and the League of Libyan Writers. He received a BA and an MA from Cairo University Law School, and a PhD in Law, Economics and Social Science from Mohamed V University, Rabat. Ali's stories have been translated into several languages.

Wahbi Bouri (1916–2010) Widely considered the 'original' Libyan short story writer, Wahbi Bouri is one of the most accomplished of the post-war civil servants. Bouri's government appointments included Minister of Foreign Affairs (1957), Minister of Petroleum (1960) and Ambassador to the UN (1963). Bouri's university years were spent in Rome and Naples, during which time he translated Arabic articles and broadcasts for the Italian Ministry of Culture. In 1947, he returned to Benghazi. Bouri received an MA in African Studies from St Johns University in New York. In 2005, he published *Benghazi*, an extensive non-fiction portrait of a city under Italian colonization. Other literary credits include a number of stories for *Libya Al-Musawwara*. His first short story was 'A Wedding Night'.

Ramadan Abdalla Bukheit (1935–) Born in the Ahrebeesh quarter of Benghazi, Bukheit developed a following as a storywriter in the 1960s, when a number of his pieces appeared in local newspapers. To support his writing career, Bukheit worked for the Department of Training and the General Electricity Board in Benghazi. Over the years, Bukheit's fiction has appeared in popular magazines like *Al-Rawa'id*. In the nineties he wrote for the Libyan newspaper *Al-Jamahiriya* and the journal *Al-Fusul al Arbi'a* (*The Four Seasons*), in addition to *Al- Naqd*, a London-based literary magazine. In addition to short stories, Bukheit has published works of literary criticism, focused on the art of the short story.

Ahmed Ibrahim Fagih (1942–) Born in the village of Mizda, 100 miles south of Tripoli, Ahmed Ibrahim Fagih is perhaps the best known of the 'sixties generation' of Libyan writers, among which are Ibrahim Koni, Kamel Maghur, Ramadan Bukheit and Sadiq Neihoum. He worked as a journalist in Tripoli until 1962, when he won a scholarship to study theatre at London's New Era Academy of Drama and Music. In 1972 Fagih returned to Libya to head the National Institute of Music and Drama. In the same year he became editor of the influential *Al-Usbu'Ath-Thaqafi* (*Cultural Weekly*). Fagih's Magnum Opus, a trilogy with the

English titles *I Shall Present You With Another City, These are the Borders of My Kingdom* and *A Tunnel Lit by a Woman*, won the prize for best novel at the 1991 Beirut Book Fair. Fagih's first collection of stories, *Al-Bahr La Ma' Fih* (*No Water in the Sea*), won Libya's Royal Commission for Fine Arts' highest award in 1965. Collections of Fagih's short stories include: *Fasten Your Seat Belts* (1968), *The Stars Disappeared* (1976), *A Woman of Light* (1985) and *Mirrors of Venice* (1997). Several of Fagih's novels have been translated into English, including *Maps of the Soul* (Darf, 2014) and *Homeless Rats* (Quartet, 2011). Fagih has had a long, parallel diplomatic career, having previously headed Libya's missions in Greece and Romania. In the wake of the 2011 Revolution, Fagih defected to the Rebel government and continued as Libya's Ambassador to the Arab League, based in Cairo. Fagih holds a Ph.D. in the Libyan Short Story from the University of Edinburgh.

Abdullah Ali Al-Gazal (1965–) Gazal established himself in the Libyan literary community in 2003 with the publication of *Al- Tabut* (The Ark), which won first prize in the 2003 Sharjah Literary Innovators Competition. A collection of stories under the title *Aswat* won first prize at the subsequent Sharjah Competition. The Libyan newspaper *Al-Jamahir* published a series of Gazal's essays under the title *Reflections Upon the Greatest Secret*. Another anthology, *Al- Qawqa'a*, was published in 2006 by the Arab Publishing Corporation. Gazal received a BA in Mechanical Engineering in 1987; he is a member of the Mechanical Engineering Teaching Faculty at the Institute for Higher Professional Studies in Misurata, Libya.

Meftah Genaw (1958–) Born in Tripoli, Genaw graduated from a flight engineering academy in Czechoslovakia in 1984, after which he worked as a mechanic for the Libyan Air Force. In 2001, Genaw became editor of *Al-Fonoon* (*The Arts*) magazine, published by the General Secretariat of the League of Libyan Artists, and his first book of short stories was published in 2004 under the name of *Caesar's Return*. In addition to short stories, Genaw has published various pieces of literary criticism. He is one of the founders of the Libyan Story and Novel Club, and a member of the General Union of Libyan Lawyers and the League of Libyan Writers. Genaw claims to have been heavily influenced by the Czech satirist Jaruslav Hasek, whose *The Good Soldier Svejk* has been called a 'cynical and satirical treatment of all forms of ideology'. Genaw holds a degree in law from the University of Libya.

Ahmed Mohammed Lannaizy (1929–) Born in Benghazi, Lannaizy studied the Qur'an at Az-Zawiya Mosque before entering one of the Arab-only schools established by the Italian colonizers. His studies cut short by the start of World War II, Lannaizy was appointed to the appeals court of Barqa, then became an administrator at the Libyan University. Lannaizy began writing short stories in the early 1950s. His stories, translations and commentary have appeared in the periodicals *Tarabulus Al-Gharb*, *Barqat Al Jadid*, *Majallat An-Nour* and *Majallat Al-Rawad*. Two collections of short stories have been published as books. Lannaizy has been a judge in Libyan literary competitions and participated in a number of North African literary conferences.

Azza Kamel Maghur (1964–) has emerged in the last decade as a recognized name in Arabic short fiction, and one of the prominent chroniclers of the first year of Revolution. She has has published two collections of short stories with Dar Al Rowad Press: *Tripoli: Thirty Stories of My City* (2013) and *Fashloum* (2012), from which the short story *The Olive Tree* is taken. Some of her stories have been translated into English, including *The Bicycle*, (*Banipal Magazine*, #40) as part of a special issue on modern Arab literature. Critics have noted Maghur's creative vision and her ability to capture the lost world of Libyan youth in fiction about an idealistic country in the process of change. A prominent human rights lawyer, both before and after the Revolution, she was appointed by the National Transitional Council (post-Revolutionary Libya's governing body) as a member of the Libyan National Council for Civil Liberties and Human Rights. In addition to chairing the committee to draft new NGO law (2012), she was the sole woman member of the February Commission to amend the Constitutional Declaration (2014). A collection of essays entitled, *Libya: The Difficult Road Towards Democracy* is forthcoming. She is the eldest daughter of Kamel Hassan Maghur.

Kamel Hassan Maghur (1935–2002) Born in the Dahra neighbourhood of Tripoli, Maghur was one of the pioneers of the Libyan short story. Maghur graduated from Cairo University in 1957 with a degree in law. He began his career in 1959 as advisor to the State of Tripolitania; ten years later he was appointed to the Libyan Court of Appeals. By 1970, he had a seat on the Libyan Supreme Court. Maghur represented his country in most of the critical post-Independence international legal dealings, from agreements governing post-war decommissioning of foreign military bases to disputes with Tunisia over the international maritime border and with Chad over the Ouzou Strip. Maghur served alternately as Minister of Petroleum, Head of OPEC, and Minister of Foreign Affairs, as well as Libya's ambassador to the UN, Canada, France and China. Maghur's best-known titles include: *Tales From My City*, *Four Centuries of Hegemony*, *Landmarks*, *Tales from the White City*, *On Culture*, and *People's Worries*. He died in Rome on 4 January, 2002.

Lamia El-Makki (1972–) An author and teacher of Arabic as a Second Language, Ms El-Makki is a graduate of the Arabic Language and Islamic Studies Programme at Al-Fateh University, Tripoli. She holds a General Certificate of Education/'A' level in Classical Arabic from London University. Since 1991, El-Makki has worked as a translator, interpreter and Arabic language instructor for various foreign companies and diplomats serving in Libya.

Abdel Raziq Al-Mansuri (1954–) A journalist and writer, by the end of 2004 Al-Mansuri had written some fifty articles and commentaries for Internet sites. His story *My Dead Friends* was published by the Libyan news and culture website Libya Al-Yowm in 2005.

Ali Mustapha Misrati (1926–) attended Cairo's Al-Azhar University. Upon graduation he returned to a newly-independent Libya to work in print journalism and radio broadcasting. In addition to being a writer and critic, Misrati had a substantial political career, having been elected to the Libyan parliament several times during the Monarchy. One source says of Misrati that 'he occupies a notable position in the field of Libyan short stories; his protagonists take us into the core of popular struggles in his homeland of Libya. Literary critic Mohammed Khafaji said Misrati, 'writes in a splendid and loveable style.'[139] Among Misrati's best-known works are: *Libyan Landmarks*, *Literary Glimpses of Tripoli*, *Joha in Libya* and *Hufnat Min Rimad* (*Handful of Ashes*), a collection of short stories.

Sadiq Neihoum (1937–1994) Born in Benghazi, Neihoum graduated from Libya University in 1961 with a major in Arabic Language and Literature. He began his writing career in the late 1950s, writing articles for the local paper. Neihoum won a lectureship at the Faculty of Arts, and subsequently a fellowship to pursue postgraduate studies at the University of Munich, after which he returned to Benghazi and began writing for a start-up publication, *Al-Haqiqa* (*The Truth*), whose first issue featured Neihoum's essay 'This is My Experience'. Early works included *The Word and Image*, *African Lover* and a treatise on the poetry of Mohamed Fituri. In 1967, Neihoum published two books, a collection of essays under the title *Who Comes and Who Doesn't*, and *Symbolism in the Quran*, both of which established him as a leading figure in Libyan letters. Neihoum's Al-Haqiqa columns won him a loyal following, for a style that many found 'vivid and dashing'. In the mid-1970s, Neihoum moved to Beirut, where he wrote for *Al-Usbu' Al-Arabi* (*The Arab Week*) magazine. In 1976 he took up a post as lecturer in comparative religion at the University of Geneva, where he founded both Heritage House and Al-Mokhtar House. Other works include the novels *From Mecca to Here*, *Qisas Atfal* (*Children's Stories*), *Knights Without Battle*, *Hello*, *Al-Qurud* (*The Monkeys*), *The*

Animals, and *The Voices of Everyday People*. Neihoum died in Finland in 1994.

Maryam Ahmed Salama (1965–) Maryam Salama is one of the most apparent of a small but growing group of female Libyan writers. She received her undergraduate degree from the Department of Literature and Culture at Al-Fateh University in 1987, and works currently in the field of translation, with an emphasis on historical studies. Her works of prose and poetry have been published in Libyan and foreign newspapers and magazines. Ms Salama has a number of book titles to her credit, including *Ahlam Tifla Sajina* (*Dreams of a Captive Girl*).

Najwa Ben Shetwan (1968–) A specialist in narrative and the short story, Najwa Ben Shetwan was born in the Libyan town of Ajdabia. She earned her Master's degree in Literature, and is currently a professor of literature at Gar Younes University in Benghazi. Ben Shetwan's play *Al-Mat'af* won third place in the Sharjah Literary Innovators Competition in 2002. Her narrative 'Wabr Al Ahsinat' ('The Horse's Mane') won the literature prize at the Khartoum Festival in 2005. Other publications include *Al Ma' fi Sinarati* (2003), *Qisas Laesat lil Rijal* (a collection of short stories, 2004), and *Tifl Al Waw* (short stories, 2006). Laila Nayhoum described Najwa Ben Shetwan as 'one of the very best Libyan short story writers of her generation'.

Saleh Saad Younis (1975–) Born in the town of Al-Beida', Younis received a BA in Literature from Omar Al-Mohtar University in 1998. *The Yellow Rock* is his first published collection of stories.

Bibliography

Ahmida, Ali Abdullatif, 'Identity, Cultural Encounter and Alienation in the Trilogy of the Libyan Writer Ahmed Ibrahim Al-Fagih', *Arab Studies Quarterly* (ASQ), 22 March 1998.

Ahmidan, Ibrahim, "The Libyan Novel", in *Bannipal* #40, Spring, 2011, p 46–48

Ajayi, J. F. Ade, ed., *UNESCO General History of Africa: VI Africa in the Nineteenth Century until the 1880s*, Berkeley: University of California Press, 1989.

'Ajina, Saleh, *Min As-Satr Al-Awal lil Riwayat Al Libiya*, Tripoli: Dar Anamil, 2004.

Ali, Ziyad, *At-Tair Alathi Nasi Rishahu*, Libya: Dar Al Arabiya Lil Kitab, 1999.

Al-Kikli, Omar Abdulqasim, "The Short Story in Libya", in *Bannipal* #40, Spring, 2011, p 44–46

Allen, Roger, *The Arab Novel*, New York: Syracuse University Press, 1995.

Asti, Ali Sha'ban, *Mahalat Mezran: Al Madi wa al-Hadhir*, 1880–1992, Benghazi: Dar Al-Kutub Al-Wataniya, 2005.

Bazama, Mohammed Mustafa, *Al-Madina Al-Basila*, Libya: Al-Hiwar, 1994.

Bereniq, "Istishad Qai'd Al-Thuwwar, Al Sheikh Mohammed Al Madani, fi Zintan," May 2, 2011

Bey, Ahmed Hassanein, *The Lost Oases*, Cairo: American University in Cairo Press, 2006 (reprint of 1925 original).

Bin Arefa, At-Tahir, *At-Ta'reef Bil Adab Al-Libi*, Tripoli: Dar al Hikma, 1997.

Bin Taleb, Mohammed Umar, *Lebda Al-Hadara*, Benghazi: Dar Al Kutub Al-Wataniya, 2001.

Birley, Anthony, *Septimius Severus, The African Emperor*, New Haven: Yale University Press, 1972.

Bouri, Wahbi, *Benghazi fil Fitrat Al-Isti'mar Al-Italiya*, Benghazi: Majlis Tanmiya Al-Ibda' Ath-Thaqafi, 2004.

——*Al-Milh Hayat Benghazi*, Benghazi: Bank Tijara Wa Tanmiya, no. 3, 2005.

——*Al-Bawakeer Al-Qissat Al-Libiya Al-Qasira*, Tripoli: Mu'tammar, 2004.

Brett, Michael, and Fentress, Elizabeth, *The Berbers*, Massachusetts: Blackwell Publishing, 2005.

Bukheit, Ramadan Abdalla, *Hikayat Al-Madi Al-Qarib*, Benghazi: Dar Al-Kutub Al-Wataniya, 1996

Bushnaf, Mansour, *Chewing Gum*: London: Darf Publishers: 2012

Chouraqui, Andre N., *Between East and West, A History of the Jews of North Africa*, Philadelphia: Jewish Publication Society of America, 1968.

Cohen-Mor, Dalya, *Arab Women Writers, An Anthology of Short Stories*, New York: SUNY, 2005.

Cowan, J. M., and Wehr, Hans, eds, *Dictionary of Modern Arabic*, New York: Spoken Language Services, Inc., 1976.

Deeb, Marius K. and Mary Jane, *Libya Since the Revolution: Aspects of Social and Political Development*, New York: Praeger, 1982.

Djaziri, Moncef, *Etat et société en Libye*, Paris: L'Harmattan, 1996.

Elnaili, Safa, *A Stylistic Analysis of Libyan Short Stories: The Connotation of Adjectives*, Unpublished MA Thesis, Louisiana State University, May, 2013
http://etd.lsu.edu/docs/available/etd-03042013-113651/unrestricted/thesis.pdf

Fagih, Ahmed Ibrahim, 'Background Notes on Modern Libyan Literature,' in *Majmu'a al-A'maal Al Kamila* (CD), Tripoli: self-published, 2004.

——'The Libyan Short Story: The Realistic Approach', in *Majmu'a al- A'maal Al Kamila*, CD, Tripoli: self-published, 2004.

——*Libyan Stories*, New York: Columbia University Press, 2000.

Faludi, Susan, *Stiffed: The Betrayal of the American Man*, New York: HarperCollins, 2000.

Fathaly, Omar, and Palmer, Monte, *Political and Social Change in Libya*, New York: Lexington Books, 1980.

Fontaine, Jacques, 'La population libyenne, un demi-science de mutations', in Pliez, Olivier, ed., *La Nouvelle Libye: Sociétés, espaces et* géopolitique au lendemain de l'embargo, Paris: Karthala, 1991.

Gellner, Ernest, *Saints of the Atlas*, Chicago: University of Chicago Press, 1969.

Genaw, Meftah, *'Awdat Caesar, Qisas Qasira*, Tripoli: Majlis Tanmiyya Al-Ibda'a Ath-Thaqafi, 2004.

Ghadamsi, Mohammed Ali, *An-Naft Al-Libi*, Beirut: Dar Al-Jeel, 1998.

Glubb, John Bagot, *The Great Arab Conquests*, London: Quartet Books, 1980.

Goldberg, Harvey, *Jewish Life in Muslim Libya*, Chicago: University of Chicago Press, 1990.

Goodchild, R. G., *Tarikh Benghazi* (A History of Libya), translated into Arabic by Saleh Jabariel, 2nd edition, Benghazi: Dar Al Kutub Al-Wataniya, 2003.

——*Byzantines, Berbers and Arabs in Seventh-Century Libya*, Antiquity 41, 1967

Graeff-Wassink, Maria, 'Les relations hommes-femmes en Libye, hier et aujourd'hui', in Olivier Pliez, *Villes du Sahara*, Editions CNRS, 2003.

Greene, Molly, *A Shared World: Christians and Muslims in the Early Modern Mediterranean*, Princeton, N.J.: Princeton University Press, 2000.

Ham, Anthony, *Libya*, Melbourne: Lonely Planet, 2002.

Hasek, Jaroslav, *The Good Soldier Svejk*, New York: Penguin Books, 1973.

Holcome, Knut, *Rihlat Fis-Sahra' Al-Libiya* (Arabic Translation), London: Dar Al-Fergiani, 1992.

Hussain, Hussain Sakran, ed., *Dalil Al-Wahat As-Siyahi*, Tripoli, WTR Centre, 2006.

Al-Janzouri, Abdel Rahman, *Rihlat Sanawat At-Tawila:Waqa'i wa Ta'amilaat fi Sirat Mawatin Libi*, Tripoli: Markaz Jihad Al-Libiyeen lil Dirasaat At Tarihiya, 2000.

Jayyusi, Salma, *Modern Arabic Fiction*, New York: Columbia University Press, 2005.

Jeffreys, Andrew, ed., *Emerging Morocco*, London: Oxford Business Group, 2006.

Johnson-Davies, Denis, *Modern Arabic Short Stories*, Oxford, UK: Oxford University Press, 1967.

Kashlaf, Suleiman, *Dirasaat fil Qissat Al-Libi Al-Qasira*, Tripoli: Al-Mansha'at Al-Aama Lil Nashar wa Al-Tawziy'a wa Al-I'lanaat, 1979.

Keith, Agnes Newton, *Children of Allah: Between the Sea and Sahara*, London: Michael Joseph, 1966.

Khafaji, Mohammed Abdel Munim, *Qisat Al-Adab fi Libi Al-Arabi*, Beirut: Dar Al Jeel, 1992.

Kostiner, Joseph, and Khoury, Philip S., *Tribes and State Formation in the Middle East*, Berkeley: University of California Press, 1990.

Kovach, Thomas H., 'Sidelights' (biography of Jaroslav Hasek – Matej Frantisek, 1883–1923) in *Contemporary Authors*, 2004.

Kurlansky, Mark, *Salt: A World History*, New York: Penguin, 2002.

Libya National Report on Human Development 2002, 2003, Tripoli,

National Authority of Information and Documentation, 2002, 2003.

Maghur, Azza Kamel, *Fashloum: Qisas Februaee*, Tripoli: Dar Al-Ruwad, 2012

Maghur, Kamel Hassan, *Qisas Qasira*, Tripoli: Dar Al-Ruwad, 2003.

Mahmood, Saba, *Politics of Piety: The Islamic Revival and the Feminist Subject*, Princeton: Princeton University Press, 2005.

Maliki, Hussain Naseeb, *Qira'at fi Al-Qissat Al-Qasira*, Benghazi: Dar Al Kutub Al-Wataniya, 2006.

Mallat, Chibli, *Philosophy of Nonviolence: Revolution, Constitutionalism, and Justice Beyond the Middle East*, London: Oxford University Press, 2015.

Mernissi, Fatima, *The Veil and the Male Elite, A Feminist Interpretation of Women's Rights in Islam*, New York: Basic Books, 1991.

——*Beyond the Veil: Male–Female Dynamics in Modern Muslim Society*, Bloomington: Indiana University Press, 1987.

Moorehead, Alan, *African Trilogy: The Desert War 1940–1943*, London: Cassell, 2000.

Mufti, Muhammad Muhammad, *Hadraza fis-Souk*, Libya: Dar Al Saqiya, 2006.

——*Sahaari Derna*, Benghazi: Dar Al Kutub Al-Wataniya, 2007.

——*Ghamq Zallat*, Benghazi: Dar Al Kutub Al-Wataniya, 2005.

——*Hadraza fi Benghazi*, Benghazi: Dar Al Kutub Al-Wataniya, 2004.

Neihoum, Sadiq, *Qisas Atfal*, Beirut: Tala Books, 2002.

——*Al-Hadith 'An Al-Mar'a Wa Al Diyanaat*, Beirut: Tala Books, 2002 (reprint).

Oliver, Roland, and Atmore, Anthony, *Medieval Africa, 1250–1800*, Cambridge, UK: Cambridge University Press, 1981.

Otayek, Rene, *La politique africaine de la Libye, 1969–1985*, Paris: Karthala, 1986.

Pacho, Jean-Raimond, *Relation d'un voyage dans la Marmarique, la Cyrenaique et les Oasis d'Audjelah et de Maradeh*, Beirut, Dar Al Jeel, 1999.

Pliez, Olivier, ed., *La Nouvelle Libye: Sociétés, espaces et* géopolitique au lendemain de l'embargo, Paris: Karthala, 1991.

——*Villes du Sahara: Urbanisation et urbanité dans le Fezzan libyen*, Paris: Editions CNRS, 2003.

Qasim Youshni', Bashir, *Ghadames, Malamih wa Suwwar*, Tripoli, self-published, 2001.

Qathafi, Muammar, *The Green Book, Part One: The Solution of the Problem of Democracy*, Tripoli: World Centre for the Study and Research of the Green Book, 1984.

Reynolds, Joyce, ed., 'Select Papers of the Late R. G. Goodchild', *Libyan Studies*, London: Paul Elek, 1976.

Roumani, Maurice, *The Case of the Jews from Arab Countries: A Neglected Issue*, Tel Aviv: World Organization of Jews from Arab Countries (WOJAC), 1983.

Salama, Maryam Ahmed, *The Way to the White City: A Guide Book*, Tripoli: Dar al Kalima, 2004.

Salih, Mohammad Fagih, *Ufuq Ahar*, Tripoli: Dar Al Kutub Al- Wataniya, 2002.

Shalabi, Salim Salim, *Tarablus Al-Qadima, Anaween Ala Nawaasi al Mahrusa*, Tripoli: Dar Fergiani, 1994.

Sourdel, Janine and Dominique, *Dictionnaire historique de l'Islam*, Paris: PUF, 1999.

Souriau, Christiane, *Libye: L'économie des femmes*, Paris: L'Harmattan, 2002.

Staub, Vincent, *La Libye et Les Migrations Subsahariennes*, Paris: L'Harmattan, 2006.

Stolz, Joelle, *Les Ombres de Ghadames*, Paris: Bayard, 1999.

Tatsios, Theodore George, *The Megali Idea and the Greek–Turkish War of 1897: The Impact of the Cretan Problem on Greek Irredentism, 1866–1897*, East European Monographs, Boulder: distributed by Columbia University Press, 1984.

Technical Mission to Libya on Illegal Immigration, 27 November to 6 December 2004, Brussels: European Union Occasional Reports, 2004.

Thierry, Jacques, *Tarikh As-Sahra' Al-Libi Fi Al-Usur Al-Wusta*, Tripoli: Al Dar Al-Jamahiriya Lil Nashar Wa Attawzi' Wa Al-I'lan, Beirut: Dar Al Jeel, 2004.

Tijani, Deriko, *Benghazi fi Al-Aqd Al-Thani Min Al-Qarn Al-Ishreen*, Benghazi: Dar Kutub Al-Wataniya Benghazi, 2003.

Tillich, Paul, *The Courage To Be*, New Haven: Yale University Press, 2000.

Lannaizy, Ahmed Mohammed, *Hadith Al-Madina*, Tripoli: Dar Al Kutub Al-Wataniya, 2005.

Vandewalle, Dirk, *A History of Modern Libya*, Cambridge, UK: Cambridge University Press, 2006.

Vandewalle, Dirk, ed., *Gaddafi's Libya, 1969–1994*, New York: St Martin's Press, 1995.

Vandewalle, Dirk, *Libya Since Independence: Oil and State Building, Ithaca*: Cornell University Press, 1998.

Ward, Philip, *Touring Libya: The Western Provinces*, London: Faber, 1969.

Werner, Louis, 'Libya's Forgotten Desert Kingdom', in *Saudi Aramco World*, May/June, 2004.

Williams, Gwyn, *Green Mountain*, Tripoli: Dar Al Fergiani, 1963.

Woodhouse, C., *Modern Greece: A Short History* (paperback), Boston and London: Faber and Faber, 1968.

Mattawa, Khaled, Preface to the Libya Issue, Words Without Borders, July 2006: http://www.wordswithoutborders. org/article/preface-to-the-libya-issue-of-words-without-borders-july-2006

Wright, John, *Libya: A Modern History*, Baltimore: Johns Hopkins University Press, 1983.

Younis, Saleh Saad, *Al-Hajar Al-Asfar*, Benghazi: Dar Al Kutub Al-Wataniya, 2006.

(unattributed), *Al-Mu'alifoon al-Libyoon al Mu'asiroon*, Tarajim wa Mu'alifaat, Benghazi: Dar Al-Kutub Al-Wataniya, 2002.

Footnotes

1. For an excellent exposition of modern Libyan fiction, including translations of Libyan short stories, see *Banipal, the Magazine of Modern Arab Literature*, #40, Spring 2011.

2. This was the topic of my second book, *Exit the Colonel: The Hidden History of the Libyan Revolution*, which was published in October, 2012, shortly after the attack on the U.S. Mission in Benghazi.

3. Salih, Mohammad Fagih, *Ufuq Ahar*, Tripoli: Dar Al-Kutub Al-Wataniya, 2002, page 69.

4. During the sanctions years, one of the only ways in and out of Libya was by ferry to Malta.

5. http://naohama.blogspot.com

6. Bouri, Wahbi, 'Al Milh Hayat Benghazi', Benghazi: *Bank Tijara Wa Tanmiya*, no. 3., p. 37.

7. Kurlansky, Mark, *Salt: A World History*, New York: Penguin, 2002. p. 47.

8. Bouri, p. 36.

9. Tripoli was the other.

10. Goodchild, R., *Tarikh Benghazi (A History of Libya)*, 2nd edition, Benghazi: Dar Al-Kutub Al-Wataniya, 2003, p. 50.

11. Author's note: Buraq did return Mohammed to Earth. *The Qur'an*, (17:1).

12. Zanj: an archaic, derogatory term for a person of African descent.

13. *Abdel Milh*: Literally, the 'salt slave'.

14. *Assabri, Sabri:* A suburb of Benghazi.

15. Sadiq Neihoum died in Finland in 1994.

16. Souk al-Jarid, Maidan al-Haddad and Souk al-Dhalam: Market of palms, Ironmongers' Square, and Market of Shadows, respectively.

17. Author's email correspondence with Dr. Muhammad Mufti, 18 October 2006.

18. *Bitaka*: Identity card.

19. A hillside cave in North Hammama.

20. *Mrabet, Marabet, or Marabout*: itinerant mystic.

21. *Ghibli/Qibli*: a blazing south-westerly wind.

22. Williams, Gwyn, *Green Mountain*, Tripoli: Dar Al Fergiani, 1963, p. 40.

23. Ibid. p. 79.

24. *Ras Al-Hilal:* Literally, 'head of the crescent'.

25. The village of Bauhareshma is located on the Libyan coast about 130 kilometres East of Benghazi.

26. *Baladiya*: Municipality.

27. *Sharmoula*: a Libyan salad made of green pepper, tomatoes, cucumber, onions, salt, lemon and olive oil; *Shakshouka*: a local dish made with fried eggs and tomatoes, green peppers, garlic and dried meat.

28. *Barakat:* Divine blessing.

29. *Houri*: a nymph, one of the virgins that await the Believer in Paradise.

30. *Ayat*: verses of the Qur'an.

31. *Qibla*: Direction of prayer, facing Mecca.

32. *Saliheen*: pious and virtuous men.

33. *Issawiya*: an ascetic Sufi movement popular after the Islamic conquest of North Africa.

34. *Jalbaba:* long dress worn primarily in Egypt, but also seen in Libya.

35. *Djinn:* Ghosts, spirits.

36. Mufti, Muhammad Muhammad, *Sahaari Derna*, Benghazi: Dar Al Kutub al-Wataniya, 2007. p. 7.

37. Williams, Gwyn, *Green Mountain*, Tripoli: Dar Al-Fergiani, 1963, p. 98.

38. Jean-Raimond Pacho, a French traveller and author of *Relation d'un voyage dans la Marmarique, la Cyrenaique et les Oasis d'Audjelah et de Maradeh*, Beirut, Dar Al Jeel, 1999.

39. Mufti, *Sahaari Derna*, p. 12.

40. Williams, *Green Mountain*, p. 98.

41. Mufti, *Sahaari Derna*, p. 14.

42. Williams, *Green Mountain*, p. 98.

43. Mufti, *Sahaari Derna*, p. 16.

44. *Fagih*: learned man.

45. *Mawlai*: My Lord.

46. One of the attributes of Allah.

47. *Amir al-Haras*: Commander of the Guards.

48. Ghadamsi, Mohammed Ali, *An-Naft Al-Libi*, Beirut: Dar Al-Jeel, 1998, p. 177.

49. Bey, Ahmed Hassanein, *The Lost Oases*, Cairo: American University in Cairo Press, 2006 (reprint of 1925 original). p. viii.

50. Ibid., p. 93.

51. According to Bey, camels instinctively know not to stop in a sandstorm, lest they be buried.

52. The artifacts displayed at the fair do not match the pictures of the crash site, however.

53. *Jawa incense, loban* and *fasukh*: All varieties of incense.

54. *Shabab*: Youth.

55. *Balah:* Early-harvest dates.

56. 2003 Libyan census.

57. *Sabah Al-Khayr*: Good morning.

58. Qasim Youshni', Bashir, *Ghadames, Malamih wa Suwwar*, Tripoli, self-published, 2001, p. 11.

59. *Kalbek*: A Libyan hat.

60. *Aaraeb Al-Abeed:* Literally, 'cattle pens for slaves'.

61. *Wallahi*: 'By God!'

62. Vandewalle, Diederik, *A History of Modern Libya,* Cambridge, UK: Cambridge University Press, 2006, p. 197.

63. NASCO, the National Supply Company, provided most of Libyans' consumer needs during the sanctions era.

64. Salama, Maryam Ahmed, *The Way to the White City: A Guide Book*, Tripoli: Dar al Kalina, 2004, pp.22-3.

65. Salem, Ali, Tripoli's Iconic Gazelle and Mermaid Statue Destroyed by Vandals, 4 november 2014, Libya Herald

66. Theoretically, Gaddafi's governing system was built upon Basic People's Congresses, of which there were more than 1,000 country-wide. The People's Congresses proposed and reviewed legislation, which was ultimately referred to the General People's Committee for approval and enactment.

67. Birley, Anthony, *Septimius Severus, The African Emperor*, New Haven: Yale University Press, 1972, p. 42.

68. Ibid., p. 200.
69. Ibid., p. 198.
70. Ibid., p. 35.
71. *Wali:* Leader, crown prince.
72. *Hara*: Arabic term for an exclusively Jewish quarter.
73. *Morcante*: Italian for merchant.
74. *Shahada*: Attestation that Allah is the One and Only God, and Mohammed is His Messenger.
75. *Quffa*: A basket made of palm leaves.
76. *Fajri*: Adjective for dawn.
77. *Haraymi*: A spicy Libyan fish soup, strongly associated with Libyan Jewish tradition.
78. *Farashiya*: A North African shawl or body-wrap, worn typically by older women. Today it is often seen as low-class, as beggars wear it to conceal their identity.
79. *Arsa*: A column, Libyan slang for 'tall woman'.
80. Ward, Philip, *Touring Libya: The Western Provinces*, London: Faber, 1963, p. 49.
81. *Souk Al-Noflieen*: Market near Tripoli's Fashloum neighbourhood.
82. *Eid As-Saghir*: the three-day festival that marks the end of the holy month of Ramadan, Eid Al-Fitr; Eid Al-Adha (sacrifice), also known widely in North Africa as Eid Al-Kebir, commemorates God's sparing Ibrahim (Abraham, in the Bible) the sacrifice of his son Ismail (Issac).
83. *Naqaalat*: Cell phones.
84. *Zimzamaat*: A group of women singers who play private events using the tabla, tambourine and other instruments.
85. *Shakboot:* A reference to the United Arab Emirates.
86. Eminent Colonel: referring to Gaddafi, not without sarcasm.
87. *Sooriya*: A white, long dress shirt; and summer *farmala*: a Libyan vest; *hooli:* a wollen wrap for men.
88. Calm Coral Sea: The Red Sea.
89. Black gold: Oil.
90. *Shabab*: Youth
91. *Macarona Ambaka:* A Libyan pasta with tomato sauce.
92. *Allahu Akbar*: God is great.
93. *Qibla:* Direction of prayer, facing Mecca.
94. *Fatiha*: The first chapter of the Qur'an.

ETHAN CHORIN

95. Fagih, Ahmed Ibrahim, *Majmu'a al-A'maal Al Kamila* (CD), Tripoli: self-published, 2004, Chapter 21, p. 6.

96. Bin Arefa, At-Tahir, *Al-Ta'reef Bil Adab Al Libi*, Tripoli: Dar al-Hikma, 1997, p. 9.

97. The 1949 Bevin-Sforza plan, named for the foreign secretaries of the U.K. and Italy, articulated a ten-year trusteeship for the three Libyan provinces of Tripolitania, Cyrenaica and Fezzan, by Italy, Britain and France, respectively. The proposal failed by one vote to gain the necessary 2/3 required for adoption by the U.N. General Assembly, a situation that ultimately led to the independence of a united Libya.

98. *Sai'qa/ Sawa'iq*: Thunderbolt(s), a group of militias based in Zintan and the Jebel Nafousa that participated in the fall of Tripoli, September, 2011.

99. Bouri, Wahbi, *Al-Bawakeer Al-Qissat Al-Libiya Al-Qasira*, Tripoli: Mu'tammar, 2004, p. 2.

100. Salih, Mohammad Fagih, *Ufuq Ahar*, Tripoli: Dar Al Kutub, p. 69.

101. Bouri, Wahbi, *Al-Bawakeer Al-Qissat Al-Libiya Al-Qasira*, Tripoli: Mu'tammar, 2004.

102. Djaziri, Moncef, *Etat et Société en Libye*, Paris: L'Harmattan, 1996. p. 52.

103. Mufti, *Ghamq Zallat*, Benghazi: Dar Al Kutub Al-Wataniya, 2005, p. 25.

104. Ibid. p. 33.

105. Fontaine, Jacques, 'La population libyenne, un demi-science de mutations', in Pliez, Olivier, ed., *La Nouvelle Libye: Sociétés, espaces et géopolitique au lendemain de l'embargo*, Paris: Karthala, 1991, p. 165.

106. Libya National Report on Human Development 2002, p. 62; shaabiya (pl. shaabiyat), an administrative district unique to Libya.

107. Woodhouse, C., *Modern Greece: A Short History* (paperback), Boston and London: Faber and Faber, 1968, p. 177.

108. Greene, Molly, *A Shared World: Christians and Muslims in the Early Modern Mediterranean*, Princeton, N.J.: Princeton University Press, 2000. p. 155.

109. For good reason: Of more than 15,000 who attempted the journey in 2003, more than 2,000 died in transit. [By 2015, the numbers had soared to over 250,000 per year, of which a more than 20,000 have died at sea].

110. Staub, Vincent, *La Libye et Les Migrations Subsahariennes*, Paris: L'Harmattan, 2006. p. 59.

111. Ibid., p. 52.

112. Michael Brett and Elizabeth Fentress, *The Berbers*, Massachusetts: Blackwell Publishing, 2005, p. 3.

113. Mufti, Mohammad Mohammed, *Ghamq Zallat*, Benghazi: Dar Al Kutub Al-Wataniya, 2005, p. 21.

114. Jeffreys, Andrew, ed., *Emerging Morocco*, London: Oxford Business Group, 2006, p 10.

115. Brett and Fentress, *The Berbers*, Massachusetts: Blackwell Publishing, 2005, p. 88.

116. Ibid., p. 143.

117. Gellner, Ernest, *Saints of the Atlas*, Chicago: University of Chicago Press, 1969, p. 225.

118. In Morocco, Jewish quarters were known as 'mellah'.

119. Chouraqui, Andre N., *Between East and West, A History of the Jews of North Africa*, Philadelphia: Jewish Publication Society of America, 1968, p. 123.

120. Pacho, Jean-Raimond, *Relation d'un voyage dans la Marmarique, la Cyrenaique et les Oasis d'Audjelah et de Maradeh*, Beirut, Dar Al Jeel, 1999, p. 147.

121. Bouri, Wahbi, *Benghazi Fil Fitrat Al-Isti'mar Al-Italiya*, Benghazi: Majlis Tanmiya al Ibda' Al-thaqafi, 2004. p. 64.

122. Ibid., p. 36.

123. Chouraqui, André N., *Between East and West, A History of the Jews of North Africa*, Philadelphia: Jewish Publication Society of America, 1968. p. 281.

124. Jayyusi, Salma, *Modern Arabic Fiction*, New York: Columbia University Press, 2005. p. 32.

125. Ibid., p. 33.

126. Mufti, Muhammad Muhammad, *Hadraza fis Souk*, Libya: Dar Al Saqiya, 2006, p. 200.

127. Tillich, Paul, *The Courage To Be*, New Haven: Yale University Press, 2000, p. 106.

128. Mufti, Muhammad Muhammad, *Hadraza fi Benghazi*, Benghazi: Dar Al Kutub Al-Wataniya, 2004. p. 93.

129. Deeb, Marius K. and Mary Jane, *Libya Since the Revolution: Aspects of Social and Political Development*, New York: Praeger, 1982, p. 69.

130. Souriau, Christiane, *Libye: L'economie des femmes*, Paris: L'Harmattan, 2002, p. 131.

131. Ibid.

132. Ibid., p. 100.

133. Faludi, Susan, *Stiffed: The Betrayal of the American Man*, New York: HarperCollins, 2000, p. 9.

134. Mernissi, Fatima, *Beyond the Veil: Male–Female Dynamics in Modern Muslim Society*, Bloomington: Indiana University Press, 1987, p. 171.

135. Faludi, *Stiffed*, p. 599.

136. Ibid., p. 594.

137. Mahmood, Saba, *Politics of Piety: The Islamic Revival and the Feminist Subject*, Princeton: Princeton University Press, 2005, p. 16.

138. https://www.youtube.com/watch?v=_Jx8tz3an1o

139. Khafaji, Mohammed Abdel Munim, *Qisat Al-Adab fi Libi Al-Arabi*, Beirut: Dar Al-Jeel, 1992, p. 268.